Threshold Shift

ERIC BROWN

With a Foreword by Stephen Baxter

GOLDEN GRYPHON PRESS • 2006

"The Children of Winter," first published in *Interzone* 163, January 2001.
"Thursday's Child," first published in *Spectrum SF* 9, October 2002.
"Ascent of Man," first published in *Interzone* 167, May 2001.
"Ulla, Ulla," first published in *The Mammoth Book of Science Fiction*, 2001.
"The Kéthani Inheritance," first published in *Spectrum SF* 7, November 2001.
"Instructions for Surviving the Destruction of Star-Probe X-11-57," first published in *Spectrum SF* 6, July 2001.
"Eye of the Beholder," first published in *Interzone* 119, May 1997.
"The Touch of Angels," copyright © 2006 by Eric Brown.
"The Spacetime Pit," (with Stephen Baxter) first appeared in *Interzone* 107, May 1996.
"Hunting the Slarque," first published in *Interzone* 141, March 1999.

LIBRARY OF CONGRESS CATALOGING–IN–PUBLICATION DATA

Brown, Eric, 1960–
   Threshold shift / Eric Brown. — 1st ed.
     p.   cm.
   ISBN 1-930846-43-6 (hardcover : alk. paper)
    I. Title.
PR6102.R684T47   2006
823'.92—dc22   2006005440

Contents

To Finn and Freya, with love

I'd like to thank the editors of the magazines and the anthology where these stories first appeared: Mike Ashley, Paul Fraser and David Pringle

Foreword

"**I**'VE HEARD IT CALLED THRESHOLD SHIFT. YOUR consciousness of what is possible undergoes a shift, a moment of conceptual breakthrough, and nothing is ever the same again . . ."

So says a character in "Ulla, Ulla," one of ten fine science fiction short stories in this new collection by Eric Brown. In the case of this story the threshold shift is endured by a NASA astronaut who travels to Mars, only to discover something much stranger than a new world, something stranger than he could have imagined . . . For connoisseurs of vintage sf the story's title may be a clue as to what that is. Suffice to say that in the best tradition of sf—and Eric's work has always been in that best tradition—the threshold shift we share with Eric's protagonist takes us not just to a place we never knew we could believe in, but to a place we suddenly realise we always *wanted* to believe in.

Eric has long been one of his (our) generation's finest writers of short science fiction. His reputation was already established when I first met him, at a small convention in Britain in the late 1980s. We were introduced by David Pringle, then editor of *Interzone*, the magazine that "discovered" us both. I knew Eric's work, of course. But I found it hard to believe that the kind, charming, shy man I met that night could already have been responsible for a nerve-tingling body of work that included the justly famous "The Time-Lapsed Man" (later published, along with several other examples of Eric's earlier work, in a collection of the same name). These stories played a significant part in germinating the much-talked-about "British boom" in science fiction that followed.

Science fiction is one of the few literary fields in which the short story form continues to flourish. In fact, some aficionados would say that it is in the short form that sf is at its best, with startling ideas polished to an economical brilliance—as in several of Eric's pieces here. "Ascent of Man," for example, couldn't be more high-concept. Its few pages tell a strange, far-future tale, almost a parable, of an impossibly crowded world, but even here, as in all Eric's work, a sympathy for the human shines through. "Instructions for Surviving the Destruction of Star-Probe X-11-57" is a tale of an interstellar stranding that recalls classics of the genre's golden age such as Tom Godwin's "The Cruel Equations." Eric shows his command of style in this piece, which is narrated by the calm tones of an automated emergency system—and yet we are moved by the plight of the hapless astronaut whom we glimpse only indirectly.

"The Eye of the Beholder" is perhaps more affecting yet. It is another startlingly high-concept piece, in this case a story of subjective and objective invisibility. But this story is set in the present day, and its protagonist, close to Eric's own heart, is a novelist. It takes a rare command of the material to make such a striking concept believable against such a mundane background—and perhaps the deeper themes of the work are dramatised more affectingly in the absence of special effects. Similarly in an extraordinary scene in "The Touch of Angels" Eric has his protagonists sitting around in a West Yorkshire pub, yet discussing the long-term destiny of mankind, for a galactic culture has folded down into their lives.

Many of Eric's short works are clustered into series. There is one excerpt here from his justly popular "Tartarus" series, "Hunting the Slarque." These stories are set against the widescreen disaster of a planet whose star is soon to go supernova. It is a simple, compelling concept against which any number of human dramas can be spun.

There are also three samples of Eric's "Kéthani" tales here. In this case the concept is just as simple, but utterly startling. The Kéthani are aliens who descend to present-day Earth and offer us a technological resurrection, a literal restoration from death, in return for service. These stories are well served by their setting in a most familiar of landscapes, Eric's birthplace of West Yorkshire, where amid pubs which serve liberal quantities of Timothy Taylor's "Landlord" ale a strange alien architecture rises, and every night the sky is full of beams of light, human souls being delivered up to an orbiting starship.

When I first read a Kéthani tale I was struck by the profundity of the concept, capable of being expressed in a few words but with implications that unravel the more you think about them, like the edges of a fractal diagram. As H. G. Wells taught us, a sf idea may come from answering the question, "What if? . . ." But such a rich idea begs supplementaries: "Yes, but what then? And what then? . . ." A story series, as opposed to a novel, is perhaps the best way to explore all the facets and depth of such ideas. Such a series of interconnected tales is precisely what Eric has proceeded to develop around his Kéthani concept in recent years, and the idea seems to get richer with the telling.

But the best sf, Eric's sf, is not just about ideas but how they make you feel. How would you *feel* to be the parent of a dying daughter, unable to agree with your spouse about the rightness of allowing aliens to "save" your child ("Thursday's Child")? How would you *feel* if the abusive parent whose senescence and death you secretly longed for were to be restored to your life ("The Kéthani Inheritance")? And, in a world where death is a mere incident, what of murder ("The Touch of Angels")?

There is one tale here which gives me pleasure of a different sort: "The Spacetime Pit," one of my three collaborations with Eric. I've given a short account of how we went about this (in *Omegatropic*, British Science Fiction Association, 2001). Since that first meeting more than fifteen years ago we had stayed good friends, and when Eric visited my home some years ago we cooked up this story, from a seed idea of Eric's, over several pints of real ale (regrettably not "Landlord"). It was a joyous process; looking at the story again now I think a sense of playfulness about the ideas comes through.

I've saved to last my personal favourite of the pieces collected here. "The Children of Winter" is a classic sf set-up, a lucid tale of a hopeless love affair between alien kinds on a remote world, off in the far future. And it is classic in its telling too, with more golden-age echoes. Eric's other-worldly "Blues" are reminiscent of Ray Bradbury's golden-eyed Martians, perhaps, and the seamless elegance and sincerity of Eric's prose recalls Bradbury too. And you won't anticipate the twist at the end, which, in a few perfectly chosen words, not just transforms our perspective on the story itself but also offers us glimpses of still stranger possibilities lying beyond. Only science fiction at its best can offer us such marvellous threshold shifts. This story is in the very best traditions of the genre, and able to hold its head up beside any of the classics which it recalls.

Since our first meeting Eric's life has changed greatly. He still lives in his beloved West Yorkshire, but now he is married, and a family man. He has continued to produce short fiction of enviably high quality, over seventy published pieces at time of writing, ten of which are now collected here. His first novel was published in 1992, he has developed a parallel career in children's fiction, and at time of writing he has five more books due out in the future.

"The Children of Winter" alone would be enough to cement a reputation, but there is much more here. If you have read Eric Brown before you will know the pleasures that await you. But if this is your first introduction to Eric's work, I envy you; you have a memorable journey ahead. Long may Eric Brown's prolific talent, and our friendship, flourish.

Stephen Baxter
July 2004

Threshold Shift

The Children of Winter

IN MY EIGHTEENTH TERM, WHICH WAS ALSO THE last term of winter, I fell in love with a Blue, lost my youth, and learned the truth—and to learn the truth, after so long living in ignorance, can be a terrible revelation.

The three of us were inseparable, then. After lessons we skated the ice-canals of Ak-helion beneath the sable skies of winter. At night we'd huddle around the brazier of an itinerant food-vendor, chewing on roasted tubers. The square was a scintillating sheet of ice, framed on three sides by the ugly stone buildings of the city; the fourth side looked down into the mountain valley, or would do so when the sun arrived to light the view.

We were swaddled in protective clothing like lagged boilers, so that it was an effort to bend our arms to eat the tubers. Nani giggled as she tried to nibble the long, steaming root. Oh, she was so beautiful, her every gesture a delight. She was, also, inaccessible: we had been friends for most of our lives, but she was in love with Kellor, and how could I begrudge my best friend the love of the girl I also secretly cherished?

The vendor closed his brazier, picked up its reins and dragged it away on its skates to another venue, leaving behind a puddle of slush that froze over within seconds.

Kellor whooped with the delight of being young and skated away on one leg, showing off to Nani. I looked around the square, at the dark buildings that merged with the night, and then I saw it. Between the Governor's manse and the library building, a tiny, bright pin-prick in the dark sky, the Star.

"Kellor!" I cried. "Nani! Come here!"

They skated to my side, each catching a shoulder to halt themselves, and almost dragged me to the ground.

"What is it, Jen?" Nani panted.

"Look," I said, "the Star . . ."

We stared, our breaths clouding the air before us.

Nani whispered something to herself. Kellor said, "To the city wall!"

We set off pell-mell. We careered down ice-canals and alleys, taking corners at speed with little thought for other skaters. The city wall was a long dam-like structure built across the valley, where often after lessons we met to stare in wonder at the fiery magnificence of the galactic spiral as it flung its starry arms high overhead.

Today it was as if our Star had detached itself from the shoal and was drifting towards us—but that was just my poetic imagination.

When we were nine terms old, Kellor, a practical-minded scientist even then, had explained to me the physics of our celestial situation.

He had taken me to the square and skated in a long oval around the brazier of a food-vendor, tilting his blades to score an ellipse in the ice. Then he returned and took my arm, dragging me with him.

"I thought you were going to show me—" I began.

He laughed in indulgent reprimand and explained. "We—us two—are our planet, Fortune," he said. "That—" pointing to the distant brazier "—is the Star. We move around it in an oval orbit. Now we are far away, so far away that we cannot feel the heat of the Star. But, as we approach—see, the coals grow brighter. We move closer and feel the heat, and as we pass by the heat is intense, but only briefly. The period of our summer is just four terms—any longer and Fortune would burn to a cinder. And then we begin the long, slow arc into winter again, the Star diminishing behind us as we move away. The winter lasts for eighteen terms, the cold and ice descends, the Star virtually disappears—until, in time, we swing back towards the Star for another short and fiery summer . . . Now do you understand, you dreamer?"

I was dumb-struck with the wonder of it. "But," I began, com-

ing to understand something for the very first time, "that is why
they call us the Children of Winter. We were born with the coming of winter, and will be initiated when winter ends!"

Kellor, even at nine, managed an adult's patronising smile.
"When we are eighteen terms old," he said grandly, "the ice will
melt and our initiation will coincide with the emergence of the
starship."

Now we were eighteen, that magical age, and it seemed to me
that life had never been so rich and full of promise.

Our initiation was just one week away.

We screamed down a steep conduit that in spring would drain the
melt-water from the city and into the valley, but which now was a
near vertical channel of breakneck ice. The conduit levelled out
and we raced on to the span of the wall. To our right was the lambent arch of the galaxy; straight ahead, low in the night sky, the
lone light of the setting Star.

We huddled in a niche in the wall, out of the rapier-keen wind
from the north. Nani stared down the valley, her big eyes high-
lighting the glow of the galactic aura, and I felt my heart leap with
love. She shook her head with finality. "I can't see the starship,"
she reported.

"The sun's not bright enough, yet," Kellor said. "It sheds little
light. And anyway, the ship's a mile or more away, and hidden in
a ravine. Only when the ice melts . . ."

I felt my heart hammer with another emotion. How fortunate
we were! We were the Children of Winter, and our initiation
ceremony would take place with the emergence of the starship
—actually within the hallowed vault of the ship itself. Other citizens, those born either side of winter, would not share our luck:
either their eighteenth term would come about when the starship
was still entombed in layers of ice, or when the molten heat of high
summer made a pilgrimage to the ship impossible.

I felt Nani's mittened hand on mine. "Jen," she whispered.
"Recite your poem."

Kellor snorted. He had little time for my sentimental verse.

I cleared my throat and stared at the distant light of the Star.
"We are Winter's Children," I began, "Conceived with Summer's
last breath/ Born to the first steel-hard frosts of Winter/ Our char-
acters, our very souls, forged in sunless hardship and sleeting snows/
To learn the Truth when Summer unveils the ship . . ."

"The Truth," Kellor laughed. "Mark my word, it'll be nothing but political mumbo-jumbo. Our elders exhorting us to high morals and good citizenship."

"I don't think so," I said. "I've watched those who've been initiated in the past. They seem . . ." I shook my head. "I don't know, somehow *changed*. As if life seems different in light of what they've learned."

Kellor was derisory. "You'd think that this so-called truth would leak out, no? That some initiate wouldn't be able to contain themselves, that they'd tell us what they've learned."

"Perhaps the truth is so . . . so shattering that they cannot bring themselves to talk—" I began.

A sound from along the wall halted our speculation. We froze, listening. From afar came the muffled chug of a steam engine. "Blues!" Kellor cried in delight.

We peered from the niche. Sure enough, below us on the road that ran parallel with the city wall, a great steam-wagon made its lumbering way. Its spiked wheels bit into the ice, clawing it forward, and two figures could be seen riding high in the uncovered cab.

The Blues were native to Fortune and it seemed to me that, by their aloof manners and insistence that they keep contact with us to a minimum, they resented our arrival here millennia ago. Even their erect postures spoke of some genetic disdain. But perhaps what I found most daunting about these creatures, similar to us though they were, was their pale blue skins and their ability to go without winter clothing. It was as if their acceptance of the cold mocked my dependency—I was winter-born, after all—on thick breeches, a quilted overcoat, hat, and gloves.

"Let's attack them!" Kellor cried, and so saying scraped up a snowball from the ground and lobbed it at the passing wagon. Nani followed suit, but I held back.

The Blues lived in the high mountains, far to the north of Akhelion. They came in their steam-wagons from time to time, trading pots and utensils for the harl-meat and the other foodstuffs we produced. A few Blues lived in the city, liaising between their kind and our traders. Whenever I saw one I was struck dumb by their otherness, their silence and grace, their strange ethereal beauty. I could never bring myself to despise these people, as we were taught to do. Still less could I bring myself to pelt them with snowballs.

They passed below, dignified in their dismissal of the missiles falling around them. As I watched, the passenger turned its head and stared up at us. She was a female of fragile beauty, her face as pale blue and translucent as the egg of a snowbird. It seemed that for a second our gazes met, and I willed into my expression an apology for the behaviour of my compatriots.

Later, when the steam-wagon had departed, we raced the length of the city wall, whooping with the fact of our being eighteen and free, and soon to be initiated.

Kellor looked up at the rearing galactic arm. From the mass of stars displayed he declared it late and time for bed. He departed with Nani, but I guessed from their manner—the almost coy propinquity of the intimate—that they would not be sleeping alone tonight.

I set off home. I skated slowly along the city wall and climbed the ice-bound stone steps to the city proper. I crossed the square where we had eaten tubers. It was late; even the food-vendors had doused their braziers and retired. Only the harl, the shaggy quadrupeds that drew passenger-sleds during the day, occupied the shadows, emitting steam and contented snores.

I was skating down the broad boulevard towards the street on which I lived, in a big government house with my mother and father, when I heard the noise.

At first I thought it was a harl in distress. I slid to a halt and listened. The sound came again, a thin, high sobbing. I moved towards its source, peering into the stone channel which flanked the road. At the foot of a steep flight of stairs to a tall town-house, I made out a figure lying in the shadows. Impeded by my skates, I climbed down.

"It's okay," I said. "I'll get help."

I stopped, then, for the face of a Blue was staring up at me. I stood and backed off.

It reached out a hand. "Please. I fell and hurt my ankle." The voice was soft, a mere breath, and feminine. "If you could assist me inside." And she gestured to the door at the top of the steps.

My first impulse was to run; my second, to my credit, was to aid the Blue as she requested. I removed my skates, then knelt and lifted her to her good foot; I put an arm around her and assisted her slowly up the steps. She leaned against me, and I was astonished at how light and insubstantial she was. At the top of the steps she pushed open the door and pointed down the corridor to another.

With my help she moved around her apartment turning on

yellow, glowing lamps. The room, revealed, was much like any other: perhaps I had expected something as alien as the Blue herself. Oils of winter landscapes adorned the walls, sculptures of winter-stark trees stood on shelves and tables. I had, in my ignorance, never credited the aliens with an appreciation of the arts.

She sat on a chair beside a glowing lamp and inspected her ankle. For the first time I became aware of what she was wearing: a thin, red dress and a slighter heavier black, hooded cape. She was probing her ankle with delicate fingers, and wincing.

I knelt and took her foot in my hand. "I . . . I don't think it's broken," I said. "Perhaps it's just badly twisted. Ah . . . maybe a bandage?" I looked up, and was shocked to behold the regard of her great black eyes.

"It *is* you," she said. "I thought so."

"Excuse me?"

"Earlier, upon the city wall. Two children cast balls of ice at our wagon. You were with them, but did not join the attack."

"You were in the wagon," I said. I recalled the cool regard of the Blue passenger, and my shame at the antics of my friends.

"I . . . I'm sorry. It was . . . they didn't mean to hurt you. It was just a game."

She regarded me with a quizzical expression. For all our differences, our far-flung origins, we had much in common. She said, "But you refrained from joining in the attack. I thought your people deemed us . . . beneath contempt. Certainly that is the impression I receive from those of you I work with from day to day."

"We aren't all like that. Some of us . . ." I stopped myself, for fear of sounding sanctimonious.

"Do you know that many of your kind would have let me lie there all night," she said. "I am indeed fortunate that you were passing."

Her stare was making me uncomfortable. She smiled and told me that I would find a bandage in the kitchen. I stood and hurried into the adjacent room.

When I returned I saw that she had taken off her cloak. I could not help but notice the delicacy of her arms and legs, her high-cheekboned face framed in a long fall of jet black hair.

Clumsily I wrapped the bandage around her swollen ankle.

"What is your name," she asked.

"Jen," I whispered, not meeting her eyes.

"And how old are you, Jen?"

"Eighteen."

"But so am I!" she declared. "And my name is Ki."

"You're eighteen? But I thought . . ." She seemed much older; something in her poise, her confidence, suggested the maturity of an adult.

"Among my people, at sixteen terms we are considered mature, and we can go about the business of the elders." Her large, black eyes seemed to bore into me. "If you are eighteen terms," she said, "then very soon you will be initiated."

"In six days," I began.

Something in her regard made me uneasy. I stood suddenly. "I must go," I said. "It's late. Be careful with the ankle. Don't put any weight on it." I hurried to the door. "Goodbye."

A half-smile played on her lips as she watched me leave the room. I put on my skates and sped home, only then realising what had occurred. I had conversed with a Blue, broken the unspoken rule that contact between our races was forbidden, except in certain circumstances. I wondered what Kellor and Nani might have to say about my encounter, not that I intended to tell them.

My mother and father were still up when I returned, reading by lamp-light in the front room. I slipped past the door and hurried up to bed. I was not close to them at the best of times, but something—was it shame?—stopped me from pausing to wish them goodnight.

That night I dreamed of Ki. It was a dream full of horror and . . . something else. I awoke in a sweat, an hour before I had to rise for college, then lay back and tried to recall the rapidly vanishing images of Ki, naked, in my arms.

The words "day" and "night," Kellor once explained to me, were derived from the time when Fortune experienced its brief, hot summer. The planet, he said, turned on its axis every twenty hours, so that for successive periods of ten hours every day during summer the sky above Ak-helion was light and then dark. During winter the sky was perpetually dark, but even so we still divided the day into periods of hours, and called one lot day and another night, for convenience. I had lived all my life in night-time darkness, and found it hard to imagine a daylight sky.

However, change was on the way. Now the Star was in the sky during the day, and at night it set. At college the following day, after my encounter with Ki, I sat at my desk and stared through the thick glass window at the small beacon of the Star, contemplating the forthcoming initiation and the changes that would follow.

In less than half a term the ice with which I was so familiar, with which I had lived all my life, would be no more. It would melt and like drinking water run off down the mountain, leaving the rocks bare and inhospitable, and then the heat would start to climb. Soon it would be impossible to live out in the open, and we would retire, the entire population of the city, to a cool sanctuary excavated deep below the mountain long ago. Four or five terms later we would re-emerge to populate Ak-helion again. I wondered if I would adapt to life underground.

I sat with Kellor and Nani in the refectory at lunch. Soon the conversation came around to the subject of the starship.

"I've been thinking," Kellor said, smiling slyly at me, "why don't we leave the city and go to the ravine of the starship ourselves, sneak a quick look before the ceremony?"

The suggestion was as foolhardy as it was profane. Nani gasped at the very idea.

I laughed. "You're not serious, are you?"

"Aren't I? Why not?"

Nani said, "Because it isn't allowed!" She made a chopping gesture with her mittened hand. "It just *isn't* allowed!"

"If we were caught . . ." I began, heartened that Nani was on my side. I had never heard of anyone trying to view the starship before the ceremony. I looked at Kellor as if he were mad.

"We'll talk about it later, okay?" Kellor said. "Meet you on the square at eight."

That evening the housemaid served me dinner and I ate alone. My parents were important civil servants, and were attending a meeting at the government assembly buildings. Afterwards I left the house and skated towards the square. On the way I passed the tall building in which Ki had her apartment. On impulse, without analysing my motives, I bought some food—bread and harl cheese—from a nearby shop, returned, and climbed the steps.

Her door at the end of the corridor was ajar, spilling yellow light. I unfastened my skates and knocked tremulously on the door. After a second or two I heard a faint, "It's open," and cautiously pushed my way inside.

She was seated upon a settee, her leg outstretched, foot resting on a cushioned stool. Her thin lips tightened into an indecipherable line at my appearance, her eyes widening.

I held up the bread and cheese. "I . . . I thought you might need something. I brought you these."

She smiled, and the sudden movement of her lips, conferring gratitude, filled me with relief.

"That is so kind of you. Please, put them here." She indicated the cushion beside her.

I could not take my eyes from that portion of her upper body not covered by her white dress, the delicate bone-work of sternum and clavicle.

I realised that it was cold in the room. I would have suffered without my thick coat. That she was happy in this environment brought home to me the fact of her alienness.

"I'm pleased that you came," she said. "I've been lonely here, with no one to talk to."

"Your people—?"

She laid her head to one side and looked at me. "They do not like to come into the city. There is just one other liaison officer in Ak-helion, but as we work shifts I rarely see him."

"Why did you become a liaison officer?" I asked.

"Because I was curious. I wanted to know whether the stories my people told me about you were true. I wanted to see if you were really as hostile as they claimed."

I wondered if she was mocking me, this young girl who was my age, but much, much older. "And are we?"

"In general, yes," she said, and I fear I blushed in shame. "I have experienced the most unwarranted acts of petty cruelty, bigotry, and ignorance during my time in Ak-helion."

I shook my head.

"And then all my assumptions, my conclusions, are thrown into confusion by the random kindness of a total stranger."

I did not know what to say, and so said nothing.

"I am curious," she said. "I want to know why—why are you not like the others? Why did you help me?"

I shook my head, and then blurted words I regretted at once. "Because I think you're beautiful," I said.

Oh, you fool, you young, besotted, inexperienced fool! I cringe when I think about the boy I was, the pain and confusion that filled me then.

But I was honest, I'll grant my young self that. I said what I felt, and to my vast relief the Blue girl did not laugh at me.

She smiled.

She must have been aware of my naivety and pain: she was experienced beyond her age. "That is one of the nicest things anyone has ever said to me, Jen. Thank you."

We talked. It seemed that a tension had been removed from our encounter, and we conversed as friends. She told me of her people, her life in the city far to the north. They were, it seemed, an advanced race—but quite how advanced she refrained from telling me. I tried to question her about the technology of her city, but with a wave of her fingers and a smile she changed the subject.

She was, like me, an only child; and also like me she had experienced no love from or for her parents. She had excelled at school and developed an interest in the people who shared her planet; she had studied hard and applied to become a liaison officer, was taken on, trained, and despatched to the city of Ak-helion.

I told her about myself, my parents and friends, my schoolwork and passion for poetry; this last was a painful admission to make—many people might have laughed at my romanticism—but Ki smiled softly and expressed a love of poetry and music, too. I think it was then that I fell in love with her.

An hour passed, then two. It was almost eight. I remembered that I had agreed to meet Kellor and Nani in the square.

I told Ki that I had enjoyed talking to her, but that I had to go.

"Do you? Do you really? Can't you stay?" She reached out, laid a soft, blue hand on mine. To my astonishment I found the touch of her fingers warm, not frost-cold as I had expected.

Her hand moved to my cheek, and drew my head as if by magic towards hers, and her kiss was the consummation of all my dreams.

She stood awkwardly and whispered something. I assisted her to the adjacent room where she undressed me until I stood, naked and shivering like some sacrificial beast. Then she slipped from her simple dress and, amazingly naked, eased me on to the bed and warmed me with her love.

I was surprised, as I grappled inexpertly with the Blue girl, that this should seem so natural. I was fearful at first, afraid of her alienness and difference—but Ki gave me pleasure I had never imagined, and I could not conceive how sex, even with my own kind, could be any better.

Later, I reached out to the bedside table and examined the glowing ball that illuminated the room. It was unlike anything I had every seen, and remarkable, but not half as remarkable as the experience bequeathed me by the alien girl who slept quietly at my side.

I replaced the lambent sphere, dressed without waking her and slipped from the apartment. I made my slow way home through the darkness, filled with a confusion of emotions: love and shame, joy and fear, elation at what I had shared with Ki, and uncertainty as to the future.

I awoke early the following morning and, unable to sleep or face breakfast, left home and skated down the deserted ice-canals. The thought of going to lessons never entered my head; last night had been special to me, had been a turning point, and I needed time in which to digest what had happened. I was drawn to Ki's apartment, even reached the corner of the boulevard, but stopped myself from going any closer. I wanted to re-acquaint myself with the pleasures of her body, but at the same time I did not want to throw myself at her. Yet, I told myself, if she felt for me what I felt for her, then surely she would be pleased to see me . . . I was a young boy in love for the first time, and confused. I was by turns elated at the thought of what we had found in each other, and then depressed at how our relationship might be viewed by my elders and so-called betters.

I explored the city three times over until exhausted, and then found a covered tea-cabin and sat with off-duty ice-trimmers and harl-jockeys as they huddled over steaming pots of spiced milk and traded ribald jokes and jibes. I watched the Star rise high into the sky, surely a little larger than it had been yesterday, and considered the future.

It was a measure of my youthful naivety that, after just one brief liaison with Ki, I considered myself in love and fearful for that love. Soon the ice would melt, daylight would come to Fortune, and the citizens of Ak-helion would migrate below ground. As for the Blues, they would leave their city and trek even further north, to the pole of the planet where they would wait out the fierce heat in the relative cool of their summer city. Next winter they would return, and Ki with them. But the thought of waiting four or five terms! I would have left college by then, and entered a profession. I would be an adult, and my parents would be looking to arrange a marriage with a suitable girl. And would Ki even remember me? I laugh to think, now, of the yearning and heartache I suffered that day, with first love still fresh in my heart.

At eight I made my way to the square.

The galactic arms were fiery and spectacular that night. Crowds thronged the ice, staring up at the umber and magenta whorls. Food-vendors and spiced milk sellers were doing a brisk trade. I found Kellor and Nani.

"Why didn't you meet us last night?" Kellor asked. "And where have you been today?"

Nani was smiling with a warm, soft glow that suggested contentment after intimacy.

"I was sick," I lied. "Must've eaten a bad tuber."

I was torn with the desire to tell them about the night I had spent with Ki, and yet chary of their ridicule. I knew they would be wrong to condemn me; what Ki and I shared was just as precious as anything between Kellor and Nani, but of course they would be unable to see that.

"We've decided to go," Kellor said proudly, as if announcing their betrothal.

I was confused, lost as I was in my own thoughts. "Go where?" I asked, and instantly recalled Kellor's boast of the day before.

He was nodding at my sudden expression of disbelief. "We made up our minds and we're going for it."

I looked to Nani, who yesterday had been as horrified as I.

Kellor had evidently talked her round. She shrugged. "Why not, Jen? If we're careful . . . Just think of it, to see the starship before anyone else!"

"But you won't," I pointed out, disappointed at her capitulation. "What about all the Church Elders preparing the ceremony, and the guards? They'll have seen it before you."

"You know what we mean," Kellor said. "We'll see it before anyone else of our age. We'll be the first."

"And if you're caught, what then? Anything might happen. You might be expelled from college, even jailed."

"We won't be caught," Kellor assured me. "We're young and fit. We can out-skate any feeble Elder."

"But you don't even know the way," I said.

"The High Elders make their way to the ravine every day," Kellor said. "We'll simply follow their tracks through the ice and snow."

"You're fools," I said. "I'll tell you now, you'll regret it."

"So you're not coming with us?" This was Nani, taunting me.

I merely shook my head and turned away.

"We leave from the square at eight tomorrow evening, if you change your mind and want to join us," Kellor said. "See you later." He took Nani's hand and tugged her off, weaving through the crowd towards her parents' place.

I skated around the square for a while, wondering who was the more foolish—Kellor and Nani for wanting to satisfy their curiosity ahead of time, or myself for loving a Blue? Perhaps my disdain for their venture was merely envy of their daring, as opposed to the cowardly doubt I felt at my own transgression.

The thought of Ki drove me from the square. I skated at speed across the city, turned down the wide boulevard and slid to a halt outside her building. Ensuring that there was no one about, I removed my skates and carefully climbed the stairs. I pushed through the outer door and knocked on the door of her apartment.

My heart leaped at the sound of her voice. "Who is it?"

"Me. Jen."

"Jen!" It was a cry. "Well, come in. Don't just stand there!" And no sooner had I pushed open the door and stepped over the threshold than she limped, wincing, into my arms.

"But where did you disappear to this morning?" she asked, all concern. "And why didn't you come earlier?"

I laughed in relief at her welcome. "I had to go home," I began. "My parents . . ."

"I missed you, Jen," she said. "I thought you were never coming back."

I carried her into the bedroom and lay with her on the bed. We held each other and talked of our respective pasts. I found myself telling her of incidents I thought I had forgotten, found that I had the ability to imbue stories with humour and excitement that had the Blue girl laughing in delight.

In the early hours I climbed from bed, and the movement woke Ki. I kissed her. "I must go. If my parents found out . . ."

"Tonight," she whispered. "Come back tonight, Jen. Please."

I promised, left her and made my way home. I slipped into the house and up to my room without disturbing the mundane sleep of my mother and father. It gave me strength and confidence to know that, for the first time in my life, I was acting without their knowledge or consent.

The following day at college I sat through the lessons in a daze, waiting only for the end of the day so that I could visit Ki. Kellor and Nani were unusually quiet, and it was awhile before I recalled what they had planned for tonight.

"You're fools if you go through with it," I whispered at lunch in the vast refectory hall. "Look, in four days it's the initiation ceremony anyway. Why not just wait?"

But they didn't even grace my concern with replies, just smiled to themselves and resumed their meal.

At five, rather than leave with them as I usually did, I strapped on my skates and sped away from the college, along the ice-canals towards Ki's boulevard. I made sure no one saw me and slipped into the building.

She was waiting for me. I lifted her from her feet and hugged her to me, as if I had been away for terms.

Her delighted laugh was the trill of a snowbird.

We made love in her bed and then lay beneath the sheets, holding each other close, and it was this period of our love-making that I preferred; animal passion spent, I lazed in the glow of intimacy with the only person I had ever loved or wholly trusted.

Ki leaned on one elbow, a sheen of sweat coating her face and breasts. She pulled back the blankets to let the air of the room cool her nakedness, while I shivered.

"Tell me about your initiation, Jen," she said.

I laughed. "That would be like telling you about . . . I don't know . . . the Star," I said. "How can I tell you about something that I've never experienced?"

She pulled a pretty face. "But you must know what happens at the ceremony. Surely your Elders have said something?"

"All I know is that on initiation day a hundred of us, maybe more, will be taken to the ravine of the starship." I realised, as I spoke, that my voice had become hushed, as if with awe.

"The starship," she said. I would recall, only later, the shadow that passed across her features then.

I nodded. "We enter the ship and the High Elder of the Church of Fortune addresses us. What he says I don't know. But it's said that he vouchsafes us the Truth."

Ki looked at me, dubious. "The Truth? Just like that? Why is it that you've never heard the Truth before now?" A smile played upon her lips.

"I don't know." I shrugged. "Initiates are sworn to secrecy."

"Jen," she said, staring at me seriously with her great, black eyes, "will you tell me the Truth when you know it?"

I kissed her high forehead. "Yes, Ki," I said.

"Promise?"

"Of course I promise." I looked about the room, at the glow-spheres that not only afforded light, I realised, but also heat. The bedroom was always warmer than the other room, though still cold to my sensibilities.

I picked up a glow-sphere from the bedside table. "I've told you what I know about the initiation. Now you tell me about these. I've never seen anything like them, Ki."

She took the ball from me and held it on her open palm; her staring eyes reflected the object. "Aren't they beautiful? But I'm no scientist, Jen. I don't know how they work."

"But you make them—the Blues, I mean?"

"Of course." She laughed. "Who else?" She frowned at me. "We aren't the savages you take us for, Jen. Who do you think sold you the invention of steam?"

I shrugged. I had always assumed that it was we who had invented steam power.

"We are a technological race, with many inventions you would never dream of," Ki said. "In time we will give you the secret of the glow-spheres, among other things."

She saw my gaze straying to the window, and the rise of the galaxy betraying the lateness of the hour. She laid a hand on my chest, pressing me to the bed. "Don't go, Jen. Stay a little longer, please."

What did it matter if I arrived home now or in three hours, just so long as my parents never discovered my absence? Ki's pleading was impossible to resist. I pulled the sheets over us, creating a scented darkness, and wrestled her into submission.

Later I considered the ceremony of the initiation, the approach of the Star, and all that this would entail.

"Ki," I said. I could hardly bring myself to broach the subject. "When the ice melts . . ."

She stilled my lips with a finger-tip. "Shhh. Don't even think about it."

"I can think of nothing else! I don't want to lose you."

"Nor do I want to lose you."

"Then stay, come with us into the mountain . . ." But even as I spoke I realised the absurdity of my words.

She smiled sadly. "You know I couldn't do that. Your people . . ." She paused. "In five terms I will be back, Jen. I'll come for you."

"But five terms? I'll go mad just waiting!"

"And so will I, but then we'll have each other to ease our madness."

Later, I dressed and tore myself away from Ki, and skated along the deserted ice-canals of Ak-helion in a dismal frame of mind. A torch burned outside my parents' house, and I wondered if my father or mother intended an early start. I crept into the hall with especial care.

They were waiting for me. They emerged from the front room as I crossed the hall, and stared at me.

"Jen," my father said, something uncompromising in his tone. I feared they had found out about my relationship with Ki.

"Where have you been?"

"I . . ." I realised I was stammering. My knees felt weak. My father seemed like a stranger to me at the best of times: now he appeared as a condemning judge. "I've been with friends."

"Who?" he asked, sharply. "Kellor and Nani?"

Something, some inkling of what had happened, made me shake my head. "No. No, someone else—"

"Who?" he asked again, unrelenting.

I stared him in the eye. "A girl," I said. "I've been with a girl I met in a tea-cabin."

My mother lowered her head and cried quietly. I burned with embarrassment at her knowing that I was no longer her innocent child.

"You're lying, Jen," my father said.

"I'm not. It's true . . . I'm sorry."

"You were with Kellor and Nina. Do not deny it!"

I repeated their names. "Why?" I managed at last. "What has happened?"

My father fixed me with a gaze colder than any northern wind. "Tonight Kellor and Nani were arrested by Church Elders close to the ravine of the starship. They are in serious trouble. If I find that you were with them . . ." His tone implied that if I were lying then he would flay me alive. "Go to your room."

I fled. I felt at first relief that my liaison with Ki had not been discovered, and then shame at that relief, and only then solicitude for my friends.

The following morning at breakfast my father did not mention the likely fate of Kellor and Nani, and I could not bring myself to ask; nor did he question me about my affair, for which I was relieved. I suspected that he would try to find out who I was seeing by other means, and I determined to ensure I was never followed to Ki's apartment.

Before I left the table, my father informed me that for the next term I must be home by seven. I agreed with good grace, secretly mourning the hours I would lose with Ki.

At college that day all talk was about the fate of Kellor and Nani, who were notable by their absence. Classmates took great delight in imagining their punishment, from lengthy incarceration to ten strokes of the lash. I absented myself from all such speculation, sickened. I wondered if, had I not been involved with Ki, I might have weakened and joined my friends on their abortive pilgrimage.

After lessons I made my way to Kellor's house, but the windows were darkened and my summons went unanswered. Then I crossed the city to Ki's boulevard, making various detours, and waited on the corner until there was not a soul in sight. I stayed with her until just before seven, and returned to share the evening meal with my parents like a dutiful son.

For the next three days, before the ceremony at the starship, I visited Ki immediately after lessons, my few hours with her at these times all the more precious for being stolen and curtailed. Of Nani and Kellor there was no word.

At college, on the day before the ceremony, an atmosphere of anticipation and excitement filled the cloisters and classrooms. The continued absence of Kellor and Nani dampened my sense of expectation, and at lunchtime in the refectory my worst fears were confirmed.

A small boy, whose father was a High Elder in the Church of Fortune, approached my table, "Are you Jen, a friend of Kellor and Nani?"

"What of it?"

"Their case is being heard today," he said with inflated self-importance. "If found guilty, their initiation will be set back six terms."

I stared at him in shock, unable to reply. The rest of the day passed in a blur, and at five I fled across the city to Ki.

Another shock awaited me at her apartment. I knocked on the door and entered. She called to me from the bedroom. I looked about the outer room, sure that something had changed. It was some seconds before I noticed that various items, tree-sculptures and paintings, were missing.

When I stepped into her bedroom I saw that she was packing. She stood gingerly on her damaged ankle, placing wrapped objects in crates.

"Ki . . . ?"

She limped across the room and took me in her arms. "Jen . . . Oh, Jen. We've been recalled. The liaison officers. The time has come for the migration north. I leave Ak-helion in two days."

"Two days?" I repeated like an idiot, disbelieving. I shook my head. "In two days you'll be gone?"

The concept was too vast and terrible to imagine.

She stared into my eyes, brushing hair from my forehead. "We have two days," she whispered. "I'll make them special, Jen, so that you'll remember me until I return."

I broke down and wept, then, like the young boy I was. She held me in her arms and tried to console me, with the care and concern of the woman she was.

I stayed with her throughout the night, regardless of my father's curfew. Damn him, I thought. I would not let him deny me precious hours with the girl I loved, no matter what the consequences. At dawn, as the Star rose in the dark sky, I made my way home and defiantly joined my parents at breakfast. That morning, the day of the ceremony, we ate in strained silence and they elected not to reprimand me for ignoring the curfew.

It seemed that the entire population of Ak-helion had gathered on the city wall to wish us on our way. Escorted by the Elders of the Church, we set off in a torch-lit procession along the downward path chiselled though the ice. The cheers of the crowd ringing in my ears, I looked round the bright, expectant faces for any sign of Kellor and Nani, but saw neither.

We left the city behind us and entered territory new to me, vast sloping fields of snow, gullies sliced through slabs of ice washed orange in the torchlight. All around us were signs of the thaw: from overhangs and lips of ice, water poured in muscled, quicksilver torrents. We seemed to trek for miles through this eerie, flame-lit landscape, our thoughts on the forthcoming initiation. For all my sorrow at my friends' absence, I was more preoccupied with what might lie ahead.

Perhaps an hour later I made out, in the distance, the rosy glow of massed torches emanating from a hollow in the ground. We approached, and as we did so the robed Church Elders in our midst began a dolorous chant. My heart set up a laboured pounding.

We neared the lip of the ravine and stared down, and I saw first the sweeping flight of steps cut into the ice, and then the starship itself.

I had had no idea what to expect. The reproduction of pictures and icons representing the ship was prohibited by the Church, and from stray comments and hints dropped by adults I had in mind that the starship might resemble a tall stalagmite of ice, an edifice of silver metal reaching for the stars.

I stopped in my tracks and gazed in slack-jawed amazement. Silver it was indeed, and tall, but I would never have guessed how silver, or how tall. It coruscated like diamond and was fully five times as high as the highest building in Ak-helion. Set into its towering, triangular length were a hundred observation nacelles and viewports, alternating with vast numerals and decals excoriated by its journey through the gulf of space. Seeing the reality of the ship for the very first time, I was filled with heart-breaking pride at the achievements of my race, at the feat of survival represented by this rearing leviathan.

Gasps and cries of wonder broke out all around me as we naive initiates stared, but no sooner had we feasted our eyes than the Church Elders hurried us down the ice steps. As we dropped into the ravine, so the starship seemed to gain height. Soon we had to crane our necks to make out the antennae bristling at its very pinnacle.

At the foot of the stairway, before the great, arched entrance of the ship, we halted. There was a commotion among our group as initiates turned and stared. I felt elation swell within me at what I saw then. Climbing down the steps after us, escorted by two stern-faced Elders, were Kellor and Nani.

I made my way back through the throng and embraced my friends under the disapproving gazes of the Elders.

"What happened?" I gasped.

"We were reprimanded," Kellor said. "That's all—just reprimanded!" He and Nani seemed dazed at the fact of their reprieve, shocked as we all were at the sight of the starship.

We were called to order by the Church High Elder, resplendent in his silver robes, and ushered into the hold of the ship.

There we stood like the worshippers we were, in this ultra-modern cathedral, while the High Elder climbed on to a podium before us and gave his speech.

I only heard fragments of what he said. It was much as Kellor had forecast: an exhortation to us, the new men and women of Ak-helion and the future of our race, to abide by established principles and prove ourselves worthy citizens.

I was disappointed that an experience of such grandeur should end like this.

"We of Ak-helion represent a proud and noble race, my friends. Through the void of space our kind came in search of new, habitable planets, came from worlds more hospitable than ours, found Fortune, and settled. We overcame hardship, intemperate seasons, and hostile climes, to survive, and not only survive, but flourish. And yet . . ." the words rang out above our heads as he paused to stare at each one of us in turn, "and yet our ancestors had much to overcome, initially."

He paused again, and Nani found my hand and gripped. Involuntarily I reached out and clasped Kellor's hand. "This is it," I said. "The Truth."

"When our forbears made landfall in the starship," intoned the High Elder, "we were met with the opposition of not only the harsh seasons, the fire of summer and the ice of winter, but an even more uncompromising foe . . ."

He went on, and I heard his words, but so benumbed was my brain by the enormity of his address that I could take in barely half of what he said. "And before our ancestors could establish contact with the natives to assure them of our peaceful intentions, we were attacked. The natives were primitive by our standards, but they had the element of surprise and vast forces, and we almost succumbed. We lost many a colonist during that first terrible week, many specialist and scientist who would have made our existence on Fortune that much less hazardous . . ."

Nausea swelled in my belly, sickening me.

"That is why," he was saying, "our relations with the natives are limited and strictly controlled. How can we trust a race who once — millennia ago, granted — did its very best to annihilate our innocent ancestors?" The High Elder stared straight at us and asked, "How can we bring ourselves to trust the Blues?"

I felt dizzy. My pulse pounded in my ears. The High Elder spoke next of an oath of silence, and allegiance to the Church. One by one we moved to the front of the gathering, knelt and received his blessing, his hand upon our heads, and repeated the oath.

Then we found ourselves outside the ship, and filing away from the hallowed vessel, up the steps towards the city that was home, but which would never again be quite the same. I recall little of the return journey, save Kellor by my side, tears streaming down his face as he cursed the Blue-skinned barbarians of this planet. Those were his exact words, and I could tell from the reaction of the group that they shared his sentiments. Our initiation had achieved its aim: never again would we look upon a Blue in quite the same light.

Except . . . I loved Ki, and knew her for a caring, compassionate being.

There was a banquet thrown for the initiates at the college, to which families and friends were invited. I went through the motions of eating the lavish meal, listening to rousing speeches by government officials and Church Elders. It was as if we had been made one by the events of the initiation, that we were unified against adversity and future hardship — except that I felt truly apart and isolated. I listened to Kellor and Nani chatter about the bravery of our intrepid ancestors, and could take no more. At the first opportunity I excused myself from the company of my parents and friends, ostensibly going outside for fresh air, and then made my escape. In the cloakroom I found my skates and raced from the college building, across the city to Ki.

She was sitting alone, surrounded by packed crates and boxes, when I pushed into the room. She looked so forlorn, and I saw that she had been crying.

She stood and limped into my arms. "Jen," she said. "I have been thinking — considering our situation. Why don't you . . ." she paused, staring at me seriously, "why don't you come with me, to the city at the pole, and wait out summer there? It would be possible."

Something in my expression stopped her words. Go with her, I thought, go with her and live among the people who had once attacked my ancestors? How might I be received, a descendant of the invaders?

"Jen? Jen, what's wrong?"

I stared at her. Did she know? Was she aware of the events of the past that had so irrevocably divided our people?

"You don't know, do you?" I said. "They never told you."

She stared, wide-eyed. "Jen?"

I took a breath. "Today was the ceremony of initiation," I said. "Today I learned the Truth. I promised that I'd tell you . . ."

She raised a hand and touched my cheek. "Tell me what?" she asked in a small voice.

"Tell you what happened when we arrived on Fortune," I said, "what happened to our ancestors."

I recounted the events of the ceremony, what the High Elder told us about what had occurred all those terms ago. I was objective in my account of the initiation, showing her that, whatever might have happened in the past, I did not agree with the Church's chauvinistic reinforcement of enmity and xenophobia.

When I finished I looked into her eyes. "So how could I go with you, Ki — how would your people accept me?"

Her face slipped into an expression of infinite pity. She kissed my lips softly, then drew away and shook her head.

"Oh, Jen," she said. "Oh, my love, can't you see . . . ?"

I stared at her, taken aback. "What?"

"Jen, please listen to me." She pushed me on to the settee, sat down by my side. "This might be hard for you to accept, but please believe me. I wouldn't lie to you—you know that. I love you, and I would not tell you one single untruth." She took my face between her palms and said, "Jen, please believe me when I say that you, your people, did not arrive on Fortune aboard the starship."

I stared at her, trying to make sense of her words.

It came to me, then, with sudden insight.

Why had I been so blind? The glow-spheres, Ki's talk of superior technology . . . It was not we who had travelled through space aboard the ship, but the Blues.

Then I wondered if it might have been *we* who had attacked the space-faring Blues. . . .

Later, to atone for our collective guilt and to maintain the status quo of life in Ak-helion, had the Church initiated the lie of the initiation ceremony?

"You . . ." I said. "You came here aboard the starship?"

She stared at me, as if pitying my ignorance.

"Jen," she said, sadly. "Jen, both our races are native to this planet. We both evolved here."

I shook my head, confused. "But the ship," I cried. "It's out there. I saw it. If we didn't come in the ship, then who did?" I stopped.

"Who else?" she asked. "A third race, who call themselves Humans. It was they who came to Fortune aboard the starship."

My mind was reeling. "Humans?" I whispered. "But . . . but I always thought that we, that my people . . ."

She was shaking her head.

"How do you know this?" I asked in a feeble whisper. "Why didn't you tell me before?"

"Because my people are sworn to secrecy—we cannot tell you the truth of the past for fear of rekindling old enmities. Before the arrival of the starship, you people of the south were at war with us. You were a terrible warrior race . . ." She paused, then went on. "Then the Humans arrived. Their ship was failing and they had to make a forced landing—they would never have chosen to settle on Fortune if not for the failure of their ship's guidance systems. And then, Jen, your people attacked. You killed many of the Humans. Only six survived. We rescued them, took them to the sanctuary of our city in the north. How do you think we gained the knowledge to develop the technology we now possess? It was the Humans, Jen, who gave us that knowledge."

I sat in silence for a long time. At last I said. "But how can you be sure, Ki? How can you *know* for certain? I mean, it's all so confusing, it all happened so long ago—how can anyone be sure?"

She was watching me with compassion. "Because, in our northern city, two Humans still live with us."

"No!" I exclaimed. "That isn't possible! The starship landed millennia ago. How could they have survived?"

She took my hand. "Jen, they live much longer than we do. They live for thousands of terms. They live with us now, as free citizens, in the north." She paused, squeezing my hand. "Jen, listen to me—you cannot stay here in this city of lies and repression. A steam-wagon leaves in three hours. Come with me and learn the truth, Jen. Come with me to the north and meet the Humans for yourself."

I left Ki then, telling her that I needed time in which to think. I skated to the city wall and sat staring into the dark sky, at the Star growing in luminosity hour by hour. I considered the initiation ceremony, and the terrible lie I had learned there.

I thought of the summer that was coming to Fortune, the claustrophobic interment that my people would be forced to undergo to escape the merciless heat of the sun. I thought of Kellor and Nani, good people diminished by conditioned ignorance.

As the Star set slowly in the east, I left the city wall and made my way to where the steam-wagon was waiting in the boulevard.

Ki was standing beside its huge front wheel, her back to me, looking nervously along the street towards my parents' house.

"Ki," I said.

She turned with speed and fear, and stared at me. I saw that she had been crying. She opened her mouth to speak, but words would not come.

At last she managed, "Jen? Have you . . . ? Will you come with me?"

Until I heard those words, the desperation in her voice, I had been undecided. Or perhaps a part of me had known what I might do all along, but had been too fearful to acknowledge the fact.

To live so long in ignorance, and then to learn the truth, can be a terrible revelation.

Slowly, without a word, I reached out and took her hand. Then we boarded the steam-wagon and began the long journey north to the polar city of the Blues.

Thursday's Child

I CRESTED THE HILL, PULLED THE RANGE ROVER into the side of the lane, and stared through the windscreen. There was something about the freezing February landscape, with the westering sun laying a gold leaf patina over the snow-covered farmland in the valley bottom, that struck me as even more beautiful than the same scene in summer.

I took a deep breath and worked to control my anger. It was always the same when I collected Lucy from Marianne. I had to stop somewhere, calm myself.

I was on call for the next hour, but calculated that the chances of being summoned during that time were slight. Marianne would object to my early arrival, but Lucy would be eager to get away. I told myself that I arrived early on these occasions so that I'd have an extra hour with my daughter, but I wondered if, subconsciously, I did it on purpose to spite Marianne.

I started the engine and cruised down the hill. Three minutes later I entered the village of Hockton and pulled up outside a row of cottages, each one quaintly bonneted with a thick mantle of snow.

A light glowed behind the mullioned window of Marianne's front room. Lucy would be watching a DVD of her latest, favourite film.

I pressed the horn twice, my signal to Lucy that I was here, and climbed out.

Lucy had hauled the door open before I reached the gate, and only the fact that she was in her stockinged feet prevented her rushing out to meet me.

She was a beautiful skinny kid, six years old, with a pale, elfin face and long black hair. My heart always kicked at the sight of her, after an absence of days.

She seemed a little subdued today: usually she would launch herself into my arms. I stepped inside and picked her up, her long legs around my waist, and kissed her nose, lips, neck, in an exaggerated pantomime of affection which made her giggle.

"Love you," I said. "Bag packed?"

"Mmm."

"Where's your mum?"

"I think in the kitchen."

"Get your bag and put some shoes on. I'll just pop through and tell her I'm here."

She skipped into the front room and I moved towards the kitchen, a psychosomatic pain starting in my gut.

Marianne was peeling carrots at the draining board, her back to me. "You're early again, Daniel," she said without turning. She knew I disliked the long form of my name.

I leaned against the jamb of the door. "I was in the area, working."

She turned quickly, knife in her hand. "You mean to say you have a body with you?"

She was a small, pretty woman, an adult version of Lucy. In the early days of our separation, alternating with the anger, I had experienced a soul-destroying sorrow that all the love I'd felt for this woman had turned to hate.

Before our marriage, I should have seen what might have happened, extrapolated from her beliefs—but at the time my love for her had allowed no doubt.

Lately she had taken to wearing a big, wooden crucifix around her neck. Her left temple was not implanted and neither, thanks to her, was Lucy's.

"Not all my work involves collection," I said. "What time should I bring her back on Thursday?"

"I'm working till five." She turned and resumed her peeling.

I pushed myself away from the door and moved to the lounge. Lucy was sitting on the floor, forcing her feet into a pair of trainers. I picked up her bag and she ran into the kitchen for a good-bye kiss. Marianne, the bitch, didn't even come to the door to wave her off.

I led Lucy to the Range Rover and fastened her into the middle section of the back seat. When I started collecting her, a year ago, she had said that she wanted to sit in the front, next to me. "But why can't I?" she had wailed.

How could I begin to explain my paranoia? "Because it's safer in case of accidents," I'd told her.

I reversed into the drive, then set off along the road back to Welling, ten miles away over the moors.

"Enjoying your holidays?" I asked.

"Bit boring."

I glanced at her in the rearview mirror. "You okay?"

She hesitated. "Feeling a bit cough," she said, and to illustrate pantomimed a hacking cough into her right fist.

"Did mum take you to the doctor's?"

I saw her nod.

"And?" I asked.

"He gave me some pills."

"Pills?" I said. "What did he say was wrong?"

She looked away, through the window. "I don't know."

"Do you have the pills with you?" Perhaps I'd be able to determine her ailment from the medication.

She shook her head. "Mummy said I didn't need them."

I decided to ring Marianne when we got back, find out what was going on. Or was this yet another manifestation of my paranoia?

We drove on in silence for a while. Cresting the snow-covered moorland, we passed the glittering obelisk of the Onward Station. It never failed to provoke a feeling of awe in me—and I saw the Station every working day. Quite apart from what it represented, it was perhaps aesthetically the most beautiful object I had ever seen.

I wondered if it was the sight of it which prompted Lucy to say, "Daddy, the girls at school have been making fun of me."

I glanced at her. "Why's that?"

"It's because I'm not implanted. They say I'll die."

I shook my head, wondering how to respond. "They're just being silly," I said.

"But if I have an accident," she began.

"Don't worry," I said, marvelling at the fact that she was only six years old, and yet had worked out the consequences of not being implanted. "You won't have an accident."

Then she asked, "Why aren't I implanted?"

It was the first time she had ever mentioned the fact, and it was a while before I replied. "Because mum doesn't want you to be," I said.

"But *why* doesn't she?"

"I think you'd better ask her that yourself," I said, and left it at that. I changed the subject. "How about a meal at the Fleece when we get back? Would you like that?"

"Mmm," she said, without her usual enthusiasm for the idea, and fell silent.

We were a couple of miles from home when the onboard mobile rang. I cursed.

"Dan Chester here," I said, hoping the collection would be nearby.

"Dan." It was Masters, the Director at the Station. "I've just had a call from someone over in Bradley. This is most irregular. They've reported a death."

I slowed down, the better to concentrate. "I don't understand. Was the subject implanted?"

"Apparently so —"

"Then why didn't it register with you?"

"Exactly what I was wondering. That's why I want you to investigate. I'm sending a team from the Station straight away, but I thought that as you're in the area . . ."

I sighed. "Okay. Where is it?"

Masters relayed the address.

"Right. I'll be in touch when I've found out what's going on," I said, and cut the connection.

Bradley was only a mile or two out of my way. I could be there in ten minutes, sort out the problem in the same time, and be at the Fleece with a pint within the half hour.

I glanced back at Lucy. She was asleep, her head nodding with the motion of the Rover.

The Grange, Bradley Lower Road, turned out to be a Georgian house tucked away in a dense copse a mile down a treacherous, rutted track. The Range Rover negotiated the pot holes with ease, rocking back and forth like a fairground ride.

Only when the foursquare manse came into view, surrounded by denuded elm and sycamore, did I remember hearing that the Grange had been bought at a knockdown price a few years ago by some kind of New Age eco-community.

A great, painted rainbow decorated the façade of the building, together with a collection of smiley faces, peace symbols, and anarchist logos.

A motley group of men and women in their thirties had gathered on the steps of the front door, evidently awaiting my arrival. They wore dungarees and over-sized cardigans and sweaters; many of them sported dreadlocks.

Lucy was still sleeping. I locked the Rover and hurried over to the waiting group, a briefcase containing release forms and death certificates tucked under my arm.

A stout woman with a positive comet's tail of blonde dreads greeted me. I was pleased to see that she was implanted—as were, so far as a brief glance could tell me, most of the other men and women standing behind her. Some radical groups I'd heard of were opposed to the intervention of the Kéthani, and openly hostile to their representatives.

"Dan Chester," I said. "I'm the ferryman from the Station."

"Dan, I'm Marsha," the woman said. "Welcome to New Haven. I'll show you to . . ."

The press parted, and Marsha escorted me across a garishly painted hallway and down a corridor.

Marsha was saying, "Sanjay was against the resurrection process, Dan. We were surprised when he decided to be implanted, a couple of weeks ago."

I nodded, wondering again why the subject's death had failed to register at the Station.

Marsha paused outside a door, pushed it open, and stood back. I stepped over the threshold and stopped in my tracks.

Sanjay lay on a mattress in the corner of the room. He had opened the vein of his left arm all the way from the wrist to the crook of his elbow.

Blood had spurted up the far wall, across the window, and soaked into the mattress around the body.

"Billy found him about thirty minutes ago," Marsha was explaining. "We knew Sanjay was depressed, but we never thought . . ."

I took in the scene, and knew immediately that there was something not quite right about the corpse. By now the nano-mechs released by the implant should have been effecting repairs on the wound. The body should have the relaxed appearance of someone asleep, not the stone-cold aspect of a corpse.

I hurried over, knelt, and placed my finger-tips to the implant beneath the skin of the young man's left temple.

The implant should have emitted a definite vibration, similar to the contented purring of a cat. I felt nothing.

I glanced over my shoulder; Marsha and half a dozen others were watching him from the door. "If I could be left alone for a minute or two . . ." I said.

They retreated, closing the door behind them.

I pulled out my mobile and got through to Masters at the Station.

"Dan here," I said. "I'm with the subject. You're not going to believe this—he's implanted, but he's dead."

"That's impossible."

"Perhaps . . . I don't know. I've never heard of a malfunction before. But there's always a first time."

"No way," Masters said. "They can't go wrong."

"Well, it looks as though this one has." I paused. "What the hell should I do?"

"The team should be with you any minute. I've called the police in. They'll take over once they arrive."

I cut the connection, moved to the window and stared out, touching my own implant. I avoided another glance at the corpse, but I knew I would see the man's pained, brown face for a long time to come. He had been implanted, and had taken his own life, fully expecting to be resurrected to begin a new life among the stars . . . How had the implant failed him?

Five minutes later I watched another Range Rover draw up beside mine, followed by a police car. Four Station officials, led by Richard Lincoln, hurried across the snow-covered drive and up the steps, two constables in their wake.

A minute later Richard appeared at the door, along with the officials and the police officers.

"What the hell's going on, Dan?" Richard said.

"I wish I knew." I indicated the corpse and went though my findings. The other officials recorded my statement and took video footage of the room.

Richard questioned Marsha and a few of the others, while the Station officials fetched a container and eased the body inside.

I followed Richard outside and climbed into the Rover. Lucy was still asleep.

Richard tramped through the snow and I wound down the window. "We'll take the body back to the Station," he said, "try to find out what happened with the implant."

I looked beyond him, to the posse of communees on the steps of the Grange, silent and watchful.

"Has anyone told them?"

Richard shook his head. "I'll come back and explain the situation when we've found out exactly what happened. See you later, Dan."

I fired the engine and headed up the track. The Fleece beckoned. I considered a rich pint of Taylor's Landlord and a hot meal, and tried to forget about what I'd seen back at the Grange.

The Fleece was one of those horse-brass and beams establishments that had resisted the tide of modernisation sweeping the country. Norman, the landlord, had the twin assets of a good publican: friendliness and the ability to keep a good pint. The food wasn't bad, either.

It was seven o'clock by the time we settled ourselves in the bar room, a little too early for the regular Tuesday night crowd. I ordered myself a pint of Landlord and steak and kidney pie with roast potatoes, and for Lucy a fresh orange juice and chicken nuggets with chips.

The food arrived. Lucy was far from her lively self tonight; she was tired and hardly talked, answered my questions with monosyllabic replies and pushed her food around the plate with a distinct lack of interest.

I put my arm around her shoulders and pulled her towards me. "Home and an early night for you, m'girl."

"Can I watch TV for a bit before I go to bed? *Please.*"

"Okay, seeing as there's no school in the morning."

I was about to suggest we leave when Khalid pushed through the door, a swirl of snow entering with him, and signalled across to me. He mimed downing a pint and pointed at my empty glass. I relented and gave him the thumbs up.

No doubt Lucy would tell Marianne that I'd kept her at the pub way past her bedtime, and I wouldn't hear the last of it the next time I picked her up. Marianne thought alcohol the tipple of the devil, and all who drank it damned.

Khalid ferried two pints from the bar and sat down across the table from me.

"Hi, sleepy-bones," he said to Lucy. Her eyelids were fighting a losing battle against sleep.

"Just the man," Khalid said to me. "I hoped you'd be here."

"It's Tuesday night," I said. "What's wrong?"

"The implanted suicide you investigated today," he said.

Khalid Azzam was a junior doctor working at Bradley General; he looked after the Implant ward. I'd met him a couple of years ago when he moved to the village from Bradford. He and his wife Zara were regulars on Tuesday nights.

"Masters contacted you?" I asked.

"They brought the body in and I inspected the implant."

I voiced what I'd been dreading since discovering the dead man. "It malfunctioned?" I asked, hard though that was to believe.

"Malfunctioned?" Khalid shook his head and accounted for the top two inches of his pint. He sighed with satisfaction. "I'd say that was well nigh impossible."

"So . . . ?"

"This is only the second case I've come across, but I've heard rumours that they're more widespread than we first believed."

He took another mouthful.

"What," I said, unable to stop myself smiling, "is more widespread?"

"This is between you and me, okay? Don't tell Masters I said anything. Your people at the Station have yet to come out with an official statement." He saw that I was about to jump in with the obvious question, and raised a hand. "Okay, okay . . ." He leaned forward, a little melodramatically—only Old Wilf was at the bar, and he was stone deaf. "Some cowboys have started pirating fake implants."

I lowered my pint and stared at him. "Why on Earth . . . ?" I began.

"It was only a matter of time," Khalid said. "Think about it. There are thousands of people out there who refuse for whatever reasons to be implanted—" his eyes flickered, almost imperceptibly, towards Lucy. "They're . . . what . . . one in a few hundred thousand? A minority, anyway. And like any minority, they occasionally suffer victimisation. Wouldn't it be easier, they reckon, if they could have something that looks like, but wasn't, an implant? They'd blend in, become one of the crowd. They would no longer stand out."

"It makes sense," I said. "And so some enterprising back-street surgeon has started offering the service?"

"Doesn't have to be a surgeon. Anyone with a little medical knowledge can perform the operation. A quick slit, insert something the same shape as an implant, and seal the wound with synthiflesh. Thirty minutes later you're back out on the street."

I thought through the implications. "But if these people don't inform friends, loved ones?"

He was nodding. "Exactly. Like today. Sanjay's friends thought he was implanted, and fully expected him to be resurrected."

"Christ," I said, "the whole thing's tragic."

"And there are thousands of people going around out there with these fake, useless implants. Masters said something about a law to make them illegal. He's talking to a few politicians tomorrow."

Lucy had stretched out on the seat next to me and was snoring away. Had she been awake and bored, guilt might have driven me homeward. As it was, I owed Khalid a pint, and at that very second Ben Knightly dashed in from the snowstorm that was evidently raging outside. I was off work for a couple of days, and I could treat myself to a lie-in in the morning.

I pointed to Khalid's empty glass. "Another?"

"You've twisted my arm."

I bought another round. Ben joined us and we stopped talking shop.

It was another hour, and two more pints, before conscience got the better of me. I refused all offers of more beer, eased the still sleeping Lucy into my arms, and carried her from the bar and along the street.

The cold had awoken her by the time I pushed through the front door. I carried her to her room, where she changed into her pyjamas. Five minutes later she was snuggling into my lap before the fire and we were watching a DVD of a French mime act, which apparently was the latest craze in kids' entertainment.

She was asleep ten minutes later, and I turned down the sound and switched over to a news programme. Half awake myself, and cradling my daughter in my arms, I allowed a succession of images to wash over me and considered how lucky I was.

So I might have married the last religious zealot in North Yorkshire, but from that match made in Hell had issued Lucy Katia Chester. And to think that, back in my twenties, I'd vowed never to have children. I sometimes shudder to think of the joy I would have missed had I stuck to my bachelor principles.

A newscaster was reporting anti-Kéthani riots in Islamabad, but by then I was fading fast.

I took Lucy to Bolton Abbey the following day. I bundled her up in her chunky pink parka, bobble hat, and mittens against the biting cold, and we walked through the trees along the riverbank. Down below, the river was frozen for the first time in living memory, its usually quicksilver torrent paused in shattered slabs of grey and silver. Later we lobbed snowballs at each other among the stark ruins of the Abbey. It was quiet—no one else had dared to venture out, with the thermometer ten below zero—and to hear her laughter echoing in the stillness was a delight. I had quite forgotten to ring Marianne last night, to enquire about Lucy's illness, but she seemed fine today so I decided not to bother.

We had lunch in the Devonshire Arms across the road from the Abbey, and in the afternoon visited Marsworld, a couple of miles north of Skipton. We wandered around the replica rockets that had carried the scientific team to the red planet a couple of years ago, then visited mock-ups of the dozen domes where the explorers were living right at that moment. I had worried that Lucy might find it boring, but she turned out to be fascinated; she'd had lessons about the mission at school, and actually knew more about it than I did.

We drove home through the narrow lanes at four, with dusk rapidly falling. I proceeded with a caution I would not have shown had I been alone: I carried a precious cargo on the back-seat . . . The only time I was truly content, and could rest easy, was when Lucy was with me: at other times, I envisaged, perhaps unfairly, the unthinking neglect with which Marianne might treat her.

"Do you know what would be nice, daddy?" Lucy said now.

"What?" I asked, glancing at her in the rearview.

"I would really like it if you and mummy would live together again."

She had said this before, and always I had experienced a hopeless despair. I would have done anything to secure my daughter's happiness, but this was one thing that I could not contemplate.

"Lucy, we can't do that. We have our separate lives now."

"Don't you love mummy anymore?"

"Not in the same way that I once did," I said.

"But a little bit?" she went on.

I nodded. "A little bit," I lied.

She was quiet for a time, and then said, "Why did you move away, daddy? Was it because of me?"

I slowed and looked at her in the mirror. "Of course not. What made you think—?"

"Mummy said that you stopped loving her because you couldn't agree about me," she said.

I gripped the wheel, anger welling. I might have hated the bitch, but I had kept that animosity to myself. Never once had I attempted to turn Lucy against her mother.

"That's not true, Lucy. We disagreed about a lot of things. What you've got to remember is that we both love you more than anything else, okay?"

We underestimate children's capacity for not being fobbed off with platitudes. Lucy said, "But the biggest thing you disagreed about was me, wasn't it? You wanted me to be implanted, and mummy didn't."

I sighed. "That was one of the things."

"Mummy says that God doesn't want people to be implanted. If we're implanted, then we don't go to heaven. She says that the aliens are evil—she says that they're in the same football league as the Devil."

I smiled to myself. I just wanted to take Lucy in my arms and hug her to me. I concentrated on that, rather than the anger I felt towards Marianne.

"That isn't true," I said. "God made everyone, even the Kéthani. If you're implanted, then you don't die. Eventually you can visit the stars, which I suppose is a kind of heaven."

She nodded, thinking about this. "But if I die, then I'll go to a different heaven?" she asked at last.

If you die without the implant, I thought, you will remain dead forever and ever, amen, and no Christian sky-god will effect your resurrection.

"That's what your mum thinks," I said.

She was relentless with her dogged, six-year-old logic. "But what do you think, daddy?"

"I think that in twelve years, when you're eighteen, you can make up your own mind. If you want, you can be implanted then." Twelve years, I thought: they seemed like an eternity.

"Hey," I said, "we're almost home. What do you want for dinner? Will you help me make it?"

"Spaghetti!" she cried, and for the rest of the journey lectured me on the proper way to make bolognese sauce.

That evening, after we'd prepared spaghetti together and eaten it messily in front of the TV, Lucy slept next to me and I tried to concentrate on a documentary about ancient Egypt.

I could not erase memories of Marianne from my mind's eye.

I had met her ten years ago, when I was thirty. She was twenty-six, and I suspected that I was her very first boyfriend. At that time her Catholicism had intrigued me, her moral and ethical codes setting her apart in my mind from the hedonism I saw all around. The Kéthani had arrived the year before, and their gift of the implants had changed society forever: in the early days, many people adopted a devil-may-care attitude towards life—they were implanted, they could not die, so why not live for the day? Others opposed the changes.

I was implanted within a year of the Kéthani's arrival. I was not religious, and had always feared extinction: it had seemed the natural thing to do to accept the gift of immortality, especially after the first returnees arrived back on Earth with the stories of their resurrection.

Not long after my implantation, I trained to become a ferry-man—and but for this I might never have met Marianne. Her mother, an atheist and implanted, had died unexpectedly of a cerebral haemorrhage, and I had collected the body.

I had been immediately attracted to Marianne's physicality, and found her worldview—during our many discussions in the weeks that followed our first date—intriguing, if absurd.

She thought the Kéthani evil, the implantation process an abomination in the eyes of the Lord, and looked forward to the day when she would die and join the virtuous in heaven.

She was appalled by my blithe acceptance of what I took to be our alien saviours.

We were married six months after our first meeting.

I was in love, whatever I thought that meant at the time. I loved her so much that I wanted to save her. It was only a matter of time, I thought, before she came to see that my acceptance of the Kéthani was sane and sensible.

She probably thought the reverse: given time, her arguments would bring about my religious salvation.

We had never spoken about what we might do if we had children. She was a successful accountant for a firm in Leeds, and told me that she did not want children. She claimed that Lucy was a mistake, but I'd often wondered since whether she had intended conceiving a child, and whether she had consciously planned what followed.

During the course of her pregnancy, I refrained from raising the topic of implants, but a couple of days after Lucy was born I presented the implantation request form to Marianne for her signature.

She would not sign, and of course, because both our signatures were required, Lucy could not undergo the simple operation to ensure her continual life.

We remained together for another year, and it was without doubt the worst year of my life. We argued, I accused my wife of terrible crimes in the name of her mythical god, while she called me an evil blasphemer. Our positions could not be reconciled. My love for Lucy grew in direct proportion to my hatred of Marianne. We separated at the end of the year, though Marianne, citing her religious principles, would not grant me a divorce.

I saw Lucy for two or three days a week over the course of the next five years, and the love of my daughter sustained me, and at the same time drove me to the edge of sanity, plagued continually by fear and paranoia.

That night, in the early hours, Lucy crept into my bed and snuggled up against me, and I dozed, utterly content.

We slept in late the following morning, lunched at the Fleece, and then went for a long walk. At five we set off for Hockton, Lucy quiet in the back seat.

I led her from the Range Rover to the front door, where I knelt and stroked a tress of hair from her face. I kissed her. "See you next week, poppet. Love you."

She hugged me and, as always, I had to restrain myself from weeping.

She hurried into the house and I left without exchanging a word with Marianne.

I threw myself into my work for the next five days. We were busy; Richard Lincoln was away on holiday for a week, and I took over his workload. I averaged half a dozen collections a day, ranging across the length and breadth of North Yorkshire.

Tuesday night arrived, and not a day too soon; I was due to pick up Lucy in the morning and keep her for the duration of my three day break. I celebrated with a few pints among congenial company at the Fleece. The regulars were present: Khalid and Rizwana, Ben Knightly, Jeff Morrow, and Richard Lincoln, the latter just back that day from the Bahamas with a tan to prove it.

It was midnight by the time I made my way home, and there was a message from Marianne on the answer-phone. Would I ring her immediately about tomorrow?

Six pints to the good, I had no qualms about ringing her when she might be in bed.

In the event, she answered the call with disconcerting alacrity. "Yes?"

"Dan here," I said. "I got the message."

"It's about Lucy. I wouldn't bother coming tomorrow. She came down with something and she'll be in bed for a couple of days."

"What's wrong?" I asked, fear gripping me by the throat.

"It's nothing serious. The doctor came, said something about a virus."

"I'll come anyway," I said. "I want to see her."

"Don't bother," Marianne said. "I really don't want to have you over here if it isn't absolutely necessary."

"I couldn't give a damn about what you want!" I said. "I want to see Lucy. I'm coming over."

But she had slammed down the receiver, leaving me talking to myself.

I considered phoning back, but didn't. It would only show her how angry I was. I'd go over in the morning anyway, whether she liked it or not.

A blizzard began just as I set off, and the road over the moors to Hockton was treacherous. It took me almost an hour to reach the village, and it was after eleven by the time I pulled up outside Marianne's cottage.

I fully expected her not to answer the door, but to my surprise she pulled it open after the first knock. "Oh," she said. "It's you."

I stepped past her. "Where's Lucy?"

She indicated the stairs with a plastic beaker full of juice. I climbed to Lucy's room, Marianne following.

"Daddy!" Lucy called out when I entered. She was sitting up in bed, a colouring book on her lap. She looked thin and pale.

I sat on the bed and took her hand. Marianne passed her the beaker of juice. I looked up at her. "What did the doctor say?"

She shrugged. She was hugging herself, and looked pinched and mean, resentful of my presence. "He just said it was a virus, that it would pass in a few days. Nothing to worry about."

"What about medication?"

"He suggested Calpol if her temperature rose."

She retreated to the door, watching me. I turned to Lucy and squeezed her hand. "How are you feeling, poppet?"

Her head against the pillow, she smiled bravely. "Bit sick," she said.

I looked up. Marianne was still watching me. "If you'd give us a few minutes alone . . ."

Reluctantly she withdrew.

I winked at Lucy. "You'll be better in no time," I said.

"Will I have to have more tests, daddy?"

"I don't know. What did the doctor say when he came?"

She shook her head. "He didn't come here. Mummy took me to the hospital. A doctor needled me and took some blood."

A hollow sensation opened up in my stomach. I smiled inanely. "What did the doctor say, Lucy? Can you remember what the doctor told mummy?"

She pulled a face in concentration. "They said something about my blood. It wasn't good enough. I think they said they might have to take it all out and put some new blood in. Then another doctor said something about my bones. I might need an operation on my bones."

My vision swam. My heart hammered.

"Was this at the hospital in Bradley?" I asked her.

She shook her head. "Mummy took me to Leeds."

"Can you remember which hospital?"

She made her concentrating face. "It was a hospital for army people," she said.

I blinked. "What?"

"I think the sign said General," she said.

"Leeds General," I said. "Was that it?"

She nodded. I squeezed her hand. My first impulse was to go downstairs and confront Marianne, find out just what the hell was going on.

Lucy had something wrong with her blood, and might need an operation on her bones . . . A bone marrow transplant, for chrissake?

I tried not to jump to the obvious conclusion.

I remained with Lucy a further thirty minutes, read her a book and then chatted about nothing in particular for a while, all the time my mind racing.

By noon, I had decided what to do. I leaned forward and kissed her. "I've got to go now, Lucy. I'll pop in and see you tomorrow, okay?"

I hurried from the room and down the stairs. I paused before the living room door, but didn't trust myself to confront Marianne just yet. I left the cottage and drove home through the snowstorm.

For the next half hour I ransacked the house for the photo-copy of Lucy's birth certificate, and my passport, for identification purposes. Then I set off again, heading towards Leeds.

It was almost three before I pulled into the bleak car-park in the shadow of the towerblock buildings. At reception I explained the situation and requested to see someone in charge. The head registrar examined my documents and spoke in hushed tones to someone in a black suit.

Thirty minutes later I was shown into the waiting room of a Mr Chandler, and told by his secretary that he would try to fit me in within the hour.

At four-thirty the secretary called my name and, heart thumping, I stepped into the consulting room.

Mr Chandler was a thin-faced, grey-haired man in his late fifties. The bulge of an implant showed at his left temple.

THURSDAY'S CHILD   **41**

He was examining a computer flat-screen on his desk, and looked up when I entered. We shook hands.

"Mr Chester," he said. "According to my secretary, you haven't been informed of your daughter's condition?"

"I'm separated from my wife. We're not exactly on speaking terms."

"This is highly irregular," he muttered to himself.

I resisted the urge to tell him that Marianne was a highly irregular woman. "Can you tell me what's wrong with my daughter, Mr Chandler?"

He consulted his files, lips pursed.

"Lucy was diagnosed one month ago as having contracted leukaemia . . ." He went on, and I heard him say that the type she was suffering from was pernicious and incurable, but it was as if I had suddenly been plucked from this reality, as if I were experiencing the events in the consulting room at a remove of miles. I seemed to have possession of my body only by remote control.

"Incurable?" I echoed.

"I'm sorry. Of course, if your daughter were implanted . . ."

I stared at him. "Don't you think I know that?" I said. "Why the hell do you think my damned wife kept her condition quiet?"

He looked away. "I'm sorry."

"Is there nothing you can do? I mean, surely under the Hippocratic oath . . . ?"

He was shaking his head. "Unfortunately I've been in this situation before, Mr Chester. It requires the consent of *both* legal guardians to allow the implantation process to be undertaken in the case of minors. I'm quite powerless to intervene, as much as I sympathise with your predicament."

I worked to calm myself, regulate my breathing. "How long might Lucy . . . ?" I began.

He said, "As things stand, perhaps one month. You see, since the advent of the Kéthani, the funding once spent on research into terminal diseases has been drastically cut back."

I listened, but heard nothing. Ten minutes later I thanked him and moved from the room in a daze.

I have no recollection whatsoever of leaving the hospital and driving away from Leeds. I recall isolated incidents: a traffic jam on the York road, passing a nasty accident on the road to Bradley, and almost skidding from the lane myself a mile outside Hockton.

Then I was parked outside Marianne's cottage, gripping the

wheel and going over and over the words I would use in an attempt to make her agree to save our daughter's life.

At last I left the Rover and hurried up the path. I had the curious sensation of being an actor on stage, and that, if I fluffed my lines now, the consequences would be dire.

I didn't bother knocking, but opened the front door and moved down the hall.

Marianne was in the living room. She sat in her armchair, legs drawn up beneath her. She was hugging herself as if cold.

"I've been to the hospital," I said. "I talked with Chandler . . ."

She looked up, showing no surprise.

Heart thumping, I sat in the armchair opposite and stared at her. "We've got to talk about this," I said. "There's more at stake than our principles or beliefs."

She looked away. She was fingering her damned crucifix. "You mean, you want me to sacrifice my principles and beliefs in order to satisfy your own?"

I leaned forward, almost insensible with rage. "I mean," I said, resisting the urge to launch myself at her, "that if we do nothing, then Lucy will be dead. Does that mean anything to you? She'll be bloody well dead!"

"Don't you think I don't know that? This isn't easy for me, you know."

I shook my head. "I don't see how you can have a moment's hesitation. The simple fact is, if you don't agree to the implantation, then Lucy will die. We won't have any second chances, no opportunity to regret. She'll be dead."

"And if I agree, I'll be damning her in the eyes of God."

I closed my eyes, controlled my breathing. I looked at her. I could not help myself, but I was crying. "Please, Marianne, for Lucy's sake."

She shook her head. "I don't know . . . I've been thinking about nothing else. I need time."

I gave a panicky nod at the thought that she might be relenting. "Chandler said she had a month, but who knows? We need to make a decision pretty damned quickly."

She stared at me, her face ashen. "I need time to think, Dan. You can't pressure me into this."

I wiped away the tears. "Lucy is all we have left, Marianne. We don't have each other anymore. Lucy is everything."

This, so far as I recall, was the gist of the exchange; I have a feeling it went on for longer, with clichés from both sides bandied back and forth, to no definite conclusion. The last thing I did before leaving the house was to climb the stairs to Lucy's bedroom, kneel beside the bed and watch my daughter as she slept.

I arrived home around midnight and, unable to sleep, stared at a succession of meaningless images passing before me on the TV screen.

I slept on the settee until ten o'clock the next morning, then showered and tried to eat breakfast. Between ten-thirty and midday I must have phoned Marianne a dozen times. She was either out, or not answering.

At one o'clock, the phone rang, startling me. Shaking, I lifted the receiver. "Hello?"

"Daniel?"

"Marianne?"

A silence, then, "Daniel. I have a form you need to sign."

"My God, you mean—?"

"I'll be in all afternoon," she said, and replaced the receiver.

I drove to Hockton, crying all the way. I pulled up before the cottage and dried my eyes, at once grateful for the decision Marianne had come to, and yet resentful that she had made me so pathetically indebted to her.

I hurried up the path, knocked, and entered. Marianne was in her usual armchair. A slip of paper sat on the coffee table before her. I sat down and read through the release form. She had already appended her signature on the dotted line at the foot of the page. Fumbling, I pulled a pen from my pocket and signed my name below hers.

I looked up. Marianne was watching me. "You won't regret this, Marianne," I said.

"I've made an appointment for the implant. I'm taking her in at one tomorrow."

I nodded. "I'll drop by to see her after work, okay?"

"Whatever . . ."

I made my way upstairs. Lucy was sitting up in bed. Intoxicated, I hugged her to me, smothering her in kisses. I stayed an hour, talking, reading her books, laughing . . .

When I made my way downstairs, Marianne was still in her armchair in the lounge. The room was in darkness.

I said goodbye before I left, but she did not respond.

It was six by the time I arrived home, and I dropped into the Fleece for a celebratory meal and a pint or three.

Khalid was there, along with Richard and Ben, and three pints turned to six as I told them the news: that, first, Lucy was going to be implanted, and second, that she was suffering from a terminal illness. My friends were a little unsure how to respond, then took my line and decided to celebrate.

It was well past one when I staggered home, and I had a raging headache all the next day at work. Fortunately, with Richard back from the Bahamas the workload was not intense, and I was finished by four.

I returned home, showered and changed, and then made my way over the moors to Hockton.

The cottage door was locked, and I thought at first that perhaps they had not returned. Then it struck me that, perhaps, Marianne had gone back on her word, decided not to take Lucy to the hospital . . .

Then the door opened.

"How is she?" I asked, pushing past Marianne and making my way upstairs.

Marianne followed me into Lucy's room. She was lying flat out, staring at the ceiling. She looked exhausted.

She beamed when she saw me. "Daddy, look. Look what I've got!"

Her small fingers traced the implant at her temple. I looked up; Marianne pushed herself away from the door and went downstairs.

I pulled Lucy to me—she seemed no more than a bundle of skin and bone—and could not stop myself from crying. "I love you," I whispered.

"Love you, too," Lucy replied, then said, "Now that I have the implant, daddy, will God love me as well?"

I lay her down, gently, and smiled. "I'm sure he will, poppet," I said.

Later, as she slept, I stroked her hair and listened to the words of the rhyme in my head: *Monday's child is fair of face, Tuesday's child is full of grace, Wednesday's child is full of woe, Thursday's child has far to go* . . .

I made my way downstairs. Marianne was in the kitchen, washing dishes.

I leaned against the jamb.

"You've made the right decision, Marianne." I said.

She turned and stared at me. "You don't know how difficult it was, Daniel," she said, without meeting my eyes, and turned back to the dishes.

I said goodbye, left the cottage and drove home.

Lucy went downhill rapidly after that.

The next time she stayed with me, she spent most of the entire two days in bed, listless and apathetic, and too drugged up even to talk much or play games. I told her that she was ill but that in time she would recover, and she gave a brave smile and squeezed my fingers.

During the course of the last two weeks, Marianne and I took time off work and nursed her at home, looking after her for alternating periods of two days.

At one point, Lucy lowered the book she was reading and stared at me from the sofa. "If I die," she said, "will the aliens take me away and make me better again?"

I nodded. "If that happens, you mustn't be frightened, okay? The Kéthani will take good care of you, and in six months you'll come back home to mum and me."

She smiled to herself. "I wonder what the aliens look like?"

Two days before Lucy died, she was admitted to Bradley General, and I was with her until the end.

She was unconscious, and dosed with pain killers. She had lost a lot of weight and looked pitifully thin beneath the crisp hospital sheets.

I held her hand during the first day and well into the night, falling asleep in my chair and waking at dawn with cramps and multiple aches. Marianne arrived shortly after that and sat with Lucy. I took the opportunity to grab a bite to eat.

On the evening of the second day, Lucy's breathing became uneven. A doctor murmured to Marianne and me that she had only a matter of hours to live.

Marianne sat across the bed from me, gripping her daughter's hand and weeping. After an hour, she could take no more.

She stood and made for the door.

"Marianne . . . ?" I said.

"I'm sorry. This is too much. I'm going."

"This is just the start," I said. "She isn't truly dying, Marianne."

She looked at me. "I'm sorry Dan," she said, and hurried out.

I returned to my vigil. I stared at my daughter, and thought of the time, six months hence, when she would be returned to me, remade. Glorious years stretched ahead.

I thought of Marianne, and her inability to see it through to the end. I was struck, then, by a thought so terrible that I was ashamed that it had occurred to me.

I told myself that I was being paranoid, that even Marianne could not do such a thing. But once the seed of doubt had been planted, it would not be eradicated.

What if I were right, I asked myself? I had to be sure. I had to know for certain.

Beside myself with panic, I fumbled with my mobile and somehow found Khalid's number.

The dial tone purred for an age. I swore at him to reply, and at last he did.

"Hello?"

"Khalid, thank god! Where are you?"

"Dan? I'm just leaving the hospital."

"Khalid, I need your help." I explained the situation, my fear. "Please, will you come over?"

There was no hesitation. "Of course. I'm on my way." He cut the connection.

He seemed to take aeons to arrive, but only two minutes elapsed before his neat, suited figure appeared around the door. He hurried over, concern etched on his face.

"I need to be sure, Khalid. It might be okay, but I need to know."

He nodded. "Fine. You don't need to explain yourself, Dan. I understand."

He moved around the bed, and I watched in silent desperation. He pulled something from his inside pocket, a device like a miniature mobile phone, and stabbed a code into the keypad.

Then he glanced at me, stepped towards Lucy, and applied the device to the implant at her temple.

He read something from the tiny screen, and shock invaded his expression. He slumped into the seat which minutes before my wife had occupied, and he said something, rapidly, in Urdu.

"Khalid?" I almost wept.

He was shaking his head, staring at me. "Dan, it's a fake. It's a fake!"

I nodded. I felt very cold. I pressed my hands to my cheeks and stared at him. I wanted to throw up, but I hadn't eaten anything for half a day. Bile rose in my throat. I swallowed it with difficulty.

"Khalid," I said. "You've got to help me."

"Dan . . ." It was a plea to make me understand the impossibility of what I was asking him.

"How long does an implantation take?" I asked. "Thirty minutes? We have time. If you can get an implant, make the cut . . ."

I realised, as I was speaking, that I was weeping, pleading with him through my tears.

"Dan, we need the signatures of both parents. If anyone found out . . ."

I recalled, then, the consent form which I had signed two weeks ago. My heart skipped at the sudden thought that there had existed a form bearing both our signatures . . . But for how long, before Marianne had destroyed it?

I said, "What's more important, Khalid? Your job or Lucy's life?"

He shook his head, staring at me. "You can't blackmail me, Dan! Marianne doesn't want this. I'm not saying that what she did was right, but you've got to understand that there are laws to obey."

"Sod the fucking laws!" I yelled. "We're talking about the life of my daughter, Khalid."

My mobile rang, and I snatched it from my pocket. "What?"

"Mr Daniel Chester?"

"What do you want? Who is it?"

The woman said her name. I cannot recall it now, but she was a police officer. "If you could make your way to Hockton police station . . ." she was saying.

I laughed at the absurdity of the situation. "Listen, I'm at Bradley hospital with my daughter. She's dying, and if you think for a second that I'm leaving her—"

"I'm sorry, Mr Chester. We'll be over right away." She cut the connection.

I sat down and gripped Lucy's hand. I looked up, across the bed at Khalid. "If this were your daughter, in this situation, what would you do? All it would take is a quick cut. Replace the implant with a genuine one."

He was shaking his head, tears tracking down his cheeks.

"For chrissake," I hissed. "We're alone. No one would see."

"Dan, I'd need to do paperwork, make a requisition order for an implant. They're all numbered, accounted for. If one went missing . . ."

I stared at him. I am not proud of what I said then, but I was driven by desperation. "You could replace the genuine implant with this fake," I said, gesturing towards Lucy.

He stared at me in shock, and only then did I realise what I'd asked him to do.

"Mr Chester?"

The interruption was unwelcome. A small, Asian WPC stood by the door. A constable, who appeared about half my age, accompanied her.

"What the hell?" I began.

"Mr Chester, it's about your wife, Marianne Chester."

"What?" I said, my stomach turning.

"If you'd kindly step out here . . ."

In a daze I left my seat and accompanied the police officers into the corridor. They escorted me to a side room, where we could be alone.

I sat down, and the WPC sat opposite me, on the end of the chair. The juvenile constable remained by the door, avoiding my eyes.

"Mr Chester," the woman said, "I'm sorry to inform you that your wife was found dead a little under one hour ago. A neighbour noticed the front door open. I'm sorry. It appears that she took her own life."

I stared at her. "What?" I said, though I had heard her clearly enough.

I've since learned that police officers are prepared to repeat bad news to people in shock. Patiently, kindly, she told me again.

Marianne was dead. What she had done to my daughter, what she had done to me, had been too much of a burden to bear. She had taken her own life. I understood the words, but not the actuality of what she had done.

I nodded, stood and moved from the room. I returned to Lucy's room. Khalid was still there, seated beside the bed, clutching my daughter's hand and quietly crying.

I sat down and told him what had happened.

One of the joys of being a father is not only the wonder of the moment, the love one feels for one's child every minute of every day, but contemplation of the future. How long had I spent daydreaming about the girl Lucy would be at the age of thirteen, and then at eighteen, on the verge of womanhood? I saw myself with her when she was twenty, and thirty, sharing her life, loving her. Such pre-emptive "memories," as it were, are one of the delights of fatherhood.

One hour later, Lucy died.

I was holding her hand, listening to her stertorous breathing and to the regular pulse of the cardiogram. Then her breathing hiccupped, rattled, and a second later the cardiogram flatlined, maintaining an even, continuous note.

I looked across at Khalid, and he nodded.

I reached out and touched the implant at her temple, the implant which Khalid had installed thirty minutes ago when, as Lucy's sole remaining parent, I had signed the consent form. The implant purred beneath my fingertips, restoring my daughter to life.

Presently a ferryman arrived and, between us, we lifted Lucy into the container, which we do not call coffins. Before she was taken away, I kissed her forehead and told her that I would be there to welcome her back in six months.

Later, I left the hospital and drove to Hockton, where I called in at the police station and read the note which Marianne had left. It was sealed in a cellophane folder, and I could not take it away with me.

Dear Dan, I read, *Please forgive me. You will never understand. I know I have done the right thing by saving Lucy from the Kéthani, even though what I have done to you is unforgivable. Also, what I am about to do to myself. It's enough to know that Lucy is saved, even if I am damned by my actions.*

Marianne.

I left the police station and drove on to the moors overlooking the towering obelisk of the Onward Station. It rose in the moonlight like a pinnacle of ice, and, as I climbed from the Rover and watched, the first of that evening's energy beams pulsed from its summit and arced through the stratosphere. Thus the dead of Earth were transmitted to the Kéthani starship waiting high above.

Thursday's child has far to go . . .

I stared up at the massed stars overhead, thought of Lucy, and gave thanks.

Ascent of Man

HE HAD ONLY A VAGUE MEMORY OF HIS BIRTH.
He recalled, fleetingly, the dizzy rush of sensory impressions
that greeted his arrival in the world: the slippery spurt of his exit,
his mother's cradling lower limbs, and then the entry into his mind
of the thousand voices. They were frightening and contradictory at
first; only later, with the passing of time and the gaining of experience, would he learn to categorise the importance of the voices,
ignore some and take note of others.

Blindly, even the dim light too strong for his newborn eyes, he
had sought purchase on his mother's legs, and then found the torso
of the person he presumed was his father. With gentle coaxing from
both, he took hold of a fleshy flank offered by one of them, and
suckled.

He felt the fingers of strangers probing his body, and heard in
his mind the welcoming words of people he later learned were
neighbours: close family and singletons adopted by the family.

"Greetings!" was the overwhelming thought. "Rejoice at new
life entering the world, for without new life there would be no
world!"

He settled down, thrilled by the attention, both physical and
mental, of those around him. In time he opened his eyes, and
beheld the wonder of his surroundings. He saw the great, munifi-

cent curve of his mother's belly, and pressed against it his father's frail lower limbs. To his immediate right were the etiolated forms of his direct family members, their flesh packed around him in tight and reassuring proximity. Only chinks of light glimmered through the family mass from above.

He thrived and grew. He alternated between sleep and learning, his life demarcated by the regularity of the feeding cycles. He sustained himself from three main sources: his mother, of course; his father, less regularly, and from the swollen flank of a woman — no family member, this, but a singleton taken in by the family many cycles ago. With difficulty he would squirm about until his prehensile lips gained hold on whoever was offering nourishment. Once, he himself gave succour. He felt lips roving over his belly, and although he knew that this was wrong, nevertheless he acceded, and the mouth from below latched on and sucked.

Seconds later the family gave vent to a great indignant blast of outrage, and the illegal feeder yelped mentally and squirmed away.

He was reprimanded, denied two cycles of food, and thus learned his lesson.

When not sleeping, he ate and learned. His father filtered the superficial thoughts from all those around him and directed into his mind those thoughts he considered edifying and worthwhile.

He marvelled at abstruse philosophies and mathematics; he wrestled with concepts way beyond the grasp of his puny infant's mind, angered at the gentle mocking humour in the thoughts of those around him.

The cycles passed, turned into mega-cycles.

He developed an aptitude for the theory of non-spatial geometry, and applied himself to the discipline.

Like this, lost in the thoughts of minds older and much wiser than his own, minds located half a world away, he grew to maturity and gained respect.

He lost his child's fascination with the physical aspect of his environment: what little his feeble eyes showed him, in the even feebler light filtering down from above, soon bored his febrile and probing imagination. The geography of packed and pressed flesh which circumscribed his dwelling place, a close horizon of fleshy protuberances, limbs and torsos and heads forming a panorama of limited variation, paled beside the vertiginous wonder offered by the free-ranging thoughts of the world's finest thinkers.

From time to time, though, as light relief from the wearying study of his discipline, he tapped into the thoughts of those individuals concerned with entirely different pursuits. He entertained himself with the images conjured by story-tellers and fabulists, by artists and musicians. He whiled away free hours listening to mindsongs, and marvelling at stories told by his favourite entertainers, the historians.

Oh, the fabulous tales they had to tell!

Immediately after study, his mind still ringing with the convoluted concepts of his calling, he sought out the school of past-tellers who captivated millions around the world with stories of How Things Once Were.

Of course, these stories were merely inventions, fictions produced to while away idle cycles . . . They could have no basis in fact, though some past-tellers vouchsafed their accuracy, and quoted learned thinkers to back the veracity of their tales. They claimed that things were not always as they were now, that change over vast epochs had resulted in this, the first truly fair and equable society, an era in which Humankind had at last learned to exist in harmony and peace.

But some of the tales they told were of the eras which preceded this, Humankind's Golden Age.

He had listened to them all, over the mega-cycles—had even strained his mind to search out the furthest and quietest of voices. His favourite tale—surely apocryphal?—was told by a shunned and limited guild of past-tellers who dwelled at the very northern pole of the planet. He had stumbled quite accidentally upon their muted musings when a mere infant, and over the mega-cycles had listened, awed, as their speculations developed and became ever more incredible.

They spoke of a time, many multi-mega-cycles before this one, which was so radically different to the world he knew that he had great difficulty in visualising how it might have been.

They spoke of a time in which Humankind did not encompass the world with their fleshy munificence. According to the past-tellers, the world then had been inhabited by only a tiny fraction of the total who lived now. In this incredibly remote era, Humans lived upon the bedrock of the planet, leading impossibly lonely lives—often going without physical contact with fellow humans for minutes on end. The mere thought filled him with a sickening nausea, a feeling of panic at such inhuman isolation. But there were more such incredible speculations: these Humans, so the story went, could move about upon their limbs and ranged around the globe for distances of several torsos (though quite why they would wish to do so was beyond him).

The past-tellers went on to claim that these people existed in isolation not just physical, but mental. They could not, it was claimed, read the thoughts of their fellows, and were forced instead to communicate their ideas through a series of strategically modulated sounds.

He found this impossible to contemplate.

Oh, the loneliness of these strange beings who, if the past-tellers were to be believed, were the ancestors of modern Humankind! The terrible isolation of their lives! For his own peace of mind, he thought that these stories had to be myth, nightmares conjured by ghouls to frighten complacent citizens. And yet, again and again, he found himself returning to the heretic thoughts formed in the minds of the shunned school half a world away.

He grew, became respected in his field. His opinion was sought on various matters concerning his recondite discipline. He arrived at the age when it was expected of him to mate and procreate and add to the bountiful richness of the Human race.

For many cycles preceding this climatic event, he fretted that the change might never eventuate, that the physical conditions reliant upon his successful mating might never come about.

He eased his mind by dwelling upon the plight of those early, lonely *Homo sapiens*, the impossible visions of a sparsely populated globe . . .

The time of his mating came around, and he could read the nervousness in the minds of those about him.

The process of finding a mate called for an unprecedented effort of movement, a rigorous physical exertion that came about only once in the lifetime of every human being.

He could hear, in his mind, the siren calls of several nearby females. He had overlooked their minds before now, not interested in their fields of endeavour, but now the urgency of their calls awoke something buried deep within him, and he responded.

One cycle, soon after waking, he sensed the stress and tenseness in the bodies around him, and then a voice in his head— the reassuring tones of his father—told him to prepare himself.

He gripped the flank of his mother with his vestigial digits, and used all his strength in concert with those about him to effect the small movement that would bring about the change.

It was over in a matter of seconds. The mass of his family

heaved, and he moved with alarming alacrity. He experienced a moment of intense, shocking pain as he squeezed between intervening bodies. Then, suddenly, he found himself miraculously aligned with one of the females who had called to him.

Their minds met, a mental coming together in harmony with the sudden and inexorable melding of their flesh.

He initiated his mate into the convoluted logic of his discipline, and she entertained him with her mindsongs. They copulated frequently, and within a dozen cycles his mate was with child.

He returned to his thoughts, sharing the fruit of his cogitation with like minds around the world—adding, he liked to think, an appreciable increment to the sum total of the knowledge available to all.

One hundred cycles later, a rare scare visited his family grouping. Above him, his mother and father fell foul of a rare and virulent disease. Their flesh thinned; their thoughts became incoherent. He called on the minds of those about him to exert healing pressure, and for many a long cycle the lives of his mother and father hung in the balance.

He feared for his parents, and the possibility that they might not attain the light. They had many mega-cycles to go before they ascended—they could not be cut off like this, so cruelly, in their prime.

The healing thoughts from his neighbours, however, proved efficacious. His concern, that his mate might give birth after the deaths of his mother and father, was unfounded. Over long cycles his parents grew strong, and their thoughts became active once again.

He gave profound thanks, and looked forward to the birth of his child.

Two hundred cycles later, his mate gave issue to a thriving girl. Great joy suffused the minds of those around him, and he called the ritual greeting to his child, and in the chorus of delight that filled his mind he was moved to hear the welcoming thoughts of his resuscitated parents.

He worked ever harder in his field of non-spatial geometry, establishing new theories and, on one momentous occasion, an entirely original line of thought which he knew would not be proven, or unproven, in the limited time he had left to him. It would fall to minds other than his to work on the conundrum he had engendered—but he could rest assured that his memory would live on.

His child grew, taking after his mate in her predilection for the arts: in time she trained to become a mindsinger like her mother, and he was gratified.

Between the hard mental toil of his calling and the appreciation of his mate and their daughter, he found time to return to that sequestered school of past-tellers. He relived again, with a shivery nostalgic frisson familiar from many cycles ago, the myths of the far distant past, the stories of how Humankind's forebears had lived alone upon the surface of the Earth.

He was older now, and wiser, and he petitioned the past-tellers with questions that as a youngster he had been too naïve, or fearful, to pose.

He asked the venerable seers about the purpose of the ancient, lonely *Homo sapiens*: he asked if they were too primitive to have evolved philosophies, too ignorant to have any idea of their eventual destination.

The past-tellers answered him with supposition only: they did not know for certain what filled the minds of their impossibly remote ancestors, but they claimed that they could make an educated guess.

The ancients, according to the past-tellers, did indeed turn their savage minds to the problem of what might await them at their eventual ends. They posited other lands into which they might be reborn, afterlives full of rewards for virtue and compassion. But they were hopelessly unevolved, the past-tellers said; they lived only upon the land, could not ascend, and therefore could have no conception of the true destiny of their kind.

It was only with evolution, the eventual attainment of their present status, that Humankind could confidently predict the glory that awaited them.

He considered the world of ignorance in which his forebears had dwelled, the terrible state of physical and mental isolation imposed upon hapless individuals born too soon to apprehend the magnificent truth.

He considered the doomed philosophies of early man, the futility of their sciences. They had lived lives of simple pleasures, of maturation, procreation, and eventual death—whiling away the mega-cycles between with fruitless speculations as to the true meaning of their plight . . . and the thought that countless generations had died in ignorance filled him with a strange and keening melancholy.

He gave thanks that he had been born into this rich and enlightened age!

*   *   *

His daughter matured, fulfilled her destiny as a fine mindsinger, and he worked less and less at his discipline, finding rewards instead in encouraging other younger, more agile minds than his own. He settled into the quiescence of old age, and looked ahead with anticipation to the time of his ascension.

The light brightened around him, a new element in the hitherto twilit world.

In time, as he knew would happen, his parents ailed. Their minds guttered, often unable to keep abreast of the thought-conversations that spanned the globe. They absented themselves for long cycles, recalling distant memories, nostalgic thoughts.

His mother thinned first, her mind full of the glorious rapture of ascension as she apprehended the light above her. She emerged before his father, and the mind-cry of joy she issued upon beholding the beauty of the light filled the family grouping with ecstasy.

His father followed shortly, adding his rhapsodic mindsong to that of his mother. *Oh, the glory*, he sang to his son, to all the world: *Oh, the ineffable effulgence of the Light!*

Any sadness he might have felt at the passing of his parents was soon purged by the evidence of their joy, and he gave thanks that they had ascended to their rightful destinies.

They passed away within a cycle of each other.

Their bodies withered and wizened in the heat, and he enjoined those members of the grouping within range to partake of the nourishment of his parents' flesh. He himself gnawed upon the skinny tendon of his mother's leg, the same leg on to which he had clung for much of his life.

As he ate, the light grew ever brighter, blinding his feeble eyes. He was aware of the clamour of the minds of those below him, asking what he could behold. He replied with the age old platitude: that only the ascending might look upon the light, and understand.

He lived for another mega-cycle, as the heat increased and his eyes grew slowly more accustomed to the once painful light.

He found his thoughts drifting then, denied the nourishment of his parents and living only on stored nutrients. He thought often of the fanciful notions of his childhood, when he had consulted past-tellers about the humans who had once inhabited the world. Ludicrous tales! Impossible fabulations! He knew this now, but was unable to stop himself from making one last call across the world to any past-teller of the old school who might remain to tell him that his memories were not those of a dying old man.

He found one aged venerable seer, so old that he too was ascending and was blessed by the inexorable light.

He asked the seer to tell him of the early humans, the beings that dwelled in terrible isolation on the surface of the world.

The past-teller gave an amiable mental chuckle. *They did indeed exist, he called: they lived their lives of materialistic excess — giving no heed to the realm of pure thought — so that eventually Humankind might evolve and learn the truth. Of course, they knew not of their sacrifice. They were but primitives who carried the burden of Humankind's long trek through time . . .*

He considered this, and gave thanks, then saluted the countless generations of unwitting *Homo sapiens* in their blind march towards an unknowable but sublime futurity.

Soon he could open his eyes and behold, without pain, the wonder that stretched out around him in every direction.

He made out, in the searing, golden light that burned down from high above, a sea of similar faces, roasted by the intensity of the radiation, as they peered about them in awe-struck wonder.

They had arrived, they had attained the highest of the high! His heart swelled to think that he was amongst them, these exalted beings, and he communicated his rapture to all around him.

As the heat increased, burning him, he considered for one last time the legions of the dead who had not lived to be granted the truth of the ultimate ascension.

He had only a vague awareness of his death.

Ulla, Ulla

AFTER THE DEBRIEFING, WHICH LASTED THREE days, Enright left the Kennedy Space Center and headed for home.

He drove south to the Keys in his '08 Chevrolet convertible, taking his time now that he was alone for the first time in three years. For that long he had been cooped up in the *Fortitude* on its voyage to Mars and back. Even on the surface of the planet, beneath the immensity of the pink sky, he had never felt truly alone. Always there were the voices of McCarthy, Jeffries, and Spirek on his com, and the prospect of the cramped living quarters on his return to the lander.

Ten miles south of Kennedy, on the coast road, he pulled into a parking lot overlooking the sea, climbed out, and stared into the evening sky.

There was Mars, riding high overhead.

He considered the mission, but he had no original take on what they had discovered beneath the surface of the red planet. He was as baffled as everyone else. One thing he knew for certain, though: everything was different now. At some point, inevitably, the news would break, and things would change forever.

He had been allowed a couple of hours with Delia after quarantine, before being whisked off to the intensive debriefing. He had not been cleared to discuss their findings with her, the one person in his life with whom he had shared everything. She had sensed something, though, detected in his manner that all was not right. She had been at mission control when the first broadcast came through from Mars, but Director Roberts had cut the transmission before anything major had leaked.

He shivered. The wind was turning cold.

He climbed back into his Chevrolet, reversed from the lot, and drove home.

He left the car in the drive and walked around the house.

The child's swing, in situ when they had bought the place four years ago, had still not been removed. Delia had promised him that she would see to it while he was away.

She was sitting in the lighted conservatory, reading. She looked up as he pushed through the door, but made no move to rise and greet him.

"You weren't due back until tomorrow," she said, making it sound like an accusation.

"Let us off a day early. Thought I'd surprise you." He was aware of the distance between them, after so long apart.

Over dinner, they chatted. Smalltalk, the inconsequential tone of which indicated that they both knew they were avoiding deeper issues. She was back teaching, three days a week at the local elementary school. Ted, her nephew, had been accepted at Florida State.

He wanted to tell her. He wanted to tell her everything that had happened on Mars. He had always shared everything with her in the past. So why not now?

Mission confidentiality? The papers he had signed seven years back on being accepted by NASA?

Or was it because what they had discovered might have been some kind of collective hallucination? And Delia might think that he was losing it, if he came out and told her?

A combination of all the above, he realised.

That night they made love, hesitantly, and later lay in a parallelogram of moonlight that cut across the bed.

"What happened, Ed?" she asked.

"Mmm?" He tried to feign semi-wakefulness.

"We were there, in mission control. You were out with Spirek. Something happened. There was a loud . . . I don't know, it sounded like a landslide. You said, 'Oh my God. . . .' Roberts cut the link and ushered us out. It was an hour before they got back to us. An hour. Can you imagine that? I was worried sick."

He reached out and stroked away her tears.

"Roberts gave us some story about subsidence," she said. "Then I heard you again, reassuring us that everything was okay."

They had staged that, concocted a few lines between them, directed by Roberts, to reassure their families back home.

He shrugged. "That's it. That's what happened. I was caught in a landslide, lost my footing." Even to his own ears, he sounded unconvincing.

Delia went on, "And then three days ago, I could tell something wasn't right. And now . . . You're hiding something."

He let the silence stretch. "I'm hiding nothing. It's hard to re-adjust. Imagine being stuck in a tin can for three years with cretins like Jeffries and McCarthy."

"You're too sensitive, Ed. You're a geologist, not an astronaut. You should have stayed at the university."

He embraced her. "Shh," he said, and fell silent.

He dreamed that night. He was back on Mars. He could feel the regolith slide away beneath his boots. The sensation of inevitable descent and imminent impact turned his stomach as it had done all those months ago. He fell, tumbling, and landed in a sitting position. In the dream he opened his eyes—and awoke suddenly, the image of what he had seen down there imprinted upon his waking consciousness.

He gasped aloud and reached out, grabbed the headboard. Then it came to him that he was no longer weightless, floating in his sleeping bag. He was on Earth. He was home. He reached out for Delia and held her.

In the morning, while Delia was at school, Enright took a walk. The open space, after so long cramped in the *Fortitude*, held an irresistible allure. He found himself on the golf course, strolling along the margin of the second fairway in the shade of maple trees.

He came to a bunker and stopped, staring at the clean, scooped perfection of the feature. He closed his eyes, and jumped. The sensation was pretty accurate. He had stepped out on to Mars again. He felt the granular regolith give beneath his boots.

When he opened his eyes he saw a young girl, perhaps twelve years old and painfully pretty. She was standing on the lip of the bunker, staring down at him.

She was clutching a pen and a scrap of paper.

Beyond her, on the green, two men looked on.

"Mr Enright, sir?" the kid asked. "Can I have your autograph?"
He reached up, took the pen and paper, and scrawled his name.
The girl stared at the autograph, as if the addition of his signature upon the paper had invested it with magical properties. One
of the watching men smiled and waved a hand.

Delia was still at school when he got back. The first thing he
did on returning was to phone a scrap merchant to take away the
swing in the back yard. Then he retired to his study and stared at
the pile of unanswered correspondence on his desk.

He leafed through the mail.

One was from Joshua Connaught, in England. Enright had cor-
responded with the eccentric for a number of years before the
mission. The man had said he was writing a book on the history of
spaceflight, and wanted Enright's opinion on certain matters.

They had exchanged letters every couple of months, moving
away from the original subject and discussing everything under the
sun. Connaught had been married, once, and he too was childless.

Enright set the envelope aside, unopened.

He sat back in his armchair and closed his eyes.

He was back on Mars again, falling. . . .

It had been a perfect touchdown.

The first manned craft to land on another planet had done so
at precisely 3.33 AM, Houston time, September 2nd, 2020.

Enright recalled little of the actual landing, other than his fear.
He had never been a good flyer—plane journeys had given him
the shakes: he feared the take-off and landings, while the bit in
between he could tolerate. The same was true of spaceflight. The
take-off at Kennedy had been delayed by a day, and then put on
hold for another five hours, and by the time the *Fortitude* did blast
off from pad 39A, Enright had been reduced to a nervous wreck.
Fortunately, his presence at this stage of the journey had been
token. It was the others who did the work—just as when they came
in to land, over eighteen months later, on the broad, rouge expanse
of the Amazonis Planitia.

Enright recalled gripping the arms of his seat to halt the shakes
that had taken him, and staring through the viewscreen at the rocky
surface of Mars which was rushing up to meet them faster than
seemed safe.

Jeffries had seen him and laughed, nudging McCarthy to take
a look. Fortunately, the air force man had been otherwise occu-

pied. Only Spirek sympathised with a smile; Enright received the impression that she too was not enjoying the descent.

The retros cut in, slamming the seat into Enright's back and knocking the wind from him. The descent of the lander slowed appreciably. The boulder-strewn terrain seemed to be floating up to meet them, now.

Touchdown, when it came, was almost delicate.

McCarthy and Jeffries were NASA men through and through, veterans of a dozen space station missions and the famous return to the moon in '15. They were good astronauts, lousy travelling companions. They were careerists who were less interested in the pursuit of knowledge, of exploration for its own sake, than in the political end-results of what they were doing—both for themselves personally, and for the country. Enright envisaged McCarthy running for president in the not too distant future, Jeffries ending up as some big-wig in the Pentagon.

They tended to look upon Enright, with his PhD in geology and a career at Miami University, as something of a make-weight on the trip.

Spirek . . . Enright could not quite make her out. Like the others, she was a career astronaut, but she had none of the brash bravado and right-wing rhetoric of her male counterparts. She had been a pilot in the air force, and was along as team medic and multi-disciplinary scientist: her brief, to assess the planet for possible future colonisation.

McCarthy was slated to step out first, followed by Enright. Fancy that, he'd thought on being informed at the briefing, Iowa farm-boy made good, only the second human being ever to set foot on Mars . . .

After the landing, Jeffries had made some quip about Enright still being shit-scared and not up to taking a stroll. He'd even made to suit up ahead of Enright.

"I'm fine," Enright said.

Spirek had backed him up. "Ed's AOK for go, Jeffries. You don't want Roberts finding out you pulled a stunt, huh?"

Jeffries had muttered something under his breath. It had sounded like "Bitch," to Enright.

So he'd followed McCarthy out on to the sun-bright plain of the Amazonis Planitia, his pulse loud in his ears, his legs trembling as he climbed the ladder and stepped on to the surface of the alien world.

There was a lot to do for the two hours he was out of the lander, and he had only the occasional opportunity to consider the enormity of the situation.

He took rock samples, drilled through the regolith to the bedrock. He filmed what he was doing for the benefit of the geologists back at NASA who would take up the work when he returned.

He recalled straightening up on one occasion and staring, amazed, at the western horizon. He wondered how he had failed to notice it before. The mountain stood behind the lander, an immense, pyramidal shape that rose abruptly from the surrounding volcanic plain to a height, he judged, of a kilometre. He had to tilt his head back to take in its summit.

Later, Spirek and Jeffries took their turn outside, while Enright began a preliminary analysis of the rock samples and McCarthy reported back to mission control.

Day one went like a dream, everything AOK.

The following day, as the sun rose through the cerise sky, Enright and Spirek took the Mars-mobile out for its test drive. They ranged a kilometre from the lander, keeping it in sight at all times.

Spirek, driving, halted the vehicle at one point and stared into the sky. She touched Enright's padded elbow, and he heard her voice in his ear-piece. "Look, Ed." And she pointed.

He followed her finger, and saw a tiny, shimmering star high in the heavens.

"Earth," she whispered, and, despite himself, Enright felt some strange emotion constrict his throat at the sight of the planet, so reduced.

But for Spirek's sighting of Earth at that moment, and her decision to halt, Enright might never have made the discovery that was to prove so fateful.

Spirek was about to start up, when he glanced to his left and saw the depression in the regolith, ten metres from the Mars-mobile.

"Hey! Stop, Sally!"

"What is it?"

He pointed. "Don't know. Looks like subsidence. I want to take a look."

Sal glanced at her chronometer. "You got ten minutes, okay?"

He climbed from the mobile and strode towards the rectangular impression in the red dust. He paused at its edge, knelt, and ran his hand through the fine regolith. The first human being, he told himself, ever to do so here at this precise location . . .

He stood and took a step forward.

And the ground gave way beneath his feet, and he was falling. "Oh, my God!"

He landed in a sitting position in semi-darkness, battered and dazed but uninjured. He checked his life-support apparatus. His suit was okay, his air supply functioning.

Only then did he look around him. He was in a vast chamber, a cavern that extended for as far as the eye could see.

As the dust settled, he made out the objects ranged along the length of the chamber.

"Oh, Christ," he cried. "Spirek . . . *Spirek!*"

He stood in the doorway of the conservatory and watched the workmen dismantle the swing and load it on to the back of the pick-up.

He'd been home four days now, and he was falling back into the routine of things. Breakfast with Delia, then a round of golf, solo, on the mornings she worked. They met for lunch in town, and then spent the afternoons at home, Delia in the garden, Enright reading magazines and journals in the conservatory.

He was due to start back at the university in a week, begin work on the samples he'd brought back from Mars. He was not relishing the prospect, and not just because it would mean spending time away from Delia: the business of geology, and what might be learned from the study of the Martian rocks, palled beside what he'd discovered on the red planet.

Roberts had phoned him a couple of days ago. Already NASA was putting together plans for a follow-up mission. He recalled what McCarthy and Jeffries had said about their discovery, that it constituted a security risk. Enright had forced himself not to laugh out loud, at the time. And yet, amazingly, when he returned to Earth and heard the talk of the back-room boys up at Kennedy, that had been the tenor of their concern. Now Roberts confirmed it by telling him, off the record, that the government was bank-rolling the next Mars mission. There would be a big military presence aboard. The disaster of bellicose US foreign policy repeating itself again, he thought: as if we hadn't learned from Oman and Burma and Venezuela. He wondered if McCarthy and Jeffries were happy now.

The workmen finished loading the frame of the swing and drove off. Delia was kneeling in the border, weeding. He watched her for a while, then went into the house.

He fetched the papers from the sitting room where he'd discovered them yesterday, slipped under the cushion of the settee.

"Delia?"

She turned, smiling.

She saw the papers and her smile faltered. Her eyes became hard. "I was just looking them over. I wasn't thinking of . . ."

"We talked about this, Delia."

"What, eight years ago, more? Things are different now. You're back at university. I can quit work. Ed," she said, something like a plea in her tone, "we'd be perfect. They're looking for people like us."

He sat down on the grass, laid the brochure down between himself and his wife. The wind caught the cover, riffled pages. He saw a gallery of beseeching faces staring out at him, soft focus shots manufactured to pluck at the heart-strings of childless couples like themselves.

He reached out and stopped the pages. He stared at the picture of a small, blonde-haired girl. She reminded him of the kid who'd asked for his signature at the golf course the other day.

And, despite himself, he felt a longing somewhere deep within him like an ache.

"Why are you so against the idea, Ed?"

They had planned to start a family in the early years. Then Delia discovered that she was unable to bear children. He had grown used to the idea that their marriage would be childless, though it was harder for Delia to accept. Over the years he had devoted himself to his wife, and when eight years ago she had first mentioned the possibility of adoption, he had told her he loved her so much that he would be unable to share that love with a child. He was bullshitting, of course. The fact was that he did not want Delia's love for him diluted by another.

And now? Now, he felt the occasional craving to lavish love and affection on a child, and he knew he would find it hard to explain his uneasiness to Delia.

Look at the world, he wanted to say to her. Look at the mess we've made of the place: it's one disaster after another, war after ecological foul-up after war . . . Was the world really any place in which to bring up a child? Even if they adopted, then how would he sleep at night knowing that the future was hideously bleak for child he loved?

He shook his head, wordlessly, and a long minute later he stood and returned to the house.

The following day Delia sought him out in his study. He'd retreated there shortly after breakfast, and for the past hour had been staring at his replica 16th century globe of the world. He considered crude, formless shapes that over the years had been redefined as countries and continents.

Terra incognita . . .

A sound interrupted his reverie. Delia paused by the door, one hand touching the jamb. She was carrying a newspaper.

She entered the room and sat down on the very edge of the armchair beside the bookcase. He managed a smile.

"You haven't been yourself since you got back."

"I'm sorry. It must be the strain. I'm tired."

She nodded, let the silence develop. "Did you know, there were stories at the time? The 'net was buzzing with rumours, speculation."

He smiled at that. "I should hope so. Humankind's first landing on Mars . . ."

"Besides that, Ed. When you fell, and the broadcast was suddenly cut."

"What were they saying? That we'd been captured by little green men?"

"Not in so many words. But they were speculating . . . said you might have stumbled across some sign of life up there." She stopped, then said, "Well?"

"Well, what?"

"What happened?"

He sighed. "So you'd rather believe some crazy press report—?"

She stopped him by holding out the morning paper. The headline of the Miami Tribune ran: *Life on Mars?*

He took the paper and read the report.

Speculation was growing today surrounding man's first landing on the red planet. Leaks from NASA suggest that astronauts McCarthy, Jeffries, Enright, and Spirek discovered ancient ruins on their second exploratory tour of the red planet. Unconfirmed reports suggest that . . .

Enright stopped reading and passed the paper back to his wife.

"Unconfirmed reports, rumours. Typical press speculation."

"So nothing happened?"

"What do you want me to say? I fell down a hole—but I didn't find wonderland down there."

Later, when she left without another word, he chastised himself for such a cheap parting shot.

He hadn't found wonderland down there, but something far stranger instead.

So the leaks had begun. Maybe he should tell Delia, before she found out from the paper.

For the rest of the morning, he went through the pile of letters that had accumulated during his absence. He replied to a few and discarded others. Just as he was about to break for lunch, he came upon the letter from Connaught in England, with its distinctive King's head stamp.

He wondered what strange theory his eccentric pen-pal might have come up with this time.

He opened the letter and unfolded a single sheet of high quality note paper. Usually there were dozens of pages in his tiny, meticulous handwriting.

Enright read the letter, no more than three short paragraphs. Then he read it again, his mouth suddenly dry. He lay the sheet on his knee, as his hands were trembling.

Dear Ed, he read, *I have been following your exploits on the red planet with interest and concern. By now you will have returned, and I hope you will read this letter at the earliest opportunity. I was watching the broadcast from the Amazonis Planitia, which was suddenly terminated in strange circumstances . . . I wondered if humankind had at last found that life once existed on Mars. Ed, my friend, if you did indeed discover something beneath the sands of Mars, I think I can furnish an explanation.*

If you would care to visit me at the manor at the earliest opportunity, I have a rather interesting story to tell.

If you need further convincing that your trip might prove worthwhile, I can but write the words: Ulla, ulla . . .

Your very good friend, Joshua Connaught.

Enright read the letter perhaps a dozen times, before folding it away and staring at the far wall for long minutes.

If the original discovery had struck him as an irresolvable enigma, then this only compounded the sense of mystery.

He reached for the phone and made immediate plans to fly to England.

Later, over lunch, he told Delia that NASA had recalled him. He'd be up at the Space Center for just under a week.

"Is it about . . . about what happened on Mars?"

How much to tell her? "Delia, when I get back . . . I think I'll be able to tell you something, okay?"

And the words Connaught had scrawled at the end of his letter came back to him.

Ulla, ulla.

*   *   *

He had fetched up on his butt at the bottom of the landslide and stared about him in wonder. The dust had settled, and bright sunlight penetrated the chamber for the first time in who knew how long?

Through the dust and the glare he made out an array of towering shapes ranged along the walls of the chamber. He had fallen perhaps fifty feet, and the shapes—the machines—were almost that tall.

"Oh, Christ," he cried. "Spirek . . . *Spirek!*"

In his ear he heard, "You okay, Ed? You hear me? Are you okay?"

"Sal! You gotta see this."

"Ed, where are you?"

He looked up. Sal was a tiny, silver-suited figure bobbing about on the lip of the drop, trying to see him.

He waved. "Get yourself down here, Sal. You've gotta see this!"

In his head-set he heard McCarthy shouting, "What's going on out there, Enright? Spirek?"

"You getting the pics, McCarthy?" Enright asked.

"Is the camera working? The picture went haywire when you fell."

He checked the camera. It had ceased filming at some point during his descent. He activated it again and swept the head-mounted lens around the chamber. He could see now that a section of the ceiling had sunk over the years, and the pressure of his weight upon it had brought the slab crashing down, and tons of sand with it.

McCarthy: "It's all hazy, Enright. Can't see much."

Enright stood, tested his limbs. He was fine. No breaks. He stepped forward, out of the direct sunlight, and stared at the ranked machinery that disappeared into the perspective.

"Hell fire in heaven!" Jeffries murmured.

Spirek was still peering down at him, unsure whether to negotiate the landslide.

"Ed, are you gonna tell me?"

He peered up at her. "Get yourself down here, Sal."

She hesitated, then stepped forward and rode the sliding sand down to him like a kid on a dune.

She lost her footing and sprawled on her back. Enright helped her up. He was still holding her hand, staring past her face plate to watch her expression, as she turned and looked down the length of the chamber.

She said nothing, but silver tears welled in her eyes.

Then, without a word, spontaneously, they embraced.

Hand in hand, like frightened kids, they walked down the chamber.

They approached the machinery, the *craft*, rather. There were dozens of them, each one tall and columnar and bulky. They were dark shapes, seemingly oiled, silent and static and yet, every one upright and aimed, seemingly poised with intent.

Then they came to a smaller piece of machinery, perhaps half the height of the columns. Enright stopped, and stared.

He could not help himself: he began weeping.

"Ed?" Sal said, gripping his hand in sudden fear.

He indicated the looming, legged vehicle.

She shook her head. "So what? I don't see . . . ?"

In his head-set, Enright heard McCarthy, "Hey, you two oughtta be heading back now. Sal, how much air you got there?"

Sal swore. "Dammit, Ed. We gotta be getting back."

He was staring at the vehicle, mesmerised. "Ed!" Sal called again.

Reluctantly, Enright turned and followed Sal back up the land-slide to the Mars-mobile.

England, in contrast to sun-soaked Florida, was caught in the grip of its fiercest winter for years. From the window seat of the plane as it came in to land, Enright stared down at a landscape sealed in an otherworldly radiance of snow. This was the first time he had seen snow for almost twenty years, and he thought the effect cleansing: it gave mundane terrain a transformed appearance, bright and pristine: it looked like a land where miracles might easily occur.

He caught a Southern Line train from Heathrow to the village of Barton Humble in Dorset, and from there a taxi to Brimscombe Manor.

For the duration of the ten mile drive, Enright stared out at a landscape every bit as alien and fascinating as the terrain of Mars. He seemed to be travelling deep into the heart of ancient countryside: everything about England, he noted, possessed a quality of age, of history and permanence, entirely lacking in the American environment to which he was accustomed. The lanes were deep and rutted, with high hedges, more suited to bullock-carts than automobiles. They passed an ancient forest of oak, the dark, winter-stark trees bearing ghostly doppelgangers of themselves in the burden of snow that limned every branch.

Brimscombe Manor, when it finally appeared, standing between the forest and a shallow rise of hills, was vast and sprawling, possessed of a tumbledown gentility that put Enright in mind of fading country houses in the quaint black and white British films he'd watched as a child.

The driver took one look at the foot-thick mantle of snow that covered the drive of the manor, and shook his head. "Okay if I drop you here?"

Enright paid him off with unfamiliar European currency, retrieved his bag from the back seat, and stood staring at the imposing façade of the manor as the taxi drove away.

He felt suddenly alone in the alien environment. He knew the sensation well. The last time he had experienced this gut-wrenching sense of dislocation, he had been on Mars.

What the hell, he wondered, am I doing here? He had the sudden vision of himself, a US astronaut, standing forlornly in the depths of the English countryside on a freezing December afternoon, and smiled to himself.

"Ulla, ulla," he said, and his breath plumed in the icy air before him, the effect at once novel and disconcerting. "I'm going mad."

He set off through the snow. His boots compacted ice crystals in a series of tight, musical squeaks.

A light burned, orange and inviting, behind a mullioned window in the west wing of the manor. He climbed a sweep of steps and found a bell-push beside the vast timber door.

Thirty seconds later the door swung open, and heat and light flooded out to greet him.

"Mr Enright, Ed, you can't imagine how delighted I am . . ."

Within seconds of setting eyes upon his long-term correspondent, Enright felt at ease. Connaught had the kind of open, amicable face that Enright associated with English character-actors of the old school: he guessed Connaught was in his early sixties, medium height, with a full head of grey hair, a wide smiling mouth and blue eyes.

He wore tweeds, and a waist-coat with a fob watch on a silver chain.

"You must be exhausted after the journey. It's appalling out there." He escorted Enright across the hall. "Ten below all week. Record, so I'm told. Coldest cold snap for sixty years. You'll want a drink, and then dinner. I'll show you to your room. As soon as you've refreshed yourself, join me in the library."

He indicated a room to the right, through an open door. Enright glimpsed a roaring, open fire and rank upon rank of books. "This is the library, and right next door is your room. I hope you don't mind sleeping on the ground floor. I live here alone now, and since Liz passed away I don't bother with the upstairs rooms. Cheaper, you see. Here we are."

He showed Enright into a room with a double bed and an *en suite* bathroom, then excused himself and left.

Enright sat on the bed, staring through the window at the snow-covered lawn and the drive. The only blemish in the snow was his footprints, which a fresh fall was already filling in.

He showered, changed, and ventured next door to the library. Connaught stood beside a trolley of drinks. "Scotch, Brandy?"

He accepted a brandy and sat on a leather settee before the open fire. Connaught sat to the right of the fire in a big, high-backed armchair.

He surprised himself by falling into a polite exchange of small-talk. His curiosity was such that all he wanted from Connaught was an explanation of the letter which he carried, folded, in his hip pocket.

Ulla, ulla . . .

He fitted sound-bites and observations around Connaught's questions and comments.

"The flight was fine—a tailwind pushed us all the way, cutting an hour and a half off the expected time . . .

"England surprises me . . . Everything seems so old, and *small* . . .

"I'm impressed by the manor . . . We don't have anything quite like this back home."

And then they were discussing the history of manned space exploration. Connaught was extremely knowledgeable, indeed more so than Enright, in his grasp of the political cut and thrust of the space race.

An hour had elapsed in pleasant conversation, and still he had not broached the reason for his visit.

Connaught glanced at the carriage clock on the mantle-shelf. "Eight already! Let's continue the conversation over dinner, shall we?"

He ushered Enright along the hall and into a comfortable lounge with a table, laid for two, in a recessed area by the window.

A steaming casserole dish, a bowl of vegetables, and a bottle of opened wine stood on the table.

Connaught gestured to a seat. "I hire a woman from the village," he explained. "Heavenly cook. Comes in for a couple of hours a day and does for me."

They ate. Steak and kidney casserole, roast potatoes, carrots, and asparagus. They finished off the first bottle and started into a second.

The night progressed. Enright relaxed, drank more wine.

The amicable tenor of their correspondence was maintained, he was delighted to find, in their conversation. He contrasted the humane Connaught with the bullish ego-maniac of McCarthy.

Ulla, ulla . . .

Suddenly, the conversation switched—and it was Connaught who instigated the change.

"Of course, I watched every second of the Mars coverage. I was glued to the 'net. I hoped and prayed that your team might discover something there, though of course I was prepared for disappointment . . . I'll tell you something, Ed. I harboured the desire to be an astronaut myself, when I was young. Just a dream, of course. Never did anything about it. I fantasised about discovering new worlds, alien civilisations."

Enright smiled. "I never had that kind of ambition. I slipped into the space program almost by accident. They wanted a geologist on the mission, and I volunteered." He hesitated. "So when I stepped out on to Mars, of course the last thing on my mind was the discovery of an alien civilisation."

"I was watching the 'cast when you fell. The moment you said those words, I knew. Your tone of disbelieving wonder told me. I just knew you'd found something." Connaught refilled the glasses. "What happened, Ed? Tell me in your own words how you came to . . ."

So he recounted the landing, his first walk on the surface of Mars, and then his second. He worked up to his fall, and the discovery, like an expert storyteller. He found he was enjoying his role of raconteur . . .

They arrived back at the lander, after the discovery, with just four minutes' air supply remaining.

McCarthy and Jeffries were standing in the living quarters when they cycled through the hatch and discarded their suits. They were white-faced and silent.

Enright looked around the group, shaking his head. Words, at this moment, seemed beyond him.

McCarthy said, "Mission control went ballistic. You should hear Roberts. Wait till this breaks!"

Sal Spirek slumped into a seat. "We're famous, gentlemen. I think that this just might be the most momentous occasion in the history of humankind, or am I exaggerating?"

They stared around at each other, trying to work out if indeed she was indeed exaggerating.

Enright was shaking his head.

"What is it?" Sal asked.

He could not find the words to articulate what even he found hard to believe. "You don't understand," he began.

Sal said, "What's wrong?"

"Those things back there," Enright said, "the cylindrical rockets and three-legged machines." He stared around at their uncomprehending faces. "Have none of you ever read *The War of the Worlds?*"

Six hours later, with the go-ahead of Roberts at mission control, all four astronauts suited up and rode the Mars-mobile to the subterranean chamber.

As he negotiated the sloping drift of red sand, Enright half-expected to find the cavern empty, the cylinders and striding machines revealed to be nothing other than a figment of his imagination.

He paused at the foot of the drift, Sal by his side, McCarthy and Jeffries bringing up the rear and gasping as they stared at the alien machinery diminishing in perspective.

He and Sal walked side by side down the length of the chamber, passing from bright sunlight into shadow. He switched on his shoulder-mounted flashlight and stared at the vast, cylindrical rockets arrayed along the chamber. They were mounted on a complex series of frames, and canted at an angle of a few degrees from the perpendicular.

They paused before a smaller machine, consisting of a cowled dome atop three long, multi-jointed legs.

McCarthy and Jeffries joined them.

"Fighting Machines," Enright said.

McCarthy looked at him. "Say again?"

"Wells called them Fighting Machines," he said. "In his book—"

He stopped, then, as the implications of what he was saying slowly dawned on him.

He walked on, down the aisle between the examples of an alien culture's redundant hardware. The atmosphere within the chamber was that of a museum, or a mausoleum.

McCarthy was by his side. "You really expect us to believe . . . ?" he began.

Spirek said, "I've read *The War of the Worlds*, McCarthy. Christ, but Wells got it right. The cylinders, the Fighting Machines . . ."

"That's impossible!"

Enright said, "It's all here, McCarthy. Just as Wells described it."

McCarthy looked at him, his expression lost in the shadow behind his faceplate. "How do you explain it, Enright?"

He shrugged. "I don't. I can't. God knows."

"Here!" Spirek had moved off, and was kneeling beside something in the shadow of a tripod.

"The hardware wasn't all Wells got right." She gestured. "Look . . ."

Mummified in the airless vault for who knew how long, the Martian was much as the Victorian writer had described them in his novel of alien invasion, one hundred and twenty years before.

It was all head, with two vast, dull eyes the size of saucers, and a beak, with tentacles below that—tentacles that Wells had speculated the aliens had walked upon. It was, Enright thought, more hideous than anything he had ever seen before.

Enright walked on, and found more and more of the dead aliens scattered about the chamber.

Jeffries said, "I'll get all this back to Roberts. We need to work out strategy."

Enright looked at him. "Strategy?"

Jeffries gestured around him. "This is a security risk, Enright. I'm talking an AI security risk, here. How do we know these monsters aren't planning an invasion right now? Isn't that what the book was about?"

Enright and Spirek exchanged a glance.

"The Martians are dead, Jeffries," Spirek said. "Their planet was dying. They lived underground, but air and food was running out. They died out before they could get away."

"You don't know that, Sal," Jeffries Said. "You're speculating."

Enright strode off. He needed isolation in which to consider his discovery.

He found other chambers through giant archways, and a series of ramps that gave access to even lower levels. He imagined an entire city down there, a vast underground civilisation, long dead.

Sal Spirek joined him. "How did Wells know?" she asked. "How could he possibly have known?"

Enright recalled the last time he had read the novel, in his teens. He had been haunted by the description of a ravaged, desolate London in the aftermath of the alien invasion. He recalled the cry of the Martians as they succumbed to a deadly Terran virus, the mournful lament that had echoed eerily across an otherwise deathly silent London. "Ulla, ulla, ulla, ulla . . ."

He had left Spirek and the others, wanting to be alone with his thoughts, and descended a ramp to another, deeper chamber. He came to a great door in the wall of the chamber, and through a wide triangular viewscreen or window had seen something which had sent his pulse racing. He turned and ran, clumsily, hardly able to believe what he had seen.

"Enright? You okay?" Jeffries was in the entrance of the chamber. "You seen something?"

Aware that he had to keep what he had seen to himself, he said, "Nothing. Just more machinery and dead Martians . . ."

And he had followed Jeffries back up the ramp.

He told Connaught everything, barring his final discovery in the chamber.

"What was it like when I looked upon those ranked machines?" Enright shook his head. "I felt more than I thought, Joshua. I was overwhelmed with disbelief, and then elation, and then later, back at the ship, when I thought about it, a little fear. But at the time, when I first saw the machines . . . it came as one hell of a shock when I realised why they were so familiar."

Connaught was nodding. "Wells," he said.

Enright let the silence stretch. "How did you know?" He leaned forward. "How did Wells know?"

Connaught stood. "How about a whiskey? I have some fine Irish here."

He moved across the room to a mahogany cabinet and poured two generous measures of Bushmills.

He returned to the table. Enright sipped his drink, feeling the mellow burn slide down his throat like hot velvet.

"My great-grandfather, James," Connaught said, "inherited the Manor from his father, who built the house in 1870 from profits made in the wine trade. James was a writer—unsuccessful and unpublished. He wrote what was known then as scientific romances. He self-published a couple of short books, to no great notice. To be honest, his imagination was his strong point—his literary ability was almost negligible. To cut a long story short, he was friendly with a young and aspiring writer at the time—this was the early 1890s. Chappie by the name of Wells. They spent many a weekend down here and swapped stories, ideas, plots, etc. . . . One story James told him was about the invasion of Earth by creatures from Mars. They came in vast cylinders, and stalked the Earth aboard great marching war machines. Apparently, my great-grandfather had tried to write it up himself, but didn't get very far. Wells took the idea, and the rest is history. *The War of the Worlds.* A classic."

Connaught paused, staring into his glass.

Enright nodded, his mind full of H. G. Wells and James Connaught discussing story ideas in this very building, all those years ago.

"How," he asked at last, "how did your great-grandfather know about the Martians?"

He realised that he was drunk, his speech slurred. The sense of anticipation he felt swelling within him was almost unbearable.

"One night way back in 1880," Connaught said, "James was out walking the grounds. This was late, around midnight. He often took a turn around the garden at this time, looking for inspiration. Anyway, he saw something in the sky, something huge and fiery, coming in from the direction of the coast. It landed with a loud explosion in the spinney to the rear of the Manor."

Enright leaned forward, reached for the whiskey bottle, and helped himself.

"James ran into the spinney," Connaught continued, "after the fallen object, and found there . . . He found a huge pit gouged into the ground, and in that pit a great cylindrical object, glowing red and steaming in the cold night."

Enright sat back in his chair and shook his head.

Joshua Connaught smiled. "You don't believe me?"

"No, it's just . . . I do believe you. It's just that it's so fantastic."

Connaught smiled. "I've heard it called threshold shift," he said. "Your consciousness of what is possible undergoes a shift, a moment of conceptual breakthrough, and nothing is ever the same again."

Enright laughed. "You can say that again."

Connaught went on, "My great-grandfather excavated the pit and built an enclosure around it, and it exists to this day. I've shown no one since Elizabeth."

Enright experienced a sudden dizziness. He made a feeble gesture.

Connaught smiled. "It's still there, Ed."

Enright shook his head. "*It*, you mean . . . ?"

"The Martian cylinder, and other things."

Enright downed the last of his whiskey, felt it burning his throat.

Connaught stood. "Shall we go?"

Enright stood also, unsteadily. "Please, after you." Swaying, he followed Connaught from the room.

He expected to be taken outside, but instead Connaught led him through a narrow door and down a flight of even narrower steps. A succession of bare, low-watt bulbs illuminated a series of vaulted cellars, the first chambers stocked with wine, the later ones empty and musty.

They walked along a narrow red brick corridor.

"We're now passing from the manor and walking beneath the kitchen garden towards the spinney," Connaught reported over his shoulder.

Enright nodded, aware that he was sobering rapidly with the effects of the cold and the notion of what might imminently be revealed.

The corridor extended for five hundred yards, and terminated abruptly at a small, wooden door.

Connaught drew a key from the pocket of his waist-coat and opened the door. He stood aside, gesturing for Enright to enter.

Cautiously, he stepped over the threshold.

He faced an abyss of darkness, until Connaught reached past him and threw a switch.

A dozen bare bulbs illuminated a vast rectangular, red-brick room. The walls were concave, bowed like the hull of a galleon. A series of rough wooden steps led down to the floor, again of red-brick.

The cylinder lay in the centre of the room, a long, gun-metal grey column identical to those he had seen in the chamber on Mars. At the facing end of the cylinder was a circular opening. Beside the cylinder, laid out lengthways, was one of the Fighting Machines.

Enright climbed down the steps, aware that his mouth was hanging open. He walked around the cylinder, its dimensions dwarfing him and Connaught. He reached out and touched the icy cold surface of the cylinder, something he had been unable to do on Mars. He inspected the tripod, marvelling at the intricacy of the metalwork—crafted far away on Mars by a race other than human.

"According to the story," Connaught said, "that night James crouched on the edge of the pit and watched fearfully as the great threaded stopper slowly unscrewed and fell out. He waited, but hours elapsed and nothing emerged other than a strange, other-worldly cry, 'Ulla, ulla, ulla, ulla.' It was day-break before he plucked up the courage to scramble down into the pit and approach the cylinder. There were three beings in the craft, he could see by the light of dawn, but they were dead. Fortunately, the spinney was on his land, and anyway the trees concealed the pit from view. Over the course of the following year, working alone, he built this construction around the craft, and then devoted the rest of his life to the study of its contents. He and his son, my grandfather, reconstructed the tripod you see there. They even attempted to preserve the dead aliens, but they rotted almost to nothing with the passage of years."

Enright looked up. "Almost nothing?"

Connaught walked over to a raised wooden platform. Upon this was a big desk, and piles of papers and manuals, illuminated by a reading lamp. He gestured to a bulbous preserving jar, floating in which was a grey-brown scrap of what looked like hide.

"This is all that remains of the first alien beings to arrive on planet Earth," Connaught said.

"Did James show Wells all this?" Enright asked.

Connaught shook his head. "It was a strict secret, at the time known only to James and his son. As I said, he gave Wells the idea as a fiction, but supplied him with detailed drawings of the cylinder and the other machinery, and even of the aliens themselves, and their death cry."

"And you've never shown anyone outside the family, until now?"

Connaught smiled. "By the time my father found out, the truth of what had happened was lost in time. My grandfather was old when he showed my father the cylinder—his memory was not what it was. My father took the story with a pinch of salt. He rationalised that James had manufactured the cylinder himself, and the tripod. My father sealed the chamber, and only showed it to me when I was down here exploring, and asked about the mysterious bricked-up door."

"And yet you believed James's story?" Enright said.

Connaught hesitated. "I was at Oxford in the seventies," he said, "studying ancient literature. Later I found myself working for the government, decrypting codes . . . When I inherited the manor, I inspected this chamber and everything it contained."

He moved to the desk and unlocked a drawer. From it he produced a thick, silver object that looked something like a book.

He laid it upon the desk and opened the cover. The pages were also silver, manufactured of some thin, metal-like material, and upon each leaf of the book Enright made out, in vertical columns, what might have been lines of script. But it was a script unlike any he had ever seen before.

"James discovered this in the cylinder. For years and years he worked at decoding the book from the stars, as he called it. He failed. When I came across it, I began where my great-grandfather had left off."

Enright stared at him. "And you succeeded?"

Connaught bent and unlocked another drawer. From this he lifted a more conventional manuscript, a ream of A4 paper in a clip folder.

"I succeeded. Last year I finished translating the book. Much of it is an encyclopaedia of their world, a history of their race. Mars was dying, Ed. Millennia ago, the beings that had dwelled on the surface of the planet were forced to move underground, out of the inhospitable cold. Their numbers dwindled, until only tens of thousands survived. They realised that they had to leave their planet."

"And invade Earth," Enright finished.

But Connaught was smiling and shaking his head. "They were a peaceful people. Only in Wells's fiction were they belligerent."

He reached out and opened the cover of his translation. "Please," he said.

Enright stepped forward, his pulse pounding, and read the first paragraph.

We of the fourth planet of the solar system, the planet we call Vularia, come to the third planet on a mission of peace. Although our kind has known enmity, and fought debilitating wars, we have outgrown this stage of our evolution. We come with the hope that our two races might join as one and explore the universe together . . .

Enright stopped reading, aware of the constriction in his throat. He leafed through over five hundred pages of closely printed text.

He thought of McCarthy, and Jeffries, and the military operation underway right at this minute.

"Over half a million words," Connaught said. "You can hardly begin to conceive what a treasure it is."

Enright turned and walked away from the desk. He stared at the cylinder, and the so-called Fighting Machine.

Behind him, Connaught was saying, "My great-grandfather guessed that they were dying before they arrived on Earth—that it was not an earthly virus that ended their existence, but one of their own. How wonderful it might have been, had they survived."

Enright smiled to himself.

He turned and looked at Connaught. "Why, Joshua? Why have you shown me all this? Your translation?"

"Why else? This has been a secret long enough. Now, my life's work is finished, the translation done—I would like to receive acknowledgement, in due course. I summoned you here so that you might take this copy of the translation back to America, to answer the mystery of what you discovered beneath the sands of Mars."

He gestured towards the door. "Come, it's cold in here. Shall we retire to the library for a nightcap?"

With one last backwards glance at the Martian machines, he followed Connaught from the chamber.

Later, before the open fire, Enright said, "They're sending a military mission to Mars, Joshua."

The old man smiled. "Forgive me if say that that is typical of your government." He laughed. "A military mission to rout the ghosts of long-dead Martians!"

Enright looked up from his whiskey and stared at Connaught. "Joshua, there's something I haven't told you. I've told no one, yet." He paused and smiled to himself, then said, "I was sickened by the thought of my government sending a hostile mission to Mars—"

"But, Ed, all they'll find is . . ."

The old man stopped, his words halted by something in Enright's expression.

"They'll find a race of Martians," he said. "The survivors. I saw them in one of the lower chambers. Dozens of them. I have no doubt that we would have rounded them up and imprisoned them, at best. Perhaps, if I take your document to the right people, that course of action might be averted."

They raised their glasses in a toast to that.

On the flight back to America, Enright dreamed. He was in London, but a London laid waste by some apocalyptic war. He strode through the ruins, listening. He was not alone. Beside him was a child, a small girl, and when he looked upon her he was filled with a strange sense of hope for the future, a hope like elation. The girl slipped a hand in to his, and at that moment Enright heard it. Faint at first, and then stronger. It was the saddest, most haunting sound he had ever heard in his life.

"Ulla, ulla, ulla, ulla . . ."

Then he saw the Martian standing amid the ruins, and it came to him that its call was not one of desolation, after all.

He awoke with a start. The sensation of the small, warm hand in his was so real that he glanced at the seat beside him, but it was empty.

The plane was banking. They were coming in to land at Orlando.

Enright checked beneath his seat to ensure that he still had the briefcase containing the Martian translation.

We of the fourth planet of the solar system, the planet we call Vularia, come to the third planet on a mission of peace . . .

He smiled to himself, closed his eyes, and thought of Delia, and home, and the future.

The Kéthani Inheritance

IN THE WINTER OF 2013, WHICH WAS THE COLDEST on record for over half a century, two events occurred which changed my life: my father died, and for the first time in thirty years I fell in love. I suppose the irony is that, but for my father's illness, I would never have met Elisabeth Carstairs.

He was sitting in the lounge of the Sunny View nursing home that afternoon, chocked upright in his wheelchair with the aid of cushions, drooling and staring at me with blank eyes. The room reeked of vomit with an astringent overlay of bleach.

"Who're you, then?"

I sighed. I was accustomed to the mind-numbing, repetitive charade. "Ben," I said. "Benjamin. Your son."

Sometimes it worked, and I would see the dull light of recognition in his rheumy eyes. Today, however, he remained blank.

"Who're you, then? What do you want?"

"I'm Ben, your son. I've come to visit you."

I looked around the morning room, at the other patients, or "guests" as the nurses called them; they all gazed into space, seeing not the future, but the past.

"Who're you, then?"

Where was the strong man I had hated for so long? Such was

his decrepitude that I could not bring myself to hate him any longer; I only wished that he would die.

I had wished him dead so many times in the past. Now it came to me that he was having his revenge: he was protracting his life purely to spite me.

In Holland, I thought, where a euthanasia law had been passed years ago, the old bastard would be long dead.

I stood and moved to the window. The late afternoon view was far from sunny. Snow covered the hills to the far horizon, above which the sky was mauve with the promise of evening.

I was overcome with a sudden and soul-destroying depression.

"What's this?" my father said.

I focussed on his apparition reflected in the plate-glass window. His thin hand had strayed to his implant.

"What's this, then?"

I returned to him and sat down. I would go through this one more time—for perhaps the hundredth time in a year—and then say goodbye and leave.

His frail fingers tapped the implant at his temple, creating a hollow timpani.

"It's your implant," I said.

"What's it doing there?"

It sat beneath the papery skin of his temple, raised and rectangular, the approximate size of a matchbox.

"The medics put it there. Most people have them now. When you die, it will bring you back to life."

His eyes stared at me, then through me, uncomprehendingly.

I stood. "I'm going now. I'll pop in next week . . ." It would be more like next month, but, in his shattered mind, all days were one now.

As I strode quickly from the room I heard him say, "Who're you, then?"

An infant-faced Filipino nurse beamed at me as I passed reception. "Would you like a cup of tea, Mr Knightly?"

I usually refused, wanting only to be out of the place, but that day something made me accept the offer.

Serendipity. Had I left Sunny View then, I might never have met Elisabeth. The thought often fills me with panic.

"Coffee, if that's okay? I'll be in here." I indicated a room designated as the library, though stocked only with a hundred Mills and Boon paperbacks, *Reader's Digest* magazines, and large print Western novels.

I scanned the chipboard bookcases for a real book, then gave up. I sat down in a big, comfortable armchair and stared out at the snow. A minute later the coffee arrived. The nurse intuited that I wished to be left alone.

I drank the coffee and gazed at my reflection in the glass: I felt like a patient, or rather a "guest."

I think I was weeping when I heard, "It is depressing, isn't it?"

The voice shocked me. She was standing behind my chair, gripping a steaming mug and smiling.

I dashed away a tear, overcome with irritation at the interruption.

She sat down in the chair next to mine. I guessed she was about my age—around thirty—though I learned later that she was thirty-five. She was broad and short with dark hair bobbed, like brackets, around a pleasant, homely face.

"I know what it's like. My mother's a guest here. She's senile."

She had a direct way of speaking that I found refreshing.

"My father has Alzheimer's," I said. "He's been in here for the past year."

She rolled her eyes. "God! The repetition! I sometimes just want to strangle her. I suppose I shouldn't be saying that, should I? The thing is, we were so close. I love her dearly."

I found myself saying, "In time, when she dies, her memory will—" I stopped, alarmed by something in her expression.

It was as if I had slapped her.

Her smile persisted, but it was a brave one now in the face of adversity. She shook her head. "She isn't implanted. She refused."

"Is she religious?"

"No," she said, "just stubborn. And fearful. She doesn't trust the Kéthani."

"I'm sorry."

She shook her head, as if to dismiss the matter. "I'm Elisabeth, by the way. Elisabeth Carstairs."

She reached out a hand, and, a little surprised at the forthright gesture, I took it. I never even thought to tell her my own name.

She kept hold of my hand, turning it over like an expert palm reader. Only later did I come to realise that she was as lonely as I was: the difference being, of course, that Elisabeth had hope, something I had given up long ago.

"Don't tell me," she said, examining my weather-raw fingers. "You're a farmer, right?"

I smiled. "Wrong. I build and repair dry-stone walls."

She laughed. "Well, I was almost there, wasn't I? You do work outdoors, with your hands."

"What do you do?" I would never have asked normally, but something in her manner put me at ease. She did not threaten. "I teach, for my sins. The comprehensive over at Bradley."

"Then you must know Jeff Morrow. He's a friend."

"You know Jeff? What a small world."

"We meet with another friend in the Fleece every Tuesday." I shrugged. "Creatures of habit."

She glanced at her watch and pulled a face. "I really should be getting off. It's been nice talking . . ." She paused, looking quizzical.

I was slow on the uptake, then realised. "Ben," I said. "Ben Knightly. Look, I'm driving into the village. I can give you a lift if you . . ."

She jangled car keys. "Thanks, anyway."

I stood to leave, nodding awkwardly, and for the first time she could see the left-hand side of my face.

She stared, something stricken in her eyes, at where my implant should have been.

I hurried from the nursing home and into the raw winter wind, climbed into my battered ten-year-old Sherpa van and drove away at speed.

The following evening, just as I was about to set off for the Fleece, the phone rang. I almost ignored it, but it might have been a prospective customer, and I was going through a lean spell.

"Hello, Ben? Elisabeth here, Elisabeth Carstairs. We met yesterday."

"Of course, yes." My heart was thudding, my mouth dry: the usual reactions of an inexperienced teenager on being phoned by a girl.

"The thing is, I have a wall that needs fixing. A couple of cows barged through it the other day. I don't suppose . . . ?"

"Always looking for work," I said, experiencing a curious mixture of relief and disappointment. "I could come round tomorrow, or whenever's convenient."

"Sometime tomorrow afternoon?" She gave me her address.

"I'll be there between two and three," I said, thanked her and rang off.

That night, in the snug of the Fleece, I was on my third pint of Timothy Taylor's Landlord before I broached the subject of Elisabeth Carstairs.

The conversation was desultory. We'd been meeting in the same pub, sitting at the same table beside the log fire, and drinking the same beer for almost five years now. As might be expected the talk had grown somewhat predictable over that time.

Jeff Morrow was forty-five, a quiet, thoughtful man who shared my interest in football and books. He'd come to the village just over five years ago, and once, after a few too many pints, had told me the reason he'd fled his last school. He'd had an affair with an eighteen-year-old pupil, which had ended in tragedy. She had not been implanted—he never said why not—and had taken her life for reasons that he had also never divulged.

He carried a photograph of her in his wallet: a slim, beautiful French girl called Claudine. Five years before that, and a year before the Kéthani came, his wife had died in a car accident.

An accretion of sadness showed in his eyes.

He had never once commented on the fact that I was not implanted, and I respected him for this.

The third member of our party was Richard Lincoln, the local ferryman. I'd always viewed people in his profession in the same light as undertakers, which in a way is what they were. He was a big, silver-haired man in his early sixties, and before taking up his present profession had edited school textbooks.

I suppose we gravitated towards each other because we were all single at the time, liked a regular pint, and enjoyed the company of quiet people to whom silences were natural.

"I met a woman called Elisabeth Carstairs yesterday," I said. "She teaches at your school, Jeff."

"Ah, Liz. Lovely woman. Good teacher. The kids love her. One of those naturals."

That might have been the end of that conversation, but I went on. "Is she married?"

He looked up. "Liz? God no."

Richard traced the outline of his implant with an absent forefinger. "Why 'God, no,' Jeff? She isn't—?"

"No, nothing like that." He shrugged, uncomfortable. Jeff is a tactful man. He said to me, "She's been looking after her mother for the past fifteen years. As long as I've known her, she's never had a boyfriend."

Richard winked at me. "You're in there, Ben."

I swore at him. Jeff said, "Where did you meet?"

I told him, and conversation moved on to the health of my

father (on his third stroke, demented, but still hanging on), and then by some process of convoluted logic to Leeds United's prospects this Saturday.

Another thing I liked about Jeff and Richard was that they never made digs about the fact that I had never had a girlfriend since they'd known me—since my early twenties, if the truth be known.

I'd long ago reconciled myself to a life mending dry-stone walls, reading the classics, and sharing numerous pints with the likes of Messrs Morrow and Lincoln.

And I'd never told anyone that I blamed my father: some wounds are too repulsive to reveal.

It was midnight by the time I made my way up the hill and across the moors to the cottage. I recall stopping once to gaze at the Onward Station, towering beside the reservoir a mile away. It coruscated in the light of the full moon like a stalagmite of ice.

As I stared, a beam of energy, blindingly white, arced through the night sky towards the orbiting Kéthani starship, and the sight, I must admit, frightened me.

"I tried repairing it myself," Elisabeth said, "but as you can see I went a bit wrong."

"It's like a jigsaw puzzle," I said. "It's just a matter of finding the right piece and fitting it in."

It was one of those rare, brilliantly sunny November days. There was no wind, and the snow reflected the sunlight with a twenty-four carat dazzle.

I dropped the last stone into place, rocked it home, and then stood back and admired the repair.

"Thirty minutes," Elisabeth said. "You make it look so easy."

I smiled. "Matter of fact, I built this wall originally, twelve years ago."

"You've been in the business that long?"

We chatted. Elisabeth wore snow boots and a padded parka with a fur-lined hood that that made her look like an Eskimo. She stamped her feet. "Look, it's bitter out here. Would you like a coffee?"

"Love one."

Her house was a converted barn on the edge of the moor, on the opposite side of the village to my father's cottage. Inside it was luxurious: deep pile carpets, a lot of low beams and brass. The spacious kitchen was heated by an Aga.

I stood on the doormat, conscious of my boots.

"Just wipe them and come on in," she said, laughing. "I'm not house-proud, unlike my mother."

I sat at the kitchen table and glanced through the door to a room full of books. I pointed. "Like reading?"

"I love books," she said, handing me a big mug of real coffee. "I teach English, and the miracle is that it hasn't put me off reading. You?" She leaned against the Aga, holding her cup in both hands.

We talked about books for a while, and I think she was surprised at my knowledge.

From time to time I caught her glancing at my left temple, where the implant should have been. I felt that she wanted to comment, to question me, but couldn't find a polite way of going about it.

The more I looked at her, and the more we talked, the more I realised that I found her attractive. She was short, and a little overweight, and her hair was greying, but her smile filled me with joy.

Romantic and inexperienced as I was, I extrapolated fantasies from this meeting, mapped the future.

"How often do you visit your mother?" I asked, to fill a conversational lull.

"Four times a week. Monday, Wednesday, Friday, and Sunday."

I hesitated. "How long has she been ill?"

She blew. "Oh . . . when has she ever been well! She had her first stroke around fifteen years ago, not long after we moved here. I've been working part time and looking after her ever since. She's averaged about . . . oh, a stroke every three years since. The doctors say it's a miracle she's still hanging on."

She hesitated, then said, "Then the Kéthani came, and offered us the implants . . . and I thought all my prayers had been answered."

I avoided her eyes.

Elisabeth stared into her cup. "She was a very intelligent woman, a member of the old Labour Party before the Blair sellout. She knew her mind. She wanted nothing to do with afterlife, as she called it."

"She was suspicious of the Kéthani?"

"A little, I suppose. Weren't we all, in the beginning? But it was more than that. I think she foresaw humanity becoming complacent, apathetic with this life when the stars beckoned."

"Some people would say that she was right."

A silence developed. She stared at me. "Is that the reason you . . . ?"

There were as many reasons for not having the implant, I was sure, as there were individuals who had decided to go without. Religious, philosophical, moral . . . I gave Elisabeth a version of the truth.

Not looking her in the eye, but staring into my empty cup, I said, "I decided not to have the implant, at first, because I was suspicious. I thought I'd wait, see how it went with everyone who did have it. A year passed, two . . . It seemed fine. The returnees came back, a little fitter, healthier, younger. Those that went among the stars later, they recounted their experiences. It was as the Kéthani said. We had nothing to fear." I looked up quickly to see how she was taking it.

She was squinting at me. She shrugged. "So, why didn't you . . . ?"

"By that time," I said, "I'd come to realise something. Living on the edge of death, staring it in the face, made life all the more worth living. I'd be alone, on some outlying farm somewhere, and I'd be at one with the elements . . . and, I don't know, I came to appreciate being alive."

Bullshit, I thought. It was the line I'd used many a time in the past, and though it contained an element of truth, it was not the real reason.

Elisabeth was intelligent; I think she saw though my words, realised that I was hiding something, and I must admit that I felt guilty about lying to her.

I thanked her for the coffee and made to leave.

"How much for the work?" she said, gesturing through the window at the repaired wall.

I hesitated. I almost asked her if she would like to go for a meal, but stopped myself just in time. I told myself that it would seem crass, as if she had to accept the invitation in payment. In fact, the coward in me shied away from escalating the terms of our relationship.

"Call it fifty," I said.

She gave me a fifty euro note and I hurried from the house, part of me feeling that I had escaped, while another part was cursing my fear and inadequacy.

I found myself, after that, visiting my father four times a week.

Sunny View seemed a suitably neutral venue in which to meet and talk to Elisabeth Carstairs.

I even found myself looking forward to the visits.

About two weeks after I repaired her wall, I was sitting in the lounge with my father. It was four o'clock and we were alone. Around four-thirty Elisabeth would emerge from her mother's room and we would have a coffee in the library.

I was especially nervous today because I'd decided to ask her if she would like to come for a meal the following day, a Thursday. I'd heard about a good Indonesian place in Harrogate.

I'd come to realise that I liked Elisabeth Carstairs for who she was, her essential character, rather than for what she might represent: a woman willing to show me friendship, affection, and maybe even more.

We had a lot in common, shared a love of books, films, and even a similar sense of humour. Moreover, I saw in Elisabeth a fundamental human decency, perhaps borne out of hardship, that I detected in few other people.

"Who're you, then?"

"Ben," I said absently, my thoughts miles away.

He regarded me for about a minute, then said, "You always were bloody useless!"

I stared at him. He had moments of lucidity: for a second, he was back to his old self, but his comment failed to hurt: I'd heard it often before, when the sentiment had been backed by an ability to be brutal.

"Dry-stone walls!" he spat.

"Is that any worse than being a bus driver?" I said.

"Useless young . . ." he began, and dribbled off.

I leaned forward. "Why don't you go to hell!" I said, and hurried from the room, shaking.

I sat in the library, staring out at the snow, and hoped that, when my father was resurrected and returned, he would have no memory of the insult.

"Hello, Ben. Nice to see you."

She was wearing her chunky primrose parka and, beneath it, a jet black cashmere jumper. She looked lovely.

"You don't look too good," she said, sitting down and sipping her coffee.

I shrugged. "I'm fine."

"Some days he's worse than others, right? Don't tell me. Mum's having one of her bad days today."

More than anything I wanted to tell her that I cared nothing for my father, but resisted the urge for fear of appearing cruel.

We chatted about the books we were reading at the moment; she had loaned me Chesterton's *Tales of the Long Bow,* and I enthused about his prose.

Later, my coffee drunk, I twisted the cup awkwardly and avoided her eyes. "Elisabeth, I was wondering . . . There's a nice Indonesian restaurant in Harrogate. At least, I've heard it's good. I was wondering—"

She came to my rescue. "I'd love to go," she said, smiling at me. "Name a day."

"How about tomorrow? And I'll pay—"

"Well, I'll get the next one, then. How's that sound? And I'll drive tomorrow, if you like."

I nodded. "Deal," I said.

I was working on a high sheep fold all the following day, and I was in good spirits. I couldn't stop thinking about Elisabeth, elation mixed equally with trepidation. From time to time I'd stop work for a coffee from my Thermos, sit on the wall I was building and stare down at the vast, cold expanse of the reservoir, and the Onward Station beside it.

Ferrymen came and went, delivering the dead. I saw Richard Lincoln's Range Rover pull in and watched as he unloaded a coffin and trolleyed it across the car park and into the Station.

At five I made my way home, showered and changed and waited nervously for Elisabeth to pick me up.

The meal was a success. In fact, contrary to my fears, the entire night was wonderful. From the time she picked me up, we began talking and never stopped.

The restaurant was quiet, the service excellent, and the food even better. We ate and chattered, and it seemed to me that I had known this friendly, fascinating woman all my life.

I could not see in Elisabeth the lonely, loveless woman, that Jeff had described; she seemed comfortable and at ease. I feared I would appear gauche and naïve to her, but she gave no indication of thinking so. Perhaps the fact was that we complemented each other: two lonely people who had, by some divine and arbitrary accident, overcome the odds and discovered each other.

Elisabeth drove back through a fierce snowstorm and stopped outside her converted barn. She turned to me in the darkness. "You'll come in for a coffee, Ben?"

I nodded, my mouth dry. "Love to," I said.

We sat on the sofa and drank coffee and talked, and the free and easy atmosphere carried over from the restaurant. It was one o'clock by the time I looked into my empty mug and said, "Well, it's getting on. I'd better be . . ."

She reached out and touched my hand with her fingers. "Ben, stay the night, please."

"Well . . . If it's okay with you."

"Christ," she said, "what do you think?" And, before I knew it, she was in my arms.

I had often wondered what the first time would be like, tried to envisage the embarrassment of trying to do something that I had never done before. The simple fact was that, when we undressed each other beside the bed, and came together, flesh to soft, warm flesh, it seemed entirely natural, and accomplished with mutual trust and affection—and I realised that I'd never really had anything to fear, after all.

I was awoken in the night by a bright flash of light. I rolled over and held Elisabeth to me, cupped her bottom in my pelvis and slipped a hand across her belly.

The window overlooked the valley, the reservoir, and the Station.

High energy pulse beams lanced into the stratosphere.

"You 'wake?" she whispered.

"Mmm," I said.

"Isn't it beautiful?" she murmured. Shafts of dazzling white light bisected the sable sky, but more beautiful to me was holding a warm, naked woman in my arms.

"Mmm," I said.

"I always keep the curtains open," she whispered. "I like to watch the lights when I can't sleep. They fill me with hope."

I watched the lights with her. Hard to conceive that every beam of energy contained the newly dead of Earth.

"Elisabeth," I said.

"Hmm?"

"Have your read much about the Kéthani?"

She turned to face me, her breasts against my chest. She stroked my face and lightly kissed my lips. "Just about everything there is to read," she said.

"Something I don't understand," I said. "Millions of humans die, and are taken away and resurrected. Then they have a choice. They can either come back and resume their lives on Earth, or they can do the bidding of the Kéthani, and go among the stars, as explorers, ambassadors . . ."

"Or they can come to Earth, live awhile, and then leave for the stars."

I nodded. "That, too," I said.

The Kéthani had discovered billions of stars in thousands of galaxies. They'd found millions of habitable, and inhabited, planets, and they needed minions to go abroad and explore, contact, report on these worlds. There were not enough Kéthani to do this, so they employed humankind, and as payment they brought us back to life.

"And we trust them?" I said.

"We do now. At first, millions of us didn't. Then the reports started to come back from those who had died, been resurrected, and gone among the stars. And the stories they told, the accounts of a wondrous and teeming universe . . ."

I nodded. "I've seen the documentaries. But—"

"What?"

"What about all those humans who are . . ." I tried to think of a diplomatic phrase, "let's say, unsuited even for life on Earth. I mean, thugs and murderers, dictators, psychopaths."

My father . . .

"Hard to imagine Pol Pot acting as an ambassador for an enlightened alien race," I said.

She stroked my hair. "They're changed in the resurrection process, Ben. They come back . . . *different*. Altered. Still themselves, but with compassion, humanity." She laughed, suddenly.

"What?" I asked.

"The irony of it," she said. "That it takes an alien race to invest some people with humanity!"

She reached down and took me in her fingers, and guided me into her. We made love, again, bathed in the blinding light of the dead as they ascended to heaven.

Our parents died the following week, within days of each other.

On the Monday afternoon I was working on the fourth wall of the sheep fold when my mobile rang. "Hello, Ben Knightly here," I called above the biting wind.

"Mr Knightly? This is Maria, from Sunny View. Your father was taken into Bradley General at noon today. The doctor I spoke to thinks that it might only be a matter of hours."

I nodded, momentarily at a loss for words.

"Mr Knightly?"

"Thanks. Thank you. I'll be there as soon . . ." I drifted off.

"Very well, Mr Knightly. I'm so sorry."

I thanked her again and cut the connection.

I finished the section of wall I was working on, placing the stones with slow deliberation, ensuring a solid foundation.

I had anticipated this day for months: it would mark the start of a temporary freedom, an immediate release from the routine of visiting the nursing home. For six months I would be free of the thought of my father on Earth, demanding my attention.

It was perhaps two hours after receiving the call that I drove into the car park at Bradley General and made my way along what seemed like miles of corridors to the acute coronary ward. My father had suffered a massive heart attack. He was unconscious when I arrived, never came round, and died an hour later.

The sudden lack of a regular bleep on his cardiogram brought me from my reverie: I was staring through the window at the snow-covered fields, thinking that a few walls out there could do with attention.

Then the bleep changed to a continuous note, and I looked at my father. He appeared as he had before death: grey, open-mouthed, and utterly lifeless.

A ferryman came for him, asked me if I would be attending the farewell ceremony — I declined — and took him away in a box they called a container, not a coffin. I signed all the necessary papers, and then made my way to Elisabeth's house.

That night, after making love, we lay in bed and watched the first energy beam leave the Onward Station at ten o'clock.

"You're quiet," she said.

I hesitated. "My father died today," I told her.

She fumbled for the light, then turned and stared at me. "Why on Earth didn't you say something earlier?"

I reached out for her and pulled her to me. "I didn't think it mattered," I said.

She stroked my hair. I had never told her of my relationship with my father, always managed to steer the subject away from our acrimony.

She kissed my forehead. "He'll be back in six months," she soothed. "Renewed, younger, full of life."

How could I tell her that that was what I feared most?

The following Thursday I finished work at five and drove to Elisabeth's. The day after my father died, she had asked me to move in with her. I felt that our relationship had graduated to another level; I often had to pause and reminded myself how fortunate I was.

We settled into a routine of domestic bliss. We took turns at cooking each other meals more daring and spectacular than we would have prepared for ourselves alone.

I was expecting, that night, to be assailed by the aroma of cooking meat when I entered the kitchen, but instead detected only the cloying fragrance of air freshener. The light was off.

Then I made out Elisabeth. She was sitting on the floor by the far wall, the receiver of the phone cradled redundantly in her lap.

I saw her look up when I came in, and I reached instinctively for the light.

Her face, revealed, was a tear-stained mask of anguish.

My stomach flipped, for I knew immediately.

"Oh, Ben," she said, reaching for me. "That was the nursing home. Mum died an hour ago."

I was across the room and kneeling and hugging her to me, and for the first time I experienced another person's heartfelt grief.

The funeral was a quiet affair at the village church—the first one there, the vicar told me, for seven years. A reporter from a national newspaper was snooping, wanting Elisabeth's story. I told him where to go in no uncertain terms. There was less I could do to deter the interest of a camera crew from the BBC, who kept their distance but whose very presence was a reminder, if any were required, of the tragedy of Mary Carstairs's death.

Every day we walked up to the overgrown churchyard, and Elisabeth left flowers at the grave, and wept. If anything, my love for her increased over the next few weeks; I had never before felt needed, and to have someone rely on me, and tell me so, made me realise in return how much I needed Elisabeth.

One evening I was cooking on the Aga when she came up behind me very quietly, slipped her arms around my body, and laid her head between my shoulder blades. "God, Ben. I would have gone mad without you. You're the best thing that's ever happened to me."

I turned and held her. "Love you," I whispered.

She joined us on Tuesday nights, and it was as if her presence injected a well-needed dose of life into the proceedings: the conversation became more varied, and others joined our table. We made friends with a ferryman who lived in the old coach house a few doors down from the Fleece; Dan Chester's daughter had died of leukaemia six months earlier, and she was returning in three days. He invited us to the party to celebrate her return, and I loved Elisabeth even more when she smiled with genuine pleasure and said we'd be delighted to attend.

Four months after my father's death, Richard Lincoln came into the Fleece one Tuesday night and handed me a package. "Special delivery from the Onward Station," he said.

I turned the silver envelope over. It was small and square, the size of the DVD I knew it would contain. My name and address were printed on both sides, below the double star logo of the Kéthani.

"A message from your father, Ben," Richard said.

I could not bring myself to enjoy the rest of the evening: the package was burning a hole in my pocket.

When we returned home, Elisabeth said, "Well?"

I laughed, wrestling her towards the bedroom. "Well, what?"

"Aren't you going to play it?"

"Don't think I'll bother."

She stared at me. "Aren't you curious?"

"Not particularly."

"Well, if you aren't, I am. Come on, we'll play it on the TV in the bedroom."

I lay in bed, staring out at the rearing obelisk of the Station, while she inserted the DVD into the television. Then, with Elisabeth in my arms, I turned and stared at the screen.

My father had decided against recording his image: only his broad, bluff Yorkshire voice came through, while the screen remained blank. I was relieved that I would be spared the sight of his new, rejuvenated image.

"Ben, Reg here. I'm well. We still haven't seen the Kéthani— can you believe that? I thought I'd catch a glimpse of them at least." He paused. The fact that his voice issued from a star three hundred light years distant struck me as faintly ridiculous. "I'm in a group with about a dozen other resurrectees, all from different countries. We're learning a lot." He paused. "I still haven't decided what I'm doing yet, when I get back . . . Well, that's about it for now." His murmured farewell was followed by a profound silence.

And that was it, as casual as a postcard from Blackpool; except, I told myself, there was something almost human in his tone, an absence of hostility that I had not heard in years.

But that did nothing to help lessen my dread of the bastard's return.

Whenever Elisabeth broached the topic of implants, however tenuously, I managed to change the subject. In retrospect, I was ashamed at how my reluctance to undergo the implantation process affected her; at the time, selfishly, I could apprehend only my own frail emotions.

More than once, late at night, when we had made love, she would whisper that she loved me more than anything in the world, and that she did not want to lose me.

A week before my father was due to return, she could no longer keep her fears to herself.

She was sitting at the kitchen table when I returned from work, staring at the letter I'd received that morning from the Onward Station. My father was returning in seven days time; he had asked to meet me at a reception room in the Station.

It was the meeting I had dreaded for so long.

She was quiet over dinner, and finally I said, "Elisabeth, what is it?" I imagined that the news of my father's return had reminded her again of her mother's irrevocable demise.

She was silent for a while.

"Please don't avoid the issue this time," she said at last. "Don't change the subject or walk off." Her hand was shaking as she pushed away her plate.

"What is it?" I asked, stupidly.

She looked up, pinned me with her gaze.

"I can't stand the thought of losing you, Ben." It was almost a whisper.

"Don't worry, you won't. I have no intention of leaving you."

"Don't be so crass!" she said, and her words hurt. "You know what I mean." She shook her head, trying to fight back the tears. "Sometimes I experience a kind of panic. I'm on my own, driving to school or whatever, and I imagine you've been in some accident . . . and you can't begin to understand how that makes me feel. I don't want to lose you."

"Elisabeth . . ."

She hit the table with the ham of her right hand. "What if you're in a car crash, or drop dead of a heart attack? What then? You'll be dead, Ben! Dead forever. There'll be no bringing you back." She was crying now. "And I'll be without you forever."

"What are the chances of that?" I began.

"Don't be so bloody rational!" she cried. "Don't you see? If you were implanted, then I wouldn't worry. I could love you without the constant, terrible fear of losing you." She paused, and then went on, "And this thing about not being implanted making you appreciate being alive all the more." She shook her head. "I don't believe it for a minute. You're hiding something. You fear the Kéthani or something."

"It's not that."

"Ben, listen to me. When you're implanted, it invests you with a wonderful feeling of liberation. Of freedom. You really do appreciate being alive all the more. We've been afraid of death for so long, and then the Kéthani came along and gave us the greatest gift, and you spurn it."

We sat in silence for what seemed an age, Elisabeth staring at me, while I stared at the table top.

She could have said, then, "If you love me, Ben, you'll have the implant," but she didn't; she was not the type of person who uses the tactics of blackmail to achieve her desires.

At last I said, "My father made my life a misery, Elisabeth. My mother died when I was ten, and from then on he dominated me. He'd hit me occasionally, but far worse was the psychological torture. You have no idea what it's like to be totally dominated, to have your every move watched, your every word criticised, whatever you do put down and made worthless." I stopped. The silence stretched. I was aware of a pain in my chest, a hollowness. "I've never been able to work out why he was like that. All I know is that, until eighteen months ago, I lived in fear of him."

I stopped again, staring at my big, clumsy hands on the table top. "His criticism, his snide comments, his lack of love . . . they made me feel worthless and inadequate. I hated being alive. I'd often fantasise about killing myself, but the only thing that stopped me was the thought that my father would gain some sick satisfaction from my death." I looked up, tears in my eyes, and stared at Elisabeth. "He turned me into a lonely, socially inept wreck. I found it hard to make friends, and the thought of talking to women . . ."

She reached out, gently, and touched my hand.

I shook my head. "Ten years ago he had his first stroke, and I had to look after him. The bastard had me just where he wanted me, and he made my life even worse. Just as I fantasised about suicide, I dreamed of the day the bastard would die, freeing me . . .

"And then the Kéthani came, with their damned gift, and he

was implanted, and the thought of my father living forever . . ."
I took a long, deep breath. "I wasn't implanted, Elisabeth, because
I wanted to die. As simple as that. I hated being alive, and I was
too weak and inadequate to leave and start a life of my own."

"But now?" she asked, squeezing my fingers.

"But now," I said, "he's coming back next week."

We went to bed, and held each other in silence as the white
light streaked into the air above the Onward Station.

At last Elisabeth whispered, "Don't be afraid any longer, Ben.
You have me, now."

I left the van in the car park and approached the Station. I had
never seen it at such close quarters before, and I had to crane my
neck in order to see its sparkling summit, a thousand metres overhead.

I felt as cold as the surrounding landscape, my heart frozen. I
wanted to get the meeting over as soon as possible, find out what
he intended to do.

I passed the letter to a blue-uniformed woman at a reception
desk, and another woman led me down a long, white corridor. A
sourceless, arctic light pervaded the place, chilling me even further.

With the fixed smile of an air-hostess, the woman ushered me
into a small, white room, furnished with two sofas, and told me that
my father would be along in five minutes.

I sat down. Then I stood up and paced the room.

I almost panicked, recalling the sound of his voice, his silent,
condemnatory look.

A door at the far side of the room slid open and a figure in a
sky blue overall walked through.

All I could do was stand and stare.

It was a version of my father I recalled from my teenage years.
He looked about forty, no longer grey and bent, but upright, with
a full head of dark hair.

For so long, in my mind's eye, I had retained an image of my
father in his sixties, and vented my hatred on that persona. Now
he was the man who had blighted my early years, and I was the
young boy again, abject and fearful.

He stepped forward, and I managed to stand my ground, though
inside I was cowering.

He nodded and held out a hand. "Ben," he said.

And the sound of his voice was enough. I had a sudden memory, a vivid flash of an incident from my youth not long after my mother's death: he had discovered me in my bedroom, crying over the faded photograph of her I kept beside my bed. He had stared at me in bitter silence for what seemed like an age, and then, with his big, clumsy hands, he had unbuckled his belt and pulled it from his waist. His first, back-handed blow had laid me out across the bed, and then he had set about me with the belt, laying into me with blows that burned red-hot in time to his words, "You're a man, now, Ben, and men do not cry!"

Perhaps, I thought now, it was his own inability to show emotion that made him hate me so much for showing grief at my mother's death.

His beatings had become regular after that; he would find the slightest excuse in my behaviour to use his belt. Later it occurred to me that my beatings were a catharsis that allowed him to vent his own, perverted grief.

But, now, when he stepped forward and held out his hand, I could take no more. I had intended to confront my father, ask him what he intended, and perhaps even tell him that I did not want him to return. Instead, I fled.

I pushed my way from the room and ran down the corridor. I was no longer a man, but the boy who had escaped the house and sprinted on to the moors all those years ago.

I left the Onward Station and stopped in my tracks, as if frozen by the ice-cold night.

I heard a voice behind me. "Ben . . ." The bastard had followed me.

Without looking round, I hurried over to the van. I fumbled with the keys, my desire to find out his intentions forgotten in the craven need to get away.

"Ben, we need to talk."

Summoning my courage, I turned and stared at him. In the half-light of the stars, he seemed less threatening.

"What do you want?"

"We need to talk, about the future."

"The future?" I said. "Wasn't the past bad enough? If you think you can come back, start again where you left off, spoil the life I've made since you died . . ." I was amazed that I had managed to say it, and shook with rage and fear.

"Ben," my father said. "My own father was no angel, but that's no excuse."

"What do you want?" I cried.

He stared at me, his dark eyes penetrating. "What do *you* want, Ben? I have a place aboard a starship heading for Lyra, if I wish to take it. I'll be back in ten years. Or I can stay here. What do you want me to do . . . ?"

He left the question hanging, and the silence stretched. I stared at him as the cold night invaded my bones. The choice was mine; he was giving me, for the first time in my life so far as he was concerned, a say in my destiny. It was so unlike my father that I wondered, briefly, if in fact the Kéthani *had* managed to instil in him some small measure of humanity.

"Go," I found myself saying at last, "and in ten years, when you return, maybe then . . ."

He stared at me for what seemed like ages, but I would not look away, and finally he nodded. "Very well, Ben. I'll do that. I'll go, and in ten years . . ."

He looked up, at the stars, and then lowered his eyes to me for the last time. "Goodbye, Ben."

He held out his hand, and after a moment's hesitation I took it.

Then he turned and walked back into the Station, and as I watched him go I felt an incredible weight lift from my shoulders, a burden that had punished me for years.

I looked up into the night sky, and found myself crying.

At last I opened the door of the van, climbed inside, and sat for a long time, considering the future.

Much later I looked at my watch and saw that it was seven o'clock. I started the engine, left the car park, and drove slowly over the moors to Bradley.

It was nine by the time I arrived at the Fleece.

I had phoned Elisabeth and told her to meet me there, saying that I had a surprise for her. I'd also phoned Jeff Morrow, Richard Lincoln, and Dan Chester, to join in the celebration. They sat at a table across the room, smiling to themselves.

Elisabeth entered the bar, and my heart leapt.

She hurried over and sat down opposite me, looking concerned and saying, "How did it go with . . . ?"

I reached across the table and took her hand. "I love you," I said.

She stared at me, tears silvering her eyes. Her lips said my name, but silently.

Then she moved her hand from mine, reached up and, with gentle fingers, traced the outline of the implant at my temple.

Instructions for Surviving the Destruction of Star-Probe X-11-57

*D*O NOT BE ALARMED.

You are Leila Kuber, Chief Biology Officer aboard Star-Probe X11-57, a faster-than-light vessel exploring the planetary systems of the Lesser Magellanic Cloud. I am the probe's matrix logic system, and you are hearing this via your sub-dermal occipital implant.

There has been a malfunction in the drive system, resulting in the destabilisation of the Probe. The extent of the damage has yet to be assessed. I will keep you informed.

The malfunction has resulted in your sudden resuscitation from deep sleep. The deep sleep unit is irreparably damaged. Otherwise, I would not have awoken you until the arrival of the rescue mission. The extent of the damage necessitated the by-passing of the usual safety procedures. Because of this, you are suffering from temporary amnesia. Your memories should return within days. Meanwhile, I will guide you through the process of safely exiting the Probe.

On the cover of the hibernation pod, directly before your eyes, you will see a series of touch-commands. Press the green light and the cover will open. Step from the pod. Take care—you will be weak after three weeks in deep sleep. Exercise caution as you move. I am running a diagnostic examination of your physical state. I will be able to appraise you of your condition in precisely one minute and eleven seconds.

Now follow the green light set into the floor of the sleep chamber. This will lead you to the rise-plate. Step upon it. To your left is the control panel. Press the touch-command bearing the numeral 3, and then hold on to the handrail while you rise.

The pain in your left leg is caused by an arterial thrombosis. Take care when you walk. Speed is not imperative at the moment. While emerging from deep sleep, you suffered temporal lobe epilepsy. This might occasion certain visual hallucinations, voices, and associated trauma. Ignore these. I am working to affect somatic and neurological repair. Do not be alarmed. The situation is under control.

I have assessed the onboard situation and can issue a status report. The drive malfunction was caused by impact with a comet, or a similar stellar object. The drive unit underwent instant decompression and subsequent detonation. There were eighty-six human fatalities. You are the sole survivor.
  We are five thousand light years from the nearest Terran outpost. I was unable to initiate standard emergency procedure and issue a mayday alarm. I estimate that it will be in the region of one month before our situation is noted and rescue effected. I am currently running analyses of the remaining supplies of air, food, and water. I will appraise you of the chances of survival once I have the information.

When the rise-plate halts, touch the exit command on the control panel, step through the door, and follow the red indicator along the corridor.

Only eleven per cent of the mass of Star-Probe X11-57 remains intact. Eighty-nine per cent of the craft was destroyed as a result of the explosion.
  The sections of the ship which remain are these: your deep sleep pod, the access chute, four hundred cubic metres of levels one and two, and various sealed corridors leading from these levels.

Error! Caution!
  Do not touch the exit command!

Remain where you are.

That area of the Probe beyond the chute hatch suffered massive structural damage in the blast, and consequently underwent decompression. The area of the Probe beyond the third deck is open to the vacuum of space.

Pause while I assess the situation and evaluate possible options.

You must drop to level two. Press the touch-command bearing the numeral 2. When the plate halts, press the exit decal and step from the chute.

Follow the blue indicator along the corridor. There is a life-support unit on the starboard side of level 2. Within the unit is an emergency deep sleep pod. If you can reach this, your survival is ensured.

Halt. Turn right. Follow the red indicator in the floor. Remember, you have time. There is no need to hurry. I appreciate that the pain in your right leg is slowing you down, but do not let this effect your concentration. The life-support unit is less than three hundred metres away. You will reach it in approximately two minutes. Slow your breathing. Concentrate on every step.

I have calculated that sufficient air remains to sustain you for approximately one day, Terran standard. Therefore it is imperative that you reach the life-support unit and attain deep sleep.

Halt. Turn left. Follow the green indicator past the viewport. Ahead, you will see the hatch that gives access to the life-support unit. Enter the following sequence into the touch-command beside the hatch: 578-099.

Enter.

Before you is the pod. Touch the blue decal on the control console to open the pod. Enter your code into the controls. Your code is: CBO-95b.

One minute will elapse, and then a chime will sound to indicate that the system is ready. Lie in the pod and press the command to close the cover. Seconds later you will enter deep sleep.

Error.

There is a systems error effecting the functioning of the deep sleep pod. I am endeavouring to diagnose the nature of the malfunction.

Please be patient while I run through the program. This might take a few minutes. Do not panic. Try to relax. Take deep breaths.

The error lies in the power supply to the life-support unit. The nuclear core was destroyed in the initial blast. The hydrogen storage cell that should provide sufficient energy for this section of the Probe is running at below twelve per cent maximum efficiency. There is enough power to maintain the lighting and air supply, but not to run the deep sleep pod. Even if I could channel the power from the air supply and lighting, it would not be enough.

Calm yourself, Leila. Do not panic.

Allow me time to assess the possibilities. Through the application of logical analysis to the situation, I will arrive at a positive solution. Together, Leila, we will survive.

This may take some time.

Expending valuable energy in a needless exhibition of anger and self-pity will not aid your survival. I advise you to leave the life-support unit and sit before the viewport.

Now look out at the scene of stellar wonder before your eyes.

You were aboard Star-Probe X-11-57 for one year before the accident occurred. In that time you assessed the suitability of five planetary bodies for potential colonisation. Of those five planets, two were deemed habitable.

Calm yourself. I am working to attain a solution to the problem.

Through the viewport to your right, beyond the ruptured sponson that once held the drive units, you can see the last planet you investigated. It proved unsuitable for colonisation, but interesting nevertheless. You cannot recall landfall, Leila, but you recorded in your notes that that planet was one of the most beautiful you had ever visited.

Ammoniacal lakes. Ice massifs towering kilometres high. Magenta skies at midnight. These are mere words to me: I cannot appreciate the beauty of what they describe.

Sleep, Leila. Sleep. . . .

Leila.

You have slept for ten hours. There is sufficient air in this sector of the Probe to last you a further twelve hours. Do not panic. While you slept, I have been working.

I have a solution.

Listen carefully.

In the section of the Probe which survived the blast, there is another life-support unit, powered by the only other remaining hydrogen storage cell. Within the unit is a deep sleep pod. If you can reach the pod, your survival is guaranteed.

However, the life-support unit cannot be reached by following the colour-coded corridors in this section of the Probe.

The unit was blasted free of the main body of the Probe, and now floats in the vacuum of space, connected to the wreckage by power cables only.

Look through the viewport. At two o'clock, partially obscured by the excoriated drive nacelle, you will observe the floating life-support unit.

Do not despair.

You will need a vacuum environment suit in order to navigate your way across the gulf to the unit. There are three VE suits stored on level one.

Stand. Follow the blue indicator back to the chute and ride down to level one. Take your time. Impatience at this stage will gain you nothing. Your pain is an impediment, but not an insurmountable obstacle. Remember, soon you will be safe.

Exit the chute and follow the green indicator along the corridor as far as the first junction. Turn right. Ahead, set into the far wall, is the VE suit storage unit. Touch the open command and take a suit. They are soma-adaptive and will automatically shrink or expand to accommodate your body size. Step into the suit and pull the seal from the abdomen to the neck-line. Now affix the helmet. On your left wrist you will find a touch-command panel. Enter the code: 778-445, to initiate air supply.

Follow the black indicator along the corridor and turn right. Stop when you reach the bulkhead. Before you is a hatch. Look at the command panel on your left wrist. The red decal will release the VE suit's support cables. Touch it.

Affix the end of the cables to the lugs on either side of the hatch. Steady yourself by holding the support to the left of the hatch.

DESTRUCTION OF STAR-PROBE X-11-57

On the panel to the right of the hatch is a green exit command. Brace yourself against the pressure of the expelled air as it leaves the Probe.

Press the exit command.

Good.

Do not be afraid. You are secured by the cables. You cannot fall.

Step through the hatch. Hold on to the projections on the outside of the probe. There are many projections, designed for just such a manoeuvre.

Orient yourself and look up. At eleven o'clock, beside the drive nacelle, is the life-support unit.

Climb over the skin of the Probe until you are diametrically opposite the unit. I estimate that twenty metres will then separate you from the unit.

Take it easy. You have plenty of time. The suit's air supply will last eight hours. Rest when you feel tired. There is no need to exhaust yourself.

I can appreciate the pain, even if I am unable to experience it.

Cursing me will achieve nothing. I am trying to save your life, Leila.

Rest. Regain your breath. You are almost there.

You must go on. You have so much to live for. You are young, and healthy, with a magnificent career ahead of you in Exploration. Although you have no memory of it, your life on Earth is full and rich. You are engaged to a Pilot in the Sol Circuit division. You are very much in love. His name is Hans, and you have known each other for two years. You met in Prague, your home city. He is applying for a transfer to the Extra-Solar Star-Probe division.

You plan to explore the universe together.

You cannot give up now. Just one more push. . . .

Good. Now rest.

Look up. Directly opposite is the drive nacelle which is concealing your goal, the life-support unit. When you feel ready, and only then, crouch and kick off from the skin of the Probe. Aim for the drive nacelle. Don't worry—even if you fail to reach it at the first attempt, you will be able to haul yourself back and try again.

*   *   *

In your own time.

Crouch, holding on to the supports. Aim yourself towards the nacelle. Kick off.

Well done. You have reached the nacelle. You are more than half-way there. Rest, and when you have recovered, crawl around the drive nacelle and observe the unit. It is now a mere five metres away.

You are almost there.

You are almost safe.

Crawl, little by little.

I know. The pain. You are doing well. And again. Another few metres. You're almost there, Leila. Don't give up, now that you have almost made it. One last effort. Go on. . . .

Okay. Halt. Take deep breaths. I am sorry I can do nothing to ease the pain. The analgesics at my disposal can do only so much. You must be conscious in order to save yourself.

Okay, again. You are almost there.

Now launch yourself towards the unit. Crouch, aim, and kick.

You've made it. Hold on to the support beside the hatch. Hold on. Regain your breath. Do not cry.

Now, when you are ready, enter the sequence: 897-335 into the control-panel.

Step into the air-lock and disconnect the support cables from your VE suit. Close the hatch behind you and enter the same code into the panel beside the entry hatch.

Step inside. You are safe.

I am sorry.

I located eighty-five casualties, from a crew of eighty-seven. I assumed that the remains of the eighty-sixth human were destroyed in the explosion.

I had no way of assessing whether or not this life-support unit was occupied.

His name is Thomas Godwin. He is forty years old, a shuttle pilot, first-class. He has a wife and three children on the colony world of Brimscombe.

I can do nothing to assist you in the removal of Pilot Godwin from the deep sleep pod. That would be murder. But I can do nothing to prevent you from taking that course of action. I would understand completely.

There is only sufficient air in the life-support unit to last approximately six hours.

I estimate that the rescue mission will reach the pod in a little under one month.

Do not cry, Leila Kuber.

———

Eye of the Beholder

MILLER SAT AT HIS DESK AND STARED THROUGH the window at the gentle contours of Hampstead Heath. He considered the fact of the city beyond, the teeming millions packed into so little space. There had been a time, not so long ago, when the population of the capital, the sheer press of humanity, had filled him with claustrophobia. He smiled to himself now at the irony of the notion.

He picked up his pen and completed the entry in his journal. "So I have no rational explanation for what is happening to me. It has crossed my mind more than once that I am going mad—or maybe that I am already mad."

He paused there, staring out at the playground that abutted the heath. Swings described precise arcs against a background of tarmac and daffodils. The roundabout turned slowly, as if moved by the wind.

"And yet," he wrote, "I cannot accept this. Madness is no explanation. What has befallen me is not, I am sure, the result of some unique mental aberration, some dysfunction on a neurological level. What is happening *must* have an external cause. It is the world out there that has gone mad, not me." He paused again, then added: "But isn't that what all madmen claim?"

He closed his journal. Beside him on the desk, the screen of his PC glowed a multi-coloured invitation to start work. He had two chapters of a children's novel to complete before the weekend, four days away. He told himself that he could do the five thousand words in a day. He would begin tomorrow, take today off. In six months he had completed three short novels—losing himself in the fantasy worlds of his creation as if in a desperate bid to deny what was happening out there in the real world.

Despite the dangers of venturing out during the daylight hours, Miller decided that this morning he would go for a walk. The alternative, to remain inside and either read or watch a film, reminding himself of the world as it had once been, did not appeal to him. He would only brood if he remained at home. At least outdoors, even though he would be surrounded by reminders of the phenomenon, he would be able to gain satisfaction from the catharsis of exercise.

He found his dark glasses and moved into the hall. From the umbrella stand by the door he pulled his white stick. He opened the door and stepped outside, met by the fragrance of roses. He left the house and moved carefully down the street, staring straight ahead and tapping his cane on the pavement before him. He would call in at the newsagents for a paper, the deli for rye bread and cheese, and then circle around to the heath and walk for a mile or two to give himself an appetite for lunch.

He kept to the centre of the pavement, moving slowly and continually steeling himself for the impact. The danger was not so much one of other people's bumping into him, but of his colliding into them. At least, with this disguise, he had a ready excuse.

He had often wondered, before the catastrophe had befallen him, what it might be like to be blind. He had considered writing a novel from the point of view of a young blind boy—but something had stopped him, some notion that he was trespassing on territory he did not fully understand and therefore could not convincingly portray. Now he thought he understood the affliction a little better.

Although he was not technically blind, there were certain things that he could not see. Did that qualify him to enter the land of the blind, or at least write on their behalf? He smiled to himself . . . He remembered the adage that in the land of the blind, the one-eyed man was king. Did that make him, with two perfectly good eyes, an uncrowned monarch? Could he write a novel about his singular blindness? Would he be believed?

He stopped, staring along the deserted street, feeling angry with himself. No! No, it was not a blindness, he told himself, it was not something wrong with *him*—but something terribly askew with the world.

He bought a copy of the *Times*, then walked with exaggerated care to the delicatessen. He stood by the counter, waited until he heard the girl's bright, "Can I help you?" before he asked for a loaf of rye and a quarter each of Stilton and Gorgonzola. To maintain his guise, he had to be careful and ignore the impulse to fetch for himself the items he could see.

A plastic bag appeared on the counter before him, and he held out a five pound note. He watched it disappear from his fingers, to be replaced seconds later by a few coins. The transaction successfully accomplished, he left the shop and walked to the heath.

He was squeezing through the narrow, iron swing gate when his stick came up against something. He had been moving with unaccustomed alacrity, eager to reach the heath, and could not stop himself in time. He hit someone, staggered, and fell to his knees.

"Oh! I am sorry! Please . . . Forgive me—miles away." He heard a woman's voice, the vowels rounded with home counties enunciation.

He climbed to his feet. "I'm fine, really. It's okay—a little fall."

She touched his elbow, and he was aware of her fragrance, and the heady rush of it almost brought tears to his eyes. Mystique . . .

He turned and hurried away. As he paced from the heath he heard the woman's concerned enquiry. "I'm so very sorry. Are you sure you are all right?"

He made his way home, all thoughts of a walk forgotten as a consequence of the encounter. The mock Tudor façade of his detached house offered blessed sanctuary.

Once inside he deposited the bag, threw off his glasses, and collapsed into a chair by the window overlooking the back garden and the orderly rows of vegetables.

He wondered what it was about the encounter that had caused him such distress: the touch of the woman's soft hand, or the smell of her perfume?

If he were honest with himself, he knew it was the Mystique, and the memories it evoked.

Six years ago, at the age of thirty-two, Miller had had his first real relationship with a woman—"real" in that it not only involved sex, itself a traumatic, first-time experience for him, but also called for a reciprocation of emotions like care and concern, which he found even harder to come to terms with.

He had met Laura at a small party to celebrate the BBC production of one of his books. She had worked in the design department of his publishers, Flynn and Moran, and they had been introduced by his editor as the party was winding down. Miller had wanted nothing more than to get away from the chattering crowd, and the thought of having to amuse this small, rather attractive but painfully shy woman had not appealed. He recalled talking at length, about himself, while getting steadily more pissed on the bottle of expensive red wine he had liberated for his own consumption. He had no recollection of saying goodbye or of getting home. A situation, he told himself next morning, par for the course on the few occasions that he did venture out.

Laura had phoned a few days later, murmuring—she had always seemed to murmur, as if to speak aloud might offend—that she had enjoyed his latest book, enjoyed talking to him and perhaps . . . well, maybe they could meet for a drink some time—if it was convenient for him, of course . . . ?

He had often since wondered what had made him say, "Why, yes. Yes, that would be nice."

He had had one other abortive relationship, in his early twenties, and the degree of emotional commitment required of him, the paradoxical desire and at the same time loathing he had felt for the woman, had made him eschew even the thought of ever becoming involved again.

He had lost himself in his work, seen a couple of friends once a month, and told himself that he was reasonably content.

He had long since reconciled himself to the life of a bachelor. He gave thanks that his sex drive was inordinately low, so that his enforced celibacy did not provoke urges that might have been seen as perverse. He had got on with his life of work, the occasional talk at a school, and trips to the theatre.

Perhaps in acceding to Laura's invitation, some buried part of him had wished for something more, something better, than the cloistered existence he had come to accept.

They had seen each other for almost a year. At first he was attracted to the idea of being seen with this young, pretty girl, enamoured with the notion of being in love. But as he came to know her, to understand that beneath the prettiness cowered someone with all the emotional maturity of a schoolgirl, he came to realise that he felt nothing at all for this lost soul. It was an indication of his own immaturity that he had been unable to bring himself to hurt her by telling her that their affair was over.

As the months passed, and her emotional dependence on him conversely matched his increasing detachment from her, he found himself loathing Laura and himself in equal measure. He realised that to relate to another human being was to hold a mirror up to your soul, a mirror that reflected back at you all your emotional shortcomings, personal foibles, and faults of character. He wished to end the affair, draw a dark veil over the mirror.

He avoided her. He would not call at her flat for weeks, would not answer when she phoned. He even pretended to be out when she came round to his house and rang the door-bell for hours on end.

To her eternal credit, and his own debit on the scale of personal decency, it was Laura who had had the courage to end the affair.

She must have followed him home from the city, for as he was closing the door she burst in and confronted him in the twilight of the hall.

"You bastard!" she wept, and both the epithet and the volume of the cry shamed Miller.

"Shall we have a coffee?" he said.

"I don't want a coffee! I want . . . I thought—I thought we were . . . I was so happy with you. Don't you understand that? What went wrong? What did I do?"

And he had tried to calm her, assure her that the fault was not hers, that he was wholly to blame. He opened up, for the first time since he had known her, and told her that he had never, in all his life, felt affection for another human being. He recalled a line he used, which caused him to redden in shame even now, "The closest I've ever come to understanding and feeling for another human is in one of my books."

They had talked for over an hour, shuttling the same old, worn out and repeated dialogue back and forth, Miller trying to come to some ultimate distillation of meaning through repetition and rephrasing, much as he might rewrite a line of fiction a dozen times before getting it right.

Laura went through periods of lucidity, when she detailed her emotions, laid herself bare for his inspection: pleading for his love, if not his love then his affection, even his friendship and company. When this elicited little response from him, she would weep and plead, and then yell with a rage that was shocking to behold.

At last, in silence, they faced each other.

Laura shook her head. "I thought I loved you. I really did. But I was mistaken." She was speaking *sotto voce*, her natural mode of delivery. She was herself again. "I could never love anyone as cold and unfeeling as you. You're empty, you're cold and unfeeling and *empty* . . ." She had turned and opened the door, pausing on the threshold to look back at him. "I've never met anyone who doesn't need other people . . . and then I met you."

And she had walked from the house, walked from his life, and following the initial sense of release—the realisation that no longer would he have to confront Laura and so admit to the failings she had so accurately catalogued—he experienced a despair at the fact of who he was, and how he had become like this.

That had been six years ago, and for that long he had managed to insulate himself, to forget the woman who had made him admit to the emptiness at the core of his being.

Then today he encountered the woman on the heath, experienced her soft touch and the scent of Mystique, Laura's perfume.

Miller noticed, on the far side of the room, the winking red light of the answer phone. He crossed to it and stabbed the play button. "Miller, m'dear!" the megaphone baritone of Selwyn Rees, his agent, set up a vibration in the plastic housing of the device. "I'm ringing at eleven-thirty—why the hell aren't you pounding away on that bloody machine of yours! Look, something's come up. You've been bloody hard to catch of late, so be a pal and meet me at Harrington's at one, okay? See you then."

Miller walked to the window and stared out. For six months he had avoided all his usual contacts, putting off meeting Selwyn and his editors and conducting business by phone. Now the thought of meeting Selwyn for lunch appealed to him; oddly, Miller liked his agent's larger-than-life, back-slapping *joie-de-vivre*. It would be the first time since *it* had happened that he had met any of his old acquaintances: he would have to think up some story to excuse his "blindness."

He phoned for a taxi and fifteen minutes later found his glasses and stick and stepped out into the street.

This was the first occasion in six months that he had travelled further afield than his own street and the heath. As the taxi carried him through the deserted streets of Highgate and Belsize Park, Miller thought back to the morning of that first fateful day.

He had awoken at seven, as usual, showered, dressed, and breakfasted while half-listening to the news on Radio Four. He had thought nothing of the fact that there was no sign of the usual procession of commuters on the street outside his house—only later did it occur to him that he should have noticed the onset of the phenomenon then.

He had climbed to the second floor and his study, meaning to get down to work on the latest book. His usual working method was to compose his thoughts while staring through the window for half an hour before putting fingers to keyboard.

This morning, as he stared out, he became increasingly aware that something was very wrong.

The paths that traversed the heath were deserted—which was perhaps not so unusual at this hour. But the playground, usually busy with children during the school holidays, and bored *au pairs* with push-chairs, was also deserted.

Then Miller noticed that there were indeed a couple of push-chairs parked on the gravel path that surrounded the playground, and he felt a stab of alarm that they seemed to be unattended.

Then, as he watched, one of the buggies, seemingly of its own volition, turned and scooted off down the path, soon disappearing from sight through the gate. He experienced a sudden dizziness that sometimes effects the senses when the brain is forced to deal with an optical illusion.

Then he became aware of more of these visual impossibilities: a rain shower had started, and a multi-coloured host of umbrellas bobbed through the air—with not a soul beneath them. A dog trotted along the path, attached to a lead but without its owner, a surreal take on those mime artists who walk invisible dogs on stiff leads. As he stared more closely at the heath, he saw the grass darken in the shape of footprints as invisible citizens took their morning walks.

Miller hurried downstairs and stared through the front window. He felt an immediate relief to see cars and vans passing down the street—then was overcome with a stomach-churning nausea when he saw that the vehicles were empty. Brief-cases and shopping bags swung through short, impossible arcs a metre off the ground. A carrier full of milk bottles shot down the neighbouring drive.

Shaken, he made his way outside. He stood in the middle of the pavement, staring up and down the deserted street, normally at this hour thronged with people making their hurried way to work. For as far as the eye could see, the street was deserted—as empty as a stage set for some end of the world film—but dotted with a tell-tale signs that people still existed: the floating bags and folded newspapers, the occasional push-chair.

A disembodied voice sounded close by: "Excuse me, please."

And another: "Do you mind?" He must have presented an unusual sight to passers-by, as he turned this way and that, his arms held up in a gesture of amazement and mute appeal.

He took a few paces along the street, brought up short as he collided with the solid bulk of a man who growled: "What the hell? What do you think—?"

Off balance, Miller fell to his knees. He reached out instinctively—grabbed a leg. A woman screamed, pulled herself away. The sensation of touching someone he could not see was at once bizarre and terrifying.

He felt rough hands on his arms, dragging him to his feet. "What do you think you're up to?" someone said in his ear.

"I'm sorry, awfully sorry. Migraine. Terrible migraine . . ." He indicated his front gate. "If you could just assist me . . ."

Invisible hands steered him on to his garden path, released him. His heart pounding, bile rising in his throat, Miller staggered back to the house and lay on the settee in the front room, trying to make some sense of what was happening to him.

One hour later he stood and crossed to the window, staring out with a sense of dread. Even as he told himself that what he had experienced earlier might have been some temporary hallucination, he knew what he would see. And sure enough: driverless cars motored down the street, dogs trotted by on ridiculously rigid leads.

He phoned Selwyn. His agent's baritone boomed in his ear, reassuring him that all was well with the world. "Miller! This is a surprise. How can I help you, m'dear?"

"Ah . . . Just a social call, Selwyn. How are things?"

"Things?" Selwyn shouted, nonplussed. "What do you mean, things?"

"Look out of your window, Selwyn."

"Eh?"

"Do it, just for me. What do you see?"

After a moment's silence: "People, Miller. Millions of bloody people. What's all this about?"

Miller replaced the receiver without replying.

He remained indoors for three days, each morning checking to see if the world had returned to normal, only to find that the strange phenomenon still maintained. It seemed that the world out there was still functioning as it always had: he monitored the news on radio and television, and if anyone else had been afflicted with this strange . . . *malaise* . . . then no mention of it was made.

On the fourth day he realised that he would have to venture

out for food and other provisions. For fear of repeating his mistake of the first day and colliding with innocent passers-by, it occurred to him that in the guise of a blind man he would be able to walk the streets in relative safety. People would avoid him, and he would have an excuse in the event of accidental collisions.

His life slipped into a manageable routine. He avoided his acquaintances in the writing world, turned down invitations to talk at libraries and schools, and made excuses when invited to the theatre.

His only visual link with his fellow humans was through the medium of live television, where he could paradoxically view people—presenters, pedestrians, athletes—without hindrance. As the weeks passed, he almost came to accept the fact of his strange condition.

Of late, though, he had been much given to wondering if what was happening was the result of some external factor, or some malfunction in his own sensory awareness. He could supply no explanation as to what might have happened to the world to make its citizens invisible to him alone, but nor could he bring himself to accept the alternative: that the aberration was within him, that, in other words, he was going mad.

Miller sat back in the padded seat of the taxi, the driver invisible and the steering wheel turning as if by remote control, and watched the empty world pass by outside.

They turned into Upper St. Martin's Lane. The taxi came to a halt, caught in the snarl of bumper to bumper traffic contrasting with the deserted pavements. It was a strange enough sight to see the streets of Hampstead and Highgate emptied, but Miller stared, his amazement renewed, at the fact of central London cleared of all its citizens. The city had about it a Sunday morning deadness. Here and there, as he stared through the window, he caught the surreal image of hamburgers and hot dogs disappearing down invisible throats, newspapers hanging open in the air like details from a canvas by Magritte.

The taxi halted outside Harrington's, his agent's unofficial office. Miller paid the driver and stepped out carefully, tapping his way across the pavement with his stick. He made it to the door of the restaurant without mishap and pushed inside.

A muted babble of conversation greeted him from a seemingly empty room: the effect was disconcerting, as if a film soundtrack had been dubbed on to the wrong scene.

Then Miller noticed the small signals that belied the emptiness of the restaurant. Knives and forks worked in precise, deliberate rhythms, the movements of the knives economical, used to cut and then laid aside, those of the forks more lavish as they were lifted from plate to mouth and back again. Miller found the trajectory of the assembled silverware mesmerising—something that, when the world had been normal, he had never really noticed.

A dessert trolley trundled across the room. Trays of food, held at head height, floated through the swing doors from the kitchen to their destinations.

Then he heard: "Miller? Good God, man! Miller, is it you?"

The conversation modulated. He imagined heads turned his way. The voice sounded again, closer this time. "Miller—what happened, for Godsake?"

He felt Selwyn's meaty grip on his forearm. He was drawn across the restaurant to the booth which over the years his agent had made his own.

Selwyn, with the misplaced solicitude of the sighted for the blind, manhandled Miller into his seat. He resumed his own seat opposite: Miller saw the plush velvet of the backrest dimple. "Out with it, man! What the hell happened? Why didn't you tell me?"

Miller shook his head, less concerned by the question than by the strange phenomenon of the disembodied baritone. For the ten years that Selwyn Rees had acted as his agent, the big Welshman had been a whole entity, a physical presence—six feet tall, built like a prop-forward, ruddy-faced—and now Miller found it almost impossible to relate to Selwyn reduced as he was to merely a voice.

He shrugged. "Just last week," he said, relaying the story he'd rehearsed in the taxi. "I fell down the stairs. Concussed myself. When I came to . . ." He shrugged. "The specialists say that my sight might return—they're still running tests."

Selwyn's brandy glass rose; a goodly quantity of the amber liquid disappeared down his gullet. "God, I don't know what to say. What about work—?"

Miller smiled. "Don't worry, Selwyn. I'm still writing. I bought a dictaphone—"

"Thank God for that. Hell, this has come as something of a shock."

They ordered lunch, Miller selecting steak and kidney pie with new potatoes from the menu which Selwyn read out. He ordered a bottle of house white, then said: "You mentioned that something had come up?"

Selwyn's brandy glass bobbed in an acknowledging gesture. "Sorry to dump bad news on you like this, Miller. Bloody Worley and Greenwood—they've reneged on the contract for the third Kid Larsen book. Payment in full, of course—but they won't be publishing the book. 'Present financial climate' and all that crap."

"Any chance of placing the third elsewhere?" Miller asked. He had to stop himself from smiling at the charade of addressing a seemingly empty room.

"Think about it, man. If you were a publisher, would you touch the third book in a trilogy that wasn't selling that well?"

"Touché."

Their meals arrived. Miller watched the plates slide across the restaurant as if by a miracle of anti-gravity. He heard the waiter murmur that the plates were hot. Selwyn tucked into his sirloin with gusto, knife and fork working like pistons.

They discussed the state of the country—for about three minutes—before conversation returned, as ever, to the small world of publishing. Miller caught up on the gossip he'd missed out on over the months, nodded absently as Selwyn recounted the merry-go-round of editorial sackings and appointments.

They were sipping coffee when Miller said, "I've almost finished the latest, so I'd appreciate it if you'd look out for more of the usual." Meaning the hackwork with which he filled the weeks between his own work.

His words were greeted with a lengthy silence.

At last Selwyn said: "Miller—I don't usually hand out advice. You're a pro, you know what you're doing. But—" A pause. "Look—how about slowing down? Being a bit more . . . how should I put it? Selective. I know it's none of my business—and tell me to keep my bloody nose out if you disagree—but do you really need all this hackwork? Slow down. Take more time over the big projects. A couple of your latest books have been bloody good—and you know me, I don't hand out compliments lightly."

Miller nodded. "I appreciate your concern. You know how I like to work—I can't stop, and I work hard even on the rubbish—"

"I know you do. And it's appreciated—you don't know how glad editors are to have more than just a competent job handed in. But . . . between you and me, you're better than all that stuff." The coffee cup tipped at lip-level. "Okay. Sermon over. I've said enough."

At that second, movement flashed on the periphery of Miller's vision.

He turned his head in time to see—to his utter amazement—the quick figure of a young woman dash past a table on the far side of the room. It happened so fast that only after seconds, when the girl had disappeared through the door, did it come to him that he had seen, for the first time in six months, actually *seen* another human being . . . In retrospect, he told himself that the girl had even paused in her escape from the restaurant, stopped briefly, and looked across the room at him—but the more he considered the episode, the more he told himself that it had been nothing other than the effects of too much white wine.

Selwyn was saying, "Well . . . I suppose duty calls—"

"Did you see anything just then?" Miller said. "I mean . . . I thought I heard . . . I don't know. Did someone just run through . . . ?" He trailed off, realising how ridiculous he was sounding.

"You must be hearing things, Miller. Now, the bill. This is on me, and no protests."

Five minutes later Selwyn escorted Miller from the restaurant and insisted on finding him a taxi. As he was carried home through the London streets jammed with traffic but devoid of people, Miller sat back and considered what he had seen in the restaurant—if, indeed, he had seen anything at all.

Over the next few days Miller lost himself in finishing the last two chapters of the novel and beginning the second draft. When he considered the episode in Harrington's, he told himself that a combination of drunkenness and some desire of his subconscious had conjured the apparition of the young woman. He concentrated on his work, immersing himself in the reality of his fiction that was more real than the world outside. His life slipped into a comfortable routine of writing, eating, and strolling across the heath at sunset.

Then, just as he had succeeded in convincing himself that the woman had been nothing more than a phantom of his imagination, he thought he saw her again.

He was emerging from the deli with provisions for the next day or two when he caught a flash of white from the corner of his eye. He turned quickly, looking across the road. He could have sworn that he glimpsed the girl's slight figure dash behind the hedge of the house opposite. He moved to the edge of the pavement, staring. His manner must have appeared odd to anyone nearby—a blind man staring intently at something on the other side of the road.

Through the foliage of the hedge, he made out a fractured pattern of white material and brown skin as the girl ran away down the side of the house and out of sight.

Paradoxically, far from convincing him of the girl's physical reality, the sighting only served to convince him further that she was the product of his own subconscious: something about her elusiveness suggested that she was a figment, like the beguiling Sirens that down the years had called to him in his dreams, only to disappear with terrible, tragic finality upon his approach.

That night, after describing his sighting of the girl, Miller wrote in his journal: "There are two possibilities, of course. Either she exists in reality, or in my imagination. The latter possibility is less worrying—the thought that she is a product of my frustrated libido is one with which I can cope, as I have coped with similar frustrations over the years. The former possibility, that she really exists out there . . . this throws up a series of worrying questions. Why is she the only human being I can see? Is she following me—as the two sightings in different parts of London tend to suggest—and, if so, why? What could she want with me? I have to admit that over the months I have come to some psychological accommodation with what is happening. The advent of the girl upon the scene would serve only to confuse matters."

Miller finished the second draft of the novel, taking time to hone it to his satisfaction before sending it off to Selwyn. A week after dining with his agent, he parcelled up the manuscript and posted it as he made his way to the heath.

It was a perfect summer's afternoon, the sky clear and blue and the heat of the day tempered by a cooling breeze. Miller sat on a bench, first ensuring that it was unoccupied, and stared across the eerily deserted heath. There was evidence that the citizens of London were taking the opportunity to enjoy the clement weather: kites dipped and jinked through the air at the command of invisible controllers; ubiquitous dogs trotted, as if pushed along, at the end of straightened leads; a fleet of empty push-chairs careered crazily across the heath like remote-controlled toys.

The murmured conversation of the unseeable citizens eddied around him, rising and falling as they approached, came alongside him, and passed away.

The girl appeared, suddenly, on the crest of a small hill about fifty yards before Miller. There could be no denying, now, the reality of her existence. The fact of her physical presence, in all the emptiness around her, struck Miller with breathtaking force. She wore a simple, short white dress and a pair of soiled pink leggings. Her long, black hair whipped around her face in the wind. She was staring, with disconcerting concentration, straight at him.

Something moved within Miller, some long-repressed longing. At the same time he told himself that he wished she had never appeared, that he could do without the complications that her arrival entailed.

She swept a tress of hair from her face in a deliberate gesture, then walked from the hillock, into the dip and up the other side towards him.

She collided with something—someone—and the effect was almost comical. The impact stopped her briefly in her tracks, rocking her on her bare feet, before she gained equilibrium and continued forward. Instead of walking with care, she seemed to take a satisfaction in moving at speed, ignoring the cries that followed her progress up the hill.

She paused before Miller, staring at him with a kind of resolved belligerence. She was older than he had first thought: perhaps in her twenties. Her face was small and weathered, not at all pretty but possessing a certain aggressive charm. Miller was aware of his heartbeat. He was amazed at the fact of her face, the sheer humanness of it: the small nose and long lips and the high, domed brow. It was the first flesh-and-blood face he had looked upon for a long time, and in its singularity it stood as a paradigm for all that was human.

He saw then that her hands were soiled, her hair matted, that her eyes glinted with a light of desperation.

She was shaking her head as if in disbelief. "I can see you," she said in an amazed whisper. "I really can see you." She had a northern accent, the harsh vowel sounds accentuating her naive disbelief.

Milled removed his dark glasses, stared at her. "And I can see you, too."

His throat was dry. There were so many questions he wanted to ask that he did not know where to start.

"I saw you in London last week, in the restaurant. Couldn't believe my eyes. Thought I was seeing things."

Miller laughed suddenly: an uncontrollable burst of hilarity that spoke of his disbelief, his inability to handle what was happening.

The girl stared at him as if he were mad. "What's up?"

He dabbed his wet eyes with a handkerchief. "I'm sorry, it's just

. . . Look, you're the first person I've seen in six months—"

"Me too. I mean, you're the first person I've seen for ages. Thought I was going loopy. But everything else seemed . . . I don't know . . . everything seemed normal, apart from me. They had me in a psychiatric ward, you know. When it happened, I just flipped. I was living rough, around King's Cross. Then I woke up and the world was empty. I ran around, crashing into things . . . people. So they locked me away." She shrugged, smiled at him. "But I got away, been on the move ever since."

She hesitated, thought about it, then joined him on the bench, drawing her legs up to her chest and hugging her nylon leggings. "Do you know what's happening to us?" There was more desperation in her tone than she wanted to admit.

He shook his head. "I honestly don't know."

She nodded, regarding him. "You seem to be doing okay for yourself, though. I've been following you—after I saw you in the restaurant. I nicked a car and followed you to Hampstead, except I lost you there. Had to wait around for days, then the other morning . . ."

"I . . ." he began. "I've adapted to the circumstances as well as can be expected."

"You've got a big house . . ."

He resented the implication in the statement, and then hated himself for feeling such mean-spirited resentment. Here he was, taking part in an encounter unique in human experience, and all he could think about was how he had to keep his distance from this strange and alien creature.

"I'm Lucy, by the way."

"Miller," he said, and forced himself to say, "Pleased to meet you, Lucy."

Staring at the twin peaks of her knees, from time to time darting a quick glance at him, she told him the story of her short and horrible life to date.

She was from Leeds, and her father had died when she was ten, and her step-father had raped her when she was twelve. At fifteen she ran away from home, came to London and lived rough for five years, begging from commuters and occasionally stealing from shops and supermarkets.

As Miller listened, he realised that the tragedy of her personal life-story was that it was a succession of clichés all too common in today's society, a series of misfortunes he, in his privileged position, had no hope of understanding. He was reduced to a series of stock responses and phrases of commiseration, which might have appeared appropriate as lines of dialogue in fiction, but which in real life sounded empty and meaningless.

She trailed off. A silence came between them.

Miller wondered how he might make his excuses and leave. It crossed his mind that he should offer her a room, at least some food. But he wanted nothing more than to be away from her, back in the familiar territory of his own company.

"It's good to talk to someone again, Miller," she said. "What are you doing tomorrow? I know you come here most days."

He nodded, relieved at the possible way out she had given him. "I'll be here tomorrow," he said, "at the same time."

She smiled. "Good. I'll see you then, okay?" She hesitated, then pointed at his glasses and cane. "I like that. Very clever."

"You could do it too, Lucy. People avoid me, and it's an excuse if I do bump into people."

Lucy palmed a hank of hair from her high forehead, staring at him with her hand still in position like a visor. "It'd be no good for me now, Miller. You see, people can't see me anymore. Two weeks ago I disappeared, just like they've disappeared." She smiled. "I just go around bumping into people, freaking them out. They must think I'm a ghost."

Miller stared at her, alarmed. "How long have you been like this—I mean, when did people first disappear?"

She shrugged. "Oh . . . more than six months ago."

He wondered if what had happened to Lucy two weeks ago, the fact that she was no longer visible to others, was yet another stage in this phenomenon, this gradual disenfranchisement of the soul? Would he, in turn, disappear in the eyes of others? The thought was appalling. How might he function, if this happened? How might he find work?

"Also," she went on, as if twisting the knife, "I can't hear people now. I'm blind and deaf to the human race. What do you think of that?"

He shook his head. Blind and deaf to the human race . . . "How terrible . . ." But he was thinking more of himself than of Lucy.

She said, "Look, I've got to be going."

He reached out—surprising himself with the gesture—and took her callused palm in his hand. "Do you have somewhere? I mean—"

She shook her head. "I'm fine, okay?" She smiled, her features showing compassion. "See you tomorrow, right?"

She jumped from the bench, hurried off in the direction of Highgate. Miller watched her as she skipped away, just once colliding with someone, the impact sending her spinning to the ground. She picked herself up, laughing out loud, and ran off into the trees.

The following day he began outlining a proposal for his next book. As he worked, he found his attention wandering. He could not erase the image of Lucy from his mind. Her face kept swimming before his vision, and her coarse, northern accent filled his head. He hated himself for being unable to forget her, resented her for her intrusion into his hitherto orderly existence.

At five he cooked himself dinner and ate alone, as he had done for the past six years. He imagined Lucy sitting on the bench on the heath, waiting for him. He remained in his armchair, staring at his empty plate. He could not bring himself to move. He knew how to handle his present circumstances, was in full command of his day to day regime; to become emotionally involved with someone with whom he had nothing in common—other than the shared experience of the strange phenomenon—would only lead to mutual hurt. He told himself that she had survived very well without him until now, and would continue to do so in the future. It would be kinder to both himself and to Lucy if he left well alone.

The next day he lost himself in the novel proposal. He was pleased to find that, come five, he had outlined half a dozen chapters with hardly a thought for the girl.

He worked hard for the next few days, managing to banish Lucy from his thoughts and in so doing keeping a rein on the complex emotions of resentment and self-loathing. He expected to see her on the odd occasions when he ventured out for food, and experienced relief when he arrived home without having had the expected encounter. He avoided his customary evening strolls, a small price to pay for the reinstatement of the emotional status quo he had enjoyed for the past few years.

He completed the outline one week after his meeting with Lucy, printed out the manuscript and posted it off to Selwyn. For the rest of the day he sat in his study and read through his notebooks, looking for something that might spur his imagination. All the ideas seemed half-baked and unimaginative. He considered what Selwyn had suggested, that he concentrate on larger projects, topics closer to his heart.

He decided to ring Selwyn. He would talk an idea over with

him, a literary novel about a man who wakes up one morning to find that the entire human race is invisible . . . Perhaps if he could not confront himself honestly through the medium of a relationship with another person, then he might come to some catharsis of his soul through the one medium of communication that he did understand: that of the novel.

Or he could always ask Selwyn to find him more hackwork.

He tapped Selwyn's number into his phone and waited. He heard the amplified click of the receiver being lifted at the other end—and then silence. He spoke, saying his name. "Hello? Hello —Selwyn? Can you hear me?"

Silence. He tried to get through again, and again the same response. He wondered if there was something wrong with his phone. He tried getting though to BT complaints, with no luck.

He decided to use the phone at the newsagents on the corner. He gathered his stick, his dark glasses, and left the house. He turned left down the street, heading towards the row of shops.

He moved slowly, sweeping his stick in a swift arc before him. Someone collided with him, almost knocking him off his feet. "I'm sorry," he began. "Please excuse me."

He expected some response, either an apology or a curse. He heard nothing, and set off again. He was approaching the newsagents when he collided with someone for the second time. "I'm awfully sorry," he said. Again his apology was greeted with silence. Sweating, hardly daring to dwell on what might be happening, he pushed into the shop. He saw, before the counter, a floating, rolled newspaper and a packet of crisps. He cocked his head to catch the sound of voices, but there was no sound whatsoever. The paper and the crisps levitated, and before Miller could move the invisible customer turned and stepped into him. The crisps and the paper fell to the floor. The door whipped open. Miller imagined the customer fleeing in fright at the experience of bumping into something invisible . . . He opened the door and hurried home, keeping to the gutter to lessen his chances of bumping into people who could no longer see him.

He arrived home without mishap, seated himself in the chair before the window, and wept.

During the long hours of the afternoon he tried to work out where this latest development left him in the scheme of things. He could hear and see no one, and no one could hear or see him. He could no longer carry out the simplest transaction with his fellow human beings. If he wished to feed himself, then he would be reduced to stealing food. If he continued to write for a living, then he could only contact Selwyn through written communication.

He wondered how long he would be able to exist like this.

At six, Miller left the house and made his way to the heath. He collided with perhaps a dozen people on the way, and slowed his walk so that he would lessen the chance of injury to himself and others.

There was no sign of Lucy on the heath. He examined the grass before the bench on the hill, looking for the tell-tale sign of trampling that would indicate that the seat was occupied.

He sat down, wondering whether he really wanted the girl to show herself.

As the sun set and a cooling wind eddied around him, Miller considered the possibility of ending his life. It was a solution he had considered from time to time before—but his life had never seemed *worth* taking, had never been that terrible to warrant bringing it to a sudden and irrevocable end. And now? That which had sustained him over the years, the unvarying and reassuring routine, was shattered. He was pitched into the traumatic territory of the unknown, and he did not know if he would be able to cope.

"Hello," a voice said behind him. "Thought you might turn up, if I waited long enough."

Lucy moved around the bench and sat down, hugging her shins to her chest. The sudden sight of her, the visual miracle of her physical reality, filled Miller with a sensation akin to joy.

He tried to keep his voice calm. "And what made you think that?"

"I've been watching you, Miller. This morning, I noticed— you've gone the same way as me. They can't see you any more." She stared at him. "We're really the same now, aren't we?"

A silence stretched between them. At last Miller said: "Why do you think . . ." Something caught in his throat. "Why do you think this happened to you, Lucy?"

She blinked, threw the question back at him. "Why do you think it happened to *you?*"

He hesitated. By telling her, he would be opening himself up for minute inspection, laying bare that part of him which he had kept protected with introversion and apathy. "Shall I tell you?" he asked. "It's only a theory, and it might not be right, but . . .

"I'm a coward, Lucy," Miller went on. "For so long I've been unable to take, because I've been unwilling to give. I could never bring myself to feel affection for another human being . . ." He paused, staring into space. "Someone once said of me that I didn't need people, and, do you know, that didn't really hurt me at the time. I was too self-centred and shallow to realise what an indictment that verdict really was." And he told her of his relationship with Laura, and the woman before that, and how he had hurt these people without really realising that he was doing so, how he had hurt these people, because he had not known how to love them.

The sun set in laminated strata of orange and blood red, like a banner declaring the birth of a new day, not the beginning of night.

"And you?" he asked at last.

She smiled sadly, forked away stray hair with the tines of her fingers. "After what my step-father did, I told myself that never, never ever again . . . So I ran away and didn't let myself be used. I didn't get close to anybody, you know? I'm twenty-one, Miller, and you know what—I've never had anyone." She stopped suddenly, shaking her head at her inability to fully articulate the degree of her pain.

Miller reached out to take her hand, and the warmth of it, the sudden electric vitality of her flesh, was like an affirmation.

They left the heath, keeping off the paths and scanning the grass for signs of trampling. They walked home along the road, stepping into the gutter to allow past the occasional driverless car, and the fact that they made it home without collision seemed to Miller a signal, an indication—despite the fear in his heart and the terrible sense of inadequacy at the core of his being—that what he was doing was right.

That night they lay side by side on the bed, holding each other and talking in whispers, as if the secrets they shared might be overheard and used against them. They talked of their pasts, of their hurts and disappointments, their failings and their guilt. They fell asleep, holding each other, as dawn lightened the sky outside.

For two days they remained in the house and talked and laughed and ate. Miller discovered a great affection deep within him, a desire to cherish and protect, and in turn be cherished and protected. On the second night their conversation halted, and they stared at each other, communication between them silent now but no less eloquent.

They moved to the bedroom and undressed and made love with the uncoordinated passion of the novices they were. In the early hours Lucy slept, her arms tight around Miller as if fearing that he might abscond.

Miller could not sleep. He extricated himself from her embrace and made his way to the study. He opened his journal and wrote of the events of past two days, taking care to describe exactly his thoughts and feelings.

Lucy was still asleep when he returned to the bedroom, her small shape curled beneath the sheets, childlike in her vulnerability. Miller lay down, amazed at the sound of her breathing, the potentiality of her being. He closed his eyes and soon slept.

He was awoken by something in the morning . . . or rather not so much by something, but by a subtle sense of absence. He blinked himself awake, recalling the events of the night before, and instinctively reached out for Lucy. As he did so, he had a terrible premonition—and his hand encountered a forbidding tundra of cool linen.

She was gone.

He dressed and hurried downstairs. The front and back doors were both locked from the inside. The windows were shut. He searched the house, but there was no sign of Lucy.

He returned to the bedroom, as if by magic he might find her restored to the bed. The sight of it, empty, reminded him of the joy they had shared—and filled him with despair.

He left the house and ran down the centre of the road, dodging the traffic. He scanned the streets, the gardens, for any sign of her. He ran on to the heath, taking pains to look out for trodden grass that would denote other people abroad at this early hour.

He sat on the bench on the hill, scanning the heath, the horizon. He remained there for a long time—certainly hours—as the sun rose over London. He thought back over his brief liaison with Lucy, and it came to him that the degree of feeling aroused in him was out of all proportion to the length of time he had known the girl. It was as if fate had played a cruel joke on him, to pay him back for all the years he had voluntarily shunned his fellow humans.

He returned home. He told himself that she would be there when he got back, cooking breakfast and oblivious of his desperation. He almost ran up the garden path, unlocked the door with fumbling haste, and barged into the kitchen. Lucy was not there. The house was empty, silent. He was, as he had been for so many years, alone.

He passed the day in a daze. He sat in a chair by the window, hugging himself and staring blindly over the heath. As six o'clock approached, he told himself that he should be out there, actively looking for Lucy, rather than incarcerating himself in the house and bemoaning his fate.

For the second time that day he made his way to the heath and the bench on the hill. He sat and stared out at the deserted landscape, his heart heavy with a grief he had never before experienced, a despair at the wasted years of his life, the opportunities foregone, chances ignored.

Miller was not sure when exactly the transformation began.

So immersed in his self-pity, his rewriting of the past, he paid little attention to the empty world around him.

Perhaps it was the sound of voices that alerted him, startled him from his reverie, or perhaps the shadows that fell across the bench beside him. He looked up, hardly daring to believe what he was seeing, as if this was yet another jest the world was playing.

He stared about him in wonder.

The heath was populated by a hundred strolling figures: couples walked hand in hand, families sat in circles and talked, groups of friends stood in quick and animated conversation. As Miller watched, he was struck by the fact that it was not so much their visual presence that was the miracle, but the fact of their interaction.

He imagined the teeming city beyond the horizon of the heath, the intricate ties of association, the web of affinity that humans wove which made existence worth the while.

He stared, hardly daring to hope that what he was beholding might endure.

A middle-aged woman smiled at him. She gazed at the setting sun, the long shadows brush-stroking the heath. "Isn't it wonderful?" she said, before walking on.

Miller smiled to himself. He felt the urge to run after the women, take her in a fierce embrace.

He would go to King's Cross, he decided, try to find Lucy among the many homeless who made the streets of the city their home. And if, as he suspected, Lucy was not there to be found, had never been there . . . ?

Then Miller realised that for him the real test would begin.

The Touch of Angels

THE SUN WAS GOING DOWN ON ANOTHER CLEAR, sharp January day when Doug Standish received the call. He had left the station at the end of his shift and was driving over the snow-covered moors towards home and another cheerless evening with Amanda. He would stop at the Dog and Gun for a couple beforehand, he decided; let a few pints take the edge of his perceptions so that Amanda's barbs might not bite so deep tonight.

His mobile rang. It was Kathy at control. "Doug. Where are you?"

"On my way home. Just passing the Onward Station." The alien edifice, a five hundred metre-tall spire like an inverted icicle, scintillated with the fire of the setting sun.

"Something's just come up."

Standish groaned inwardly. Another farmer reporting stolen heifers, no doubt.

"A ferryman just rang. There's been a murder in the area. I've called in a Scene of Crime team."

He almost drove off the road. "A murder?"

She gave him the address of a sequestered farmhouse a couple of miles away, then rang off.

He turned off the B-road and slowed, easing his Renault down a narrow lane between snow-topped, dry-stone walls. The tyres cracked the panes of frozen puddles in a series of crunching reports. On either hand, for as far as the eye could see, the rolling moorland was covered in a pristine mantle of snow.

Murder . . .

Ten years ago Standish had worked as a Detective Inspector with the homicide team in Leeds. He had enjoyed the job. He had been part of a good team and their detection and conviction rate had been high. He had viewed his work as necessary in not only bringing law and order to an increasingly crime-ridden city, but also, in some metaphorical way, bringing a measure of order to what he saw as a disordered and chaotic universe.

He had no doubt that every time he righted a wrong he was, on some deep subconscious level, putting right his own inability to cope with the hectic, modern world he was finding less and less to his taste.

And then the Kéthani came along, and bestowed upon humankind the gift of immortality. Human beings no longer died—or, rather, they died and were brought back to life on the Kéthani homeplanet. Then, they had the choice of returning to Earth to resume their lives, or living among the stars as envoys and ambassadors of their alien benefactors.

Within months, crime figures had dropped dramatically. Within a year, murders had fallen by almost ninety-five percent. Why kill someone when, six months later, they would be resurrected and returned to Earth? In the early days, of course, murderers thought they could outwit the gift of the Kéthani. They killed their victims in hideous ways, ensuring that no trace of the body remained, and attempted to conceal or destroy the implant devices. But the nanotech implants were indestructible, and emitted a signal which alerted the local Onward Station as to their whereabouts. Each implant contained a sample of DNA, and a record of the victim's personality. Within a day of discovery the device would be ferried to the Kéthani homeplanet, and the individual successfully brought back to life. And then they would return to Earth and point the finger.

Two years after the coming of the Kéthani, the Leeds homicide squad had been disbanded, and Standish shunted sideways into the routine investigation of car thefts and burglaries.

Like almost everyone he knew, he had rejoiced at the arrival of the aliens and the gift they gave to humanity. He had been implanted within a month, and tried to adjust his mind to the fact that he was no longer haunted by the spectre of death; that, when he did die, he would be brought back to life to begin a renewed existence.

Shortly before the arrival of the Kéthani, Standish married Amanda Evans, the manageress of an optician's franchise in Bradley. For a while, everything had been wonderful: love, and life everlasting. But the years had passed, and his marriage to Amanda had undergone a subtle and inexplicable process of deterioration and he had gradually become aware that he was, somewhere within himself, deeply dissatisfied with life.

And he had no idea who or what to blame, other than himself.

The farmhouse was no longer the centre of a working farm but, like so many properties in the area, had been converted into an expensive holiday-home. It sat on a hill with a spectacular view of the surrounding moorland.

Standish turned the corner of the lane and found his way blocked by the Range Rover belonging to one of the local ferry-men. He braked and climbed out, into the teeth of a bitter wind. He turned up the collar of his coat and hurried across to the vehicle.

The ferryman sat in his cab, an indistinct blur seen through the misted side window. When Standish rapped on the glass and opened the door, he saw Richard Lincoln warming his hands on a mug of coffee from a Thermos.

"Doug, that was quick. Didn't expect you people out here for a while yet."

"I was passing. What happened?"

He'd got to know Lincoln over the course of a few tea-time sessions at the Dog and Gun a year ago, both men coming off-duty at the same time and needing the refreshment and therapy of good beer and conversation.

Lincoln was a big, silver-haired man in his fifties, and unfailingly cheerful. He wore tweeds, which gave him a look of innate conservatism belied by his liberal nature. His bonhomie had pulled Standish from the doldrums on more than one occasion.

Lincoln finished his coffee. "Bloody strange, Doug. I was at the Station, on the vid-link with Sarah Roberts, a colleague. She was at home." He pointed to the converted farmhouse. "We were going over a few details about a couple of returnees when she said she'd be back in a second—there was someone at the door. She disappeared from sight, and came back a little later. She was talking to someone, obviously someone she knew. She was turning to the screen to address me when there was a loud . . . I don't quite know how to describe it. A crack. A report."

"A gunshot?"

Lincoln nodded. "Anyway, she cried out and fell away from the screen. I ran to the control room, and sure enough . . . We were being signalled by her implant. She was dead. Look."

Lincoln reached out and touched the controls of a screen embedded in the dashboard. An image flickered into life, and Standish made out the shot of a well-furnished front room, with a woman's body sprawled across the floor, a bloody wound in her upper chest.

Absently, Lincoln fingered the implant at his temple. "I contacted you people and drove straight over."

"Did you pass any other vehicles on the way here?"

Lincoln shook his head. "No. And I was on the lookout, of course. The strangest thing is . . . Well, come and see for yourself."

Lincoln climbed from the cab and Standish joined him. They moved towards the wrought-iron gate that barred their way. It was locked.

"Look," Lincoln said. He indicated the driveway and lawns of the farmhouse. A thick covering of snow gave the scene the aspect of a traditional Christmas card.

Standish could see no tracks or footprints.

"Follow me." Lincoln walked along the side of the wall that encircled the property. Standish followed, wading through the foot of snow that covered the springy heather. They climbed a small rise and halted, looking down on the farmhouse from the elevated vantage point.

Lincoln pointed to the rear of the building.

"Same again," he said, peering at Standish.

"There's not a single damned footprint to be seen," Standish said.

"Nothing. No footprints, tyre marks, tracks of any kind. The snow stopped falling around midday, so there's no way a new fall could have covered any tracks. Anyway, the killer came to the house just over forty-five minutes ago."

"But how? If he didn't leave tracks . . ." Standish examined the ground, searching for the smallest imprint.

He looked at Lincoln. "There is one explanation, of course."

"There is?"

"The killer was always in the house, concealed somewhere. He came before the snow fell and hid himself. Then he emerged, crept through the house to the door, stepped outside, and knocked."

"But that'd mean . . ."

Standish nodded. "If I'm right, then he's still in there."

"You armed?"

Standish tapped the automatic beneath his jacket.

"What do you think?" Lincoln asked. "Should we go in there?"

In the old days, before the Kéthani, he would not have risked it. Now, with death no longer the threat that it used to be, he didn't think twice.

"Let's go," he said.

They returned to the front gate and climbed over. Standish led the way, high-stepping through the deep snow.

He had the sudden feeling of being involved in one of those Golden Age whodunits he'd devoured as a teenager, stories of improbable murders carried out with devious cunning and improbable devices.

In case he was mistaken about the killer still being *in situ*, he looked out for tell-tale signs of holes in the snow that might denote the use of stilts. Or perhaps the killer had flown in on a hang-glider or micro-light? But there was no sign of a landing nearer the house, no scuffing of the snow on the roof. All was pristine, Christmas Card neat.

The front door was unlocked. Taking a handkerchief from his pocket, Standish carefully turned the handle and pushed open the door.

He drew his automatic and led the way to the lounge.

Sarah Roberts lay on her back before the flickering vid-screen. The earlier image of her, Standish thought, had done nothing to convey her beauty. She was slim and blonde, her face ethereally beautiful. Like an angel, he thought.

They moved into the big, terracotta-tiled kitchen, heated by an Aga stove, and checked the room thoroughly. They found the entrance to a small cellar and descended cautiously. The cellar was empty. Next they returned to the kitchen and moved into the adjacent dining room, but found nothing yet again.

"Upstairs?" Lincoln said.

Standish nodded. He led the way, climbing the wide staircase in silence. There were three bedrooms on the second floor, two bare and unoccupied, the third furnished with a single bed. They went though them from top to bottom, Standish ready with his automatic. He was aware of the steady pounding of his heart as Lincoln pulled aside curtains and opened wardrobes. Last of all they checked the converted attic, spartanly furnished like the rest of the bedrooms, and just as free of lurking gunmen.

"Clean as a whistle," Lincoln said. They made their way downstairs.

"I think I'd rather we'd found the killer," Standish muttered. "I don't like the alternative." What was the alternative, he wondered? An eerie, impossible murder in a house surrounded by snow . . .

They entered the lounge. Lincoln knelt beside the body, reached out and touched the woman's implant.

Ten years ago Standish had seen any number of bodies during the course of a working week, and he had never really become accustomed, or desensitised, to the fact that these once living people had been robbed of existence.

Now, when he did occasionally come across a corpse in the line of duty, he was immediately struck by the same feeling of futile waste and tragedy—only to be brought up short with the realisation that now, thanks to the Kéthani, the dead would be granted new life.

Lincoln looked up at him, his expression stricken. "Christ, Doug. This isn't right."

Standish felt his stomach turn. "What?"

Lincoln slumped back against the wall. Standish could see that he was sweating. "Her implant's dead."

"But I thought you said . . . you received the signal at the Station, right?"

Lincoln nodded. "It was the initial signal indicating that the subject had died—"

"So it should still be working?"

"Of course. It should be emitting a constant pulse . . ." He shook his head. "Look, this has never happened before. It's unknown. These things just don't pack up. They're Kéthani technology."

"Maybe it was one of those false implants? Don't people with objections to the Kéthani sometimes have them—"

Lincoln waved. "Sarah worked for the Kéthani, for chrissake! And anyway, it *was* working. I saw the signal myself. Now the damned thing's dead."

Standish stared down at the woman, a wave of nausea overcoming him. He was struck again by her attenuated Nordic beauty, and he was sickened by the thought that she would never live again . . . Amanda would have called him a sexist bastard: as if the tragedy were any the greater for the woman being beautiful.

"Can't something be done?"

Lincoln lifted his shoulders in a hopeless shrug. "I don't honestly know. The device needs to be active in the minutes immediately after the subject's death, in order to begin the resurrection process. Maybe the techs at the Station might be able to do something. Like I said, this has never happened before."

The room was hot, suffocatingly so. Standish moved to a window at the back of the room and was about to open it when he saw something through the glass.

He stepped from the lounge and into the kitchen. The back door was open a few inches. He crossed to it and, with his handkerchief, eased it open a little further and peered out.

The snow on the path directly outside the door had been melted in a circle perhaps a couple of metres across, revealing a stone-flagged path and a margin of lawn. The snow began again immediately beyond the melt, but there was no sign of footprints or any other tracks.

Some underground heating device? He'd check it out later.

He returned to the lounge. Lincoln was on his mobile, evidently talking to someone at the Onward Station. "And there's nothing at your end, either? Okay. Look, get a tech down here, fast."

Standish crossed the room and stood before the big picture window, staring out at the darkening land with his back to the corpse. He really had no wish to look upon the remains of Sarah Roberts. Her reflection, in the glass, struck him as unbearably poignant, even more angelic as it seemed to float, ghostlike and evanescent, above the floor.

Lincoln joined him. "They're sending someone down to look at the implant."

Standish nodded. "The Scene of Crime team should be here any minute." He glanced at the ferryman. "You didn't hear her visitor's voice when she returned from answering the door?"

"Nothing. I was aware that there was someone in the room by Sarah's attitude. She seemed eager to end the call. But I saw or heard no one else."

"Have you any idea which door she answered, front or back?"

Lincoln turned and looked at the vid-screen. "Let's see, she was facing the screen, and she moved off to the left—so she must have answered the back door."

That would fit with the door being ajar—but what of the melted patch?

"What kind of person was she? Popular? Boyfriend, husband?"

Lincoln shrugged. "I didn't really know her. Station gossip was that she was a cold fish. Remote. Kept herself to herself. Didn't make friends. She wasn't married, and as far as I know she didn't have a partner."

"What was her job at the Station?"

"Well, she was designated a liaison officer, but to be honest I don't exactly know what that entailed. I kept her up to date with the dead I delivered, and the returnees, but I don't know what she did with the information. She worked with Masters, the Station Director. He'd know more than me."

"How long had she been at the Station?"

"Two or three months. But before that she'd worked at others up and down the country, so I heard."

Standish nodded. "I'm just going to take another look around. I'll be down when the SoC people turn up."

He left the lounge and climbed the stairs again. He stood in the doorway of the only furnished bedroom and took in the bed—a single bed, which struck him as odd—and the bedside table with nothing upon it.

He moved to the bathroom and scanned the contents: a big shower stall, a Jacuzzi in the corner, plush white carpet . . . He stared around the room, trying to fathom precisely why he had the subtle feeling that something was not quite right. It was more a vague sensation than anything definite.

He heard the muffled groan of a labouring engine and rejoined Lincoln in the lounge.

Two minutes later Kendrick, the Scene of Crime team chief, appeared at the door with three other officers, and Standish and Lincoln went over their findings.

The tech from the Station turned up shortly after that and knelt over the corpse, examining the woman's implant with the aid of a case full of equipment, scanners and a softscreen, and other implements Standish didn't recognise.

Kendrick drew Standish to one side. "They're bringing in a chap from Manchester," he said. "I know technically this is your territory, but the Commissioner's decided he wants the big boys in."

Standish opened his mouth to complain, then thought better of it. Kendrick was merely the messenger; it would achieve nothing to vent his frustration on the SoC chief.

Twenty minutes later Lincoln clapped him on the shoulder. "Heading past the Dog and Gun? Fancy a quick one?"

"You're a mind-reader, Richard. Lead the way."

* * *

They retreated with their pints of Taylor's Landlord to the table beside the fire. The barroom of the Dog and Gun was empty but for themselves and half a dozen youngsters at the far end of the bar. The kids wore the latest silvered fashions—uncomfortably dazzling to the eye—and talked too loudly amongst themselves. As if we really want to hear their inane views of life in the twenty-first century, Standish thought.

"What is it, Doug?" Lincoln asked, reducing the measure of his pint by half in one appreciative mouthful.

"What's happened to society over the past ten years, Richard?"

Lincoln smiled. "You mean, since the coming of the Kéthani? Don't you think things have got better?"

Standish shrugged. "I suppose so, yes." How could he express his dissatisfaction without sounding sorry for himself? "But . . . Okay, so we don't die. We don't have that fear. But what about the quality of the life we have now?"

Lincoln laughed. "You've been reading Cockburn, right?"

"Never heard of him."

"A Cambridge philosopher who claims that humankind has lost some innate spark since the arrival of the Kéthani."

"I wouldn't know about that," Standish said. He took a long swallow of rich, creamy bitter. "It's just that . . . perhaps it's me. I lived so long with the certainties of the old way of life. I knew where I belonged. I had a job that I liked and thought useful . . ."

At the far end of the bar, one of the kids—a girl, Standish saw—threw her lager in the face of a friend, who didn't seem to mind. They laughed uproariously and barged their way from the pub. Seconds later he saw them mount their motorcycles and roar off, yelling, into the night.

"All the old values have gone," he said.

"The world's changing," Lincoln said. "Now that we no longer fear death, we're liberated."

Standish smiled and shook his head. "Liberated from what—what freedom have we found? The freedom to live shallow, superficial lives? Perhaps it's my fault," he went on. "Perhaps I was an old fart before the aliens came, and now I'm too set in my ways to change." That was a glib analysis, he thought, but it hinted at some deeper, psychological truth.

Lincoln was watching him. "Don't you think about the future, and feel grateful for what we've got?"

Standish considered this. "I don't know. Sometimes I'm struck by the greater uncertainty of things. Before we had the certainty of death—oblivion, if you had no faith. Now we come back to life and go among the stars . . . and that seems almost as terrifying."

Lincoln contemplated his empty glass for a second or two, then said, "Another pint?"

"You've twisted my arm."

Lincoln returned, sat down, and regarded Standish in silence for a while. "How's things with Amanda?" The question was asked with the casual precision of a psychiatrist getting to the heart of his patient's problem.

Standish shrugged. "About the same. It's been bad for a year or so now." Longer, if he were to be honest with himself. It was just that he'd begun to notice it over the course of the past year.

"Have you considered counselling?"

"Thought about it," he said. Which was a lie. Their relationship was too far gone to bother trying to save. Amanda felt nothing for him any more, and had said as much.

He felt that Lincoln wanted to talk more about Amanda, but the thought made him uneasy.

He shrugged and said, "There's really not much to say about it, Richard. It's as good as over." He buried his head in his drink and willed the ferryman to change the subject.

It was over, he knew, but something deep within him, that innate conservatism again, that fear of change, was loath to be the one to admit as much. It was as if he lived in hope that things might change between them, become miraculously better.

But in lieu of improvement, he held on to what he had got for fear of finding himself with nothing at all.

Lincoln touched his shoulder and said, "Doug, perhaps you'd feel better about life in general if you could sort things out with Amanda, one way or another."

Standish finished his pint, and said, too quickly, obviously trying to silence the ferryman, "One for the road?"

Lincoln looked at his watch. "I'm late as it is. Should have been home half an hour ago." He stood. "Keep in touch, okay? How about coming over to the Fleece one night? There's a great crowd there, and the beer's excellent."

Standish smiled. "I'll do that," he said, knowing full well that he would do nothing of the sort.

He sat for a while after Lincoln had left, contemplating his empty glass, then went to the bar for a refill. The room was empty, save for himself. He'd have a couple more after this one, then go home. Amanda would no doubt comment on the reek of alcohol, and make some barbed remark about driving while over the limit, but by that time Standish would be past caring.

He thought about Sarah Roberts, and the impossibility of her murder. The image of the woman, ethereally angelic, floated into his vision. The tech from the Onward Station had been unable to ascertain if Roberts could be saved, seemed nonplussed at the dysfunction of her implant.

The entire affair had an air of insoluble mystery that made Standish uncomfortable. The unmarked snow, the circular melt, the failure of her implant . . . Perhaps it was as well that he wouldn't be working on the case.

His mobile rang, surprising him. "Doug?"

"Amanda."

"I thought you said you'd be back by six?" Her clipped Welsh tone sounded peremptory, accusing.

"Something came up. I'm working late."

"Well, I have to go out. Kath's babysitter's let her down at the last minute. I'll be back around midnight. Your dinner's in the microwave."

"Fine. Bye—"

But she had cut the connection.

Five minutes later he finished his drink and was about to go to the bar for another when, though the window, he saw a small blue VW Electro halt at the crossroads, signal right, and then turn carefully on the gritted surface.

On impulse he stood and hurried from the bar. He was over the limit, but he gave it no thought as he slipped in behind the wheel of the Renault and set off in pursuit of the VW.

Amanda's best friend, Kath, lived in Bradley, five miles in the opposite direction to where Amanda was heading now.

Seconds later, through the darkness, he made out a set of rear lights. The VW was crawling along at jogging pace. Amanda always had been too cautious a driver. He slowed so as not to catch her up, and only then wondered why he was following her.

Did he really want to know?

He wondered if Richard Lincoln's last pearl of wisdom had provoked him into action. *"Doug, perhaps you'd feel better about life in general if you could sort things out with Amanda, one way or another."*

Perhaps he'd had long enough of feeling powerless. Who had said that knowledge was power? He shook his head. The alcohol was fuddling his thinking. He really should turn around and go home, leave Amanda to whatever petty adultery she was committing.

He hunched over the wheel and concentrated on the road ahead.

Five minutes later they entered the village of Hockton and the VW slowed to a crawl and pulled into the kerb beside a row of stone-built cottages. Standish continued, overtook the parked car, and came to a halt twenty metres further along the road.

He turned in his seat and watched as Amanda climbed out and hurried through the slush. A light came on in the porch of the cottage where she'd parked, and the figure of a man appeared in the doorway.

Amanda ran into his embrace, then slipped into the house. The light in the porch went out. The door closed. He imagined his wife in the arms of the stranger, and then whatever else they might get up to in the hours before midnight.

The strange thing was that he felt no anger. No anger at all. Instead, he experienced a dull ache in his chest, like an incipient coronary, and a strange sense of disappointment.

Now he knew, and nothing could ever be the same again.

He turned his car and drove back past the house, noting the number. He would check on its occupant later, when he had thought through the implications of Amanda's actions.

He drove home, considered stopping at the Dog and Gun for a few more, but vetoed the idea. Once home, he tried to eat the meal Amanda had left for him, managed half of it and threw the rest.

He went to bed, but not in the main bedroom. He slept in the guest room, and wondered why he hadn't had the guts to do so before now.

He was still awake well after midnight when Amanda got back. He heard her key in the front door, and minutes later the sound of her soft footsteps on the stairs. He imagined her entering the bedroom and not finding him there, and the thought gave him a frisson of juvenile satisfaction.

A minute later she appeared in the doorway, silhouetted in the landing light behind her. "Doug? Are you okay?"

She was a small woman, dark-haired and voluptuous. He recalled the first time he had seen her naked.

He wanted to ask her why, but that would be to initiate a conflict in which he could only finish second best. He knew why. She no longer loved him. It was as simple as that.

She waited a second, then said, "Pissed again are you? Well, stay there, then."

She pushed herself away from the jamb, and Standish said, "Don't worry, I fully intend to."

She hesitated, obviously suspicious, but said nothing, and moved back to the main bedroom, turning off the landing light and filling the house with darkness.

Later, in the early hours, Standish awoke suddenly, startled by the burst of white light as the Onward Station beamed its freight of dead humans to the orbiting Kéthani starship.

That night he dreamed of angels.

He awoke early next morning and left the house before Amanda got up. It was another crystal clear, dazzlingly bright day. A fierce frost had sealed the snow overnight, and the roads into Bradley were treacherous.

The desk-sergeant apprehended Standish before he reached his office and handed him a print-out.

Detective Inspector Singh wanted to see him about the Roberts case.

"He's here?" Standish asked.

The sergeant shook his head. "Up at the farmhouse with a forensic team."

He drove from Bradley and over the moors, taking his time. He crested a rise and, before him, the spun-crystal pinnacle of the Onward Station came into view. It looked at its best in a setting of snow, he thought: it belonged. He wondered at the homeworld of the Kéthani, and whether it was a place of snow and ice. The returnees had spoken only of rolling, green vales and lakes, but the consensus of opinion was that this landscape was nothing more than some virtual projection, a familiar Eden to placate the senses of the newly resurrected.

How little we know of our benefactors, he thought as he arrived at the farmhouse.

A fall of snow during the night had filled in the footsteps made by Standish, Lincoln, and the others the night before, but a new trail of prints led up the drive from two police cars parked outside the gate, now unlocked. He climbed from his car and hurried over to the house.

Detective Inspector R. J. Singh stood in the front room, arms folded across his massive stomach. He was a big man in a dark suit and a white turban, and when he spoke Standish detected a marked

Lancastrian accent. "Inspector Standish. Glad you could make it. Good to have you aboard."

"I hope I can help." They shook hands, and Standish looked down at where, yesterday, the body of Sarah Roberts had sprawled.

Today, a series of holographic projectors recreated the image. It was the first time Standish had witnessed the technology at work, and he had to admit that it was impressive. But for the presence of the three small, tripod-mounted projectors, he might have believed that the body was still *in situ*.

Even though he knew it was not the real thing, he still found it hard to look upon the ethereal beauty of the spectral image.

A couple of forensic scientists knelt in the corner of the room, minutely inspecting the carpet with portable microscopes.

Singh questioned him about the discovery of the body, and Standish recounted his impressions.

They moved across the room, to where a series of photographs littered the floor. It was the farmhouse and surrounding, snow-covered grounds, from every angle.

"Not a clue," Sigh said, gesturing at the photographs. "Nothing. The killer came and went without leaving a trace. We've thought of everything. I don't suppose you've come up with anything?"

He told Singh about his theory that the killer might have concealed himself somewhere in the house.

"Thought of that," Singh said. "We went through the place with a fine-tooth comb."

Standish shook his head. "I don't know what else to suggest. I just can't see how the killer did it."

"I've studied the recordings of Roberts on the vid to the ferry-man, Richard Lincoln," Singh said. "No clues there, either. One minute she's talking to Lincoln, and the next she goes to answer the door, comes back and . . . bang."

Standish moved to the window and looked out. The melted circle which he had noted yesterday was filled now with the night's snowfall.

"Did you see . . . ?" he began.

Singh nodded. "One of the photos picked it up. I'm check-ing things like underground pipes. I don't think it's anything significant." He looked around the room. "She certainly kept a tidy house."

He had noticed that yesterday, Standish thought now, though then he'd hardly registered the fact. The place was as unlived in as a show-house.

"I've been looking into Sarah Roberts's past," Singh said. "You might be interested in what I've discovered."

Standish nodded. "Anything that might shed light—?" he began.

Singh interrupted. "Nothing." He smiled at Standish's puzzlement. "The records go back three years, during her time with over half a dozen Onward Stations up and down the country. Before that, Sarah Roberts didn't exist, officially, that is."

"So 'Sarah Roberts' was an alias?"

"Something like that. We're checking with the Ministry of Kéthani Affairs. Chances are that the whole thing will be taken away from us and declared classified. If she was important enough to work for the Ministry in some hush-hush capacity, then the killing might be deemed too sensitive a matter for us mere workaday coppers."

"And you think the killing might have been linked to her work?"

"Impossible to tell. Between you and me, I don't think we'll ever find out."

Standish let his gaze stray again to the projected image of Sarah Roberts. "Have the techs come up with any reason for the dysfunction of her implant?"

"They're mystified. I wondered if it could have been linked to the killing—if the killer had in some way disabled it, but they simply couldn't tell me. They'd never come across anything like it."

"And she's . . . I mean, there's no way they can save her?"

Singh pulled an exaggeratedly doleful face. "I'm afraid not. Sarah Roberts is dead."

Standish averted his gaze from the ghost of the woman lying on the carpet, and asked, "Is it okay if I take another look around?"

"Be my guest. Forensic have almost finished."

Standish climbed the stairs and inspected the bedrooms again. He was struck by the improbability of a woman in her mid-twenties choosing to sleep in a single bed. He looked around the room. It was remarkable only for the lack of any personality stamped upon the room during the three months that Sarah Roberts had lived there: a brush and comb sat on a dresser, next to a closed make-up box. They looked like they had been placed there by stage-hands, to give spurious authenticity to a set.

He moved to the bathroom, where yesterday he had been aware of something not quite right. Now he realised what he'd missed: the room was bare, no toothpaste, shampoo, conditioner, hair-gels, hand creams or toiletries of any kind.

Another damned mystery to add to all the others.

He returned downstairs and found the Detective Inspector in the kitchen, peering into the fridge.

"Strange," Singh said when he saw Standish. "Empty. Nothing, not even a pint of milk."

Standish told him about the empty bathroom.

"Curiouser and curiouser," Singh said to himself.

"I might go over to the Onward Station and talk to the Director," Standish said. "If you don't mind my trespassing on your territory, that is?"

"Let's share anything we come up with, okay?" Singh said. "God knows, I need all the help I can get."

Standish took his leave of the farmhouse and motored across the moors to the looming monument of the alien Station. A new fall of snow had started, sifting down from a slate-grey sky. He found himself trailing a gritter for half a mile, delaying his arrival.

He thought about Sarah Roberts, her existence as pristine as the surrounding snow, and wondered if he would learn anything more from the Director.

Five minutes later he parked in the shadow of the Station and stepped through the sliding glass doors. The décor of the interior matched the arctic tone of the landscape outside. He'd only ever visited the Station once before, for the returning ceremony of a fellow policeman, and now he recalled the unearthly atmosphere of the place, the cool, quiet otherness of the white corridors and the spacious, minimally furnished rooms. Conditioning made him associate the place with death, and with the inscrutability of their alien benefactors, to create an ambience with which he was not wholly comfortable.

He showed his identification to a blue-uniformed receptionist and he was kept waiting for almost thirty minutes before the Director consented to see him.

The receptionist escorted him down a long, white corridor, carpeted in pale blue, and left him before a white door. It slid open to reveal a stark room with a desk like an ice-table standing at the far end, before a floor-to-ceiling window that looked out over the frozen landscape.

The room seemed hardly more hospitable than the terrain outside.

A tall, attenuated man rose from behind the desk and gestured Standish to enter. Director Masters was in his forties, severely thin and formal, as if his humanity had been leached by his involvement with such otherworldly matters as the resurrection of the dead.

They shook hands and Standish explained the reason for his visit.

"Ah," Masters said, "The Roberts case. Terrible thing."

"If it's all right with you, I'd like to ask a few questions about Ms Roberts."

"By all means. I'll assist in any way possible."

Standish began by asking what had been Sarah Roberts's function at the Station.

Masters nodded. "She was the Station's Liaison Officer."

"Which means?"

"She was the official who liaised between myself and my immediate superiors in Whitehall."

"So technically she worked for the government?"

"That is so."

"I presume you had daily contact with her?"

"I did."

"And how did you find her? I mean, what kind of person would you say she was?"

Masters eased himself back in his seat. "To be honest, I found Ms Roberts a hard person to get to know. There was the age difference, of course. But even so, she was very withdrawn and reserved. Other members of my staff thought the same."

"She didn't socialise with anyone from the Station?"

Masters smiled. "Most certainly not. She wasn't the kind of person to, ah . . . socialise."

"Intelligent?"

"Acutely so."

Standish nodded. He was forming a picture of Roberts that in all likelihood was nothing like the person she had been. No doubt somewhere there was a mother and father, perhaps even a lover.

"Were you aware of anyone who might harbour a grudge or resentment against Ms Roberts?"

"Absolutely not. She hardly interacted with anyone in any way that might have caused resentment or suchlike."

"Do you by any chance have a personnel dossier on Ms Roberts?"

Masters hesitated, then nodded. He leaned towards a microphone. "Danielle, could you bring in the Sarah Roberts file, please?"

Two minutes later Standish was leafing through a brief, very brief, document which listed Roberts's other postings at Onward Stations around the country, and little else. There was no mention of her work before she joined the Ministry of Kéthani Affairs, nothing about her background or education.

But there was a photograph. It showed a fey, fair, beautiful woman in her early twenties, and Standish found it haunting.

He pulled the picture from its clip and asked Masters, "I don't suppose I could keep this?"

"I'll get Danielle to make a copy," Masters said, and called his secretary again.

For the next ten minutes, before Director Masters rather unsubtly glanced at his watch to suggest that time was pressing, Standish questioned the Director about Roberts's work. He learned that she collected data about the day to day running of the Station, the processing of the dead from the area, and passed the information on to a government department in London. Masters could tell him no more than that, or was unwilling to do so.

Standish thanked the Director and left the Station. He sat in the Renault for ten minutes in contemplative silence, staring at the stark magnificence of the alien architecture, before starting the car and driving into Bradley.

He spent the afternoon in his office, processing what in the old days would have been called paperwork. He took time out to look up the identity of his wife's lover, then finished his shift at six.

That night he ate a steak and kidney pie in the Dog and Gun, drank more than was healthy, and at closing time was sitting by himself next to the fire and staring at the photograph of the dead woman.

She reminded him of . . . what was the name of the Elf Queen from that old film, *The Lord of the Rings?* Anyway, she looked like the Elf Queen.

Serene and fey and . . . innocent?

He replaced the photograph in his breast pocket and left the pub, walking unsteadily along a lane made treacherous by bottled ice. It was after midnight when he arrived home, and thankfully Amanda was already in bed.

He slept in the guest room again, and awoke only when the bright, white light from the Onward Station reminded him of his destiny, and the dead woman who would never live again.

The following morning he slipped from the house before Amanda got up, drove into Bradley and began work. Around eleven, R. J. Singh looked into the office and they discussed the case. Standish recounted his meeting with Director Masters, and both men agreed that they were getting nowhere fast.

He had a quick sandwich in the staff canteen and after lunch returned to the routine admin work. By four, his eyes were sore from staring at the computer screen. He was considering going down to the canteen for a coffee when his mobile rang.

It was Richard Lincoln, the ferryman.

"Richard, how can I help?"

"It's about the Roberts affair," Lincoln said. "It might not amount to much, but a friend thought he saw something in the area on the afternoon of the murder."

"Where can I contact him?"

"Well, we're meeting in the Fleece in Oxenworth tonight, around seven. Why don't you come along?"

"I'll do that. See you then. Thanks, Richard."

He refuelled himself with that promised coffee and worked for a further couple of hours. Just after six he left the station and drove over the moors to Oxenworth, a tiny village of old, converted mills, a local store-cum-post office, and a public house.

He arrived early and ordered scampi and chips from the bar menu. He was on his second pint when Richard Lincoln pushed through the swing door from the hallway, followed by a man and a woman in their forties.

Lincoln introduced the couple as Ben and Elisabeth Knightly; Ben was a dry-stone waller, Elisabeth a teacher at Bradley comprehensive. They had the appearance of newlyweds, Standish thought: they found each other's hands beneath the table when they thought no one was looking, and established eye contact with each other with charming regularity.

It reminded him of the early days with Amanda . . . Christ, was it really twenty years ago, now?

Ben Knightly said, "I read about the murder in this morning's paper . . ."

Standish nodded. "We've got no further with the investigation, to be honest. We need all the help we can get. Richard mentioned you saw something."

Ben Knightly was a big man with massive, outdoor hands. When he wasn't holding his wife's hand beneath the table, he clutched his pint, as if nervous. "I was working in the Patterson's top field on the day of the killing," he said hesitantly. "I was a couple of valleys away. It was around four, maybe a bit later."

"How far were you from the Roberts's farmhouse?" Standish asked, wondering exactly how far away a "couple of valleys" might be.

"Oh, about a mile, maybe a little bit more."

Standish halted his pint before his lips. "And you say you saw something. From that distance?"

Knightly glanced at his wife, then said, "Well, it wasn't hard to miss . . ."

A helicopter, Standish thought, his imagination getting the better of him. An air balloon?

"At first I thought it was a shooting star," Knightly said. "I see them all the time, but not quite that early. But this star just went on and on, dropping towards the Earth. Then I thought it might have something to do with the Station, though I'd never seen light approaching the Station before, always leaving it."

Standish nodded, wondering where this was leading. "And then?"

Ben Knightly shrugged his big shoulders. "Then it went down behind the crest of the hill, not far from the Roberts farmhouse."

Standish looked at Lincoln. "A meteorite? I'm not very up on these things."

"Meteorites usually come in at an acute angle," the ferryman said, "not straight down."

"I thought I was seeing things," Knightly said. "But when I read about the murder . . ."

Standish shook his head. "I really don't see how . . ." Then he recalled the melted patch outside the back door of the farmhouse.

The conversation moved on to other things, after that. A little later they were joined by more people, friends of Lincoln. Standish recognised an implant doctor from Bradley General, Khalid Azzam, with his wife Zara, and Dan Chester, another ferryman.

They were pleasant people, Standish thought. They went out of their way to make him feel part of the group. He bought a round and settled in for the evening. The ferrymen talked about why they had chosen their profession, and perhaps inevitably the topic of conversation soon moved round to the Kéthani.

"Come on, you two," Elisabeth said to Richard and Dan, playfully. "You come into contact with returnees every day. They must say something about the Kéthani homeworld?"

Lincoln smiled. "It's strange, but they don't. They say very little. They talk about the rehabilitation process in the domes, conducted by humans, and then what they call 'instructions,' lessons in Zen-like contemplation, again taught by humans."

Dan Chester said, "They don't meet any Kéthani, or leave the domes. The view through the domes is one of rolling hills and vales—probably not what the planet looks like at all."

Standish looked around the group. They were all implanted. "Have you ever," he said, marshalling his thoughts, "had any doubts about the motives of the Kéthani?"

A silence developed, while each of the people around the table considered whether to answer truthfully.

At last Elisabeth said, "I don't think there's a single person on the planet who hasn't wondered, at some point or the other. Remember the paranoia to begin with?"

That was before the returnees had returned to Earth, miraculously restored to life, with stories of the Edenic alien homeworld. These people seemed cured not only in body, but also in mind, assured and centred and *calm* . . . How could the Kéthani be anything other than a force for good?

Standish said, "I sometimes think about what's happened to us, and . . . well, I'm overcome by just how much we don't know about the universe and our place in it."

He shut up. He was drunk and rambling.

Not long after that the bell rang for last orders, and it was well after midnight before they stepped from the warmth of the bar into the sub-zero chill of the street. Standish made his farewells, promising he'd drop in again but knowing that, in all likelihood, in future he would do his drinking alone at the Dog and Gun.

He contemplated taking a taxi home, but decided he was fit enough to drive. He negotiated the five miles back to his village at a snail's pace, grateful for the gritted roads.

It was well after one o'clock by the time he drew up outside the house. The hall light was blazing, and the light in the kitchen, too. Was Amanda still up, waiting for him? Had she planned another row, a detailed inventory of his faults and psychological flaws?

He unlocked the front door, stepped inside, and stopped.

Three big suitcases filled the hallway.

He found Amanda in the kitchen.

She was sitting at the scrubbed-pine table, a glass of scotch in her hand. She stared at him as he appeared in the doorway.

"I thought I'd better wait until you got back," she said.

"You're leaving?" He pulled out a chair and slumped into it. What did he feel? Relief, that at last someone in this benighted relationship had been strong enough to make a decision? Yes, but at the same time, too, a core of real regret.

"Who is she?" Amanda asked, surprising him.

He blinked at her. "Who's who?"

She reached across the table and took a photograph from where it was propped against the fruit bowl.

"I found it in the hall this morning. Who is she?"

It was the snap of Sarah Roberts he'd taken from the Station yesterday. Instinctively he reached for his breast pocket. The photograph must have slipped out last night when he'd tried to hang his jacket up.

"Well?" She was staring at him, something very much like hatred in her eyes.

A part of him wanted to take her to task over her hypocrisy, but another part was too tired and beaten to bother.

"It has nothing to do with you," he said.

"I'm going!" she said, standing.

He watched her hurry to the kitchen door, then said, "Staying with . . . what's his name? Jeremy Croft, in Hockton?"

She stopped in the doorway, turned and stared at him. He almost felt sorry for her when she said, "I met him last year, Doug, when things were getting impossible here. I wanted someone to love me, someone I could love."

"I'm sorry you couldn't find that with me."

She shook her head. "Sometimes these things just don't work, no matter how hard you try. You know that." She hesitated, then said, "I hope you find what you want with . . ." She gestured to the snap of Sarah Roberts on the kitchen table, then hurried into the hall.

He heard her open the door and struggle out with the cases. He pushed himself upright and moved into the hall.

He pulled open the door and stepped outside. Amanda was driving away.

Strangely, he no longer felt the cold. In the silence of the night, he walked from the house and stood in the lane, staring up at the massed and scintillating stars.

Then he saw a shooting star, denoting a death, somewhere — and then he knew. It was as if he had known all along, but the sight of the shooting star had released something within him, allowing him the insight.

It made sense. Sarah Roberts, a woman without a past, living in a pristine house, empty of all the trivial products of the modern world. It made perfect sense. Perhaps, after all, she was an angel.

Laughing to himself, he staggered back inside and shut the door behind him. He moved to the lounge, collapsed on the sofa, and slept.

That night, not even the pulsing light from the Onward Station could wake him from his dreams.

He woke late the following morning, dragged from sleep by something indefinable working at the edge of his consciousness. He lay on his back and blinked up at the ceiling, recalling the events of the night before and sensing the start of a debilitating depression.

Then he became aware of what had awoken him: his phone, purring in the pocket of his jacket where he'd dropped it last night.

He pulled his jacket towards him and fumbled with the phone. "Standish here."

"Mr Standish? Director Masters at the Station. I wonder if you could spare me a little of your time?"

"Concerning Roberts . . . ?"

"Not over the phone, Mr Standish."

"Very well. I'll be right over."

The Director thanked him and rang off.

He splashed his face with cold water, brushed his teeth, and then made his way out to the car, his head throbbing from too many beers in the Fleece last night.

It was another sunny morning. He wondered what Amanda was doing now. As he drove through the quiet lanes and over the moors, towards the Onward Station, he imagined her in the arms of her lover.

At the sight of the rearing obelisk, he recalled what had come to him in the early hours, as he stood staring up at the spread of stars.

It seemed, in the harsh light of day, highly improbable.

He left his Renault in the parking lot and stepped through the sliding door. Director Masters himself was on hand to greet him.

"Mr Standish, if you'd care to step this way."

He led Standish along a white corridor. They came at last to a sliding door, but not that of Masters's office.

The door eased open without a sound, and the Director gestured Standish through.

He stepped into a small, white room, furnished only with a white, centrally located settee. He heard the door click shut behind him, and when he turned to question Masters he realised that the Director had left him alone in the room.

A minute elapsed, and then two. Vaguely uneasy, without quite knowing why, he sat on the settee and waited.

Almost immediately a concealed sliding door opposite him opened quickly, and he jumped to his feet.

Someone stepped through the opening, backed by effulgent white light, and it was a second before his vision adjusted.

When it did, he could only stare in disbelief.

A slim, blonde woman stood before him. She was dressed in a white one-piece suit. Her expression, as she stared at him, was neutral.

It was Sarah Roberts.

He opened his mouth, but no words came. Then he looked more closely at the woman before him. It was almost Roberts, but not quite; there was a slight difference in the features, but enough of a similarity for the woman and Roberts to be sisters.

Standish managed, "Who are you?"

She smiled. "I think you know that, Doug." It was the familiarity of her using his first name that shocked him, as much as what she had said.

"I was right? Roberts was . . . ?"

She inclined her head. "This soma-form, and variations upon it, is how we show ourselves on Earth."

His vision blurred. He thought he was going to pass out.

Was he one of the few people ever to knowingly set eyes on a member of the Kéthani race?

"Why . . . I mean—"

"We need to come among you from time to time, to monitor the progress of our work."

"But this—" he gestured at her "—this isn't how you appear in reality?"

She almost laughed. "Of course not, Doug."

"What do you look like?"

She regarded him, then said, gently, "You would be unable to apprehend our true selves, or make sense of what you saw."

He nodded. "Okay . . ." He took a breath. His head was pounding, with more than just the effects of the hangover. "Okay, so . . . what do you want with me? Why did you summon me here? Is it about—?"

She smiled. "The killing of the woman you knew as Sarah Roberts."

"The light from the sky," he said, "the patch of melted snow outside the farmhouse . . ." He shook his head. "Who killed her?"

"There is so much you don't know about the Kéthani," the woman said, "so much you have to learn. Like you, we have enemies. There are races out there who do not agree with what we are doing. Sometimes, these races act against us. Two nights ago, three enemy agents came to various locations on Earth to assassinate our envoys. They escaped before we could apprehend them."

He nodded, let the seconds elapse. "Why do they object to what you're doing?" he asked.

She smiled. "In time, Doug, in time. You will die, be reborn, and eventually go among the stars. Then you will learn more than you can possibly imagine."

"Why have you told me this?"

"We want you to solve the crime," she replied. "You will return to the farmhouse, and search it. You will find a concealed space behind a bookcase in the main bedroom. You will assume that the killer hid there, emerged, and killed Sarah Roberts, stole her jewellery box, then escaped a day later using the cover of the tracks in the snow made by you and your colleagues."

It was his turn to smile. "But I *know* what really happened," he began.

"You do now," she said, "but when you leave the Station you will remember nothing of our meeting."

He was overcome, then, with some intimation of the awesome power of the Kéthani, and his people's ignorance.

"You are a good person, Doug." The woman smiled at him, with something like compassion in her eyes. "Let what has happened to you of late be the start of a new life, not the end."

He was suddenly aware of his pulse. "How do you know?"

"We know everything about you," the alien said. She stepped forward, and reached up.

Her fingers touched the implant at his temple, and he felt a sudden dizziness, followed by an inexplicable surge of optimism.

"The implants allow us access to your very humanity," she said. "Goodbye, Doug. Be happy."

She stepped through the sliding door, and seconds later the door to the corridor opened and Standish passed through. Masters's secretary escorted him towards the exit.

By the time he left the Station, Standish could only vaguely recall his meeting with Director Masters. He blamed the effects of the alcohol he'd consumed last night, and headed towards his car.

It came to him that he should check the farmhouse again.

There had to be a rational explanation of what had happened there the other day. Murderers simply did not appear out of the blue, and vanish again just as inexplicably.

He paused and gazed over the snow-covered landscape, marvelling at its beauty. He recalled Amanda's leaving last night, and it came to him that it wasn't so much the end of his old life, but the beginning of a new phase of existence. He experienced a sudden, overwhelming wave of optimism. He recalled the invitation from Lincoln and the others to join them at the Fleece again, and knew in future that he would.

Smiling to himself, without really knowing why, Standish started the engine and drove slowly from the Onward Station.

The Spacetime Pit

with Stephen Baxter

SHUTTLE LURCHED. "PRIMARY SHIPBOARD SYSTEMS failure."

Wake stared through the monitor as lightning leapt between fat, cotton-wool clouds. She was deep inside this remote gravity well, *inside* a storm, and fast falling further in.

"Switch to secondary, Shuttle. Affirm."

Shuttle bucked through turbulent air.

"I said, 'Affirm.' "

"Crew loss scenario."

She felt sweat prickle her skin beneath her flight suit. "Detail."

"Ninety per cent likelihood of secondary shipboard systems failure."

Shit. That was non-survivable, all right, according to the book.

"Switch to manual. Tell Mother I'm aborting the landing and coming home."

"Boosters inoperable. No pressure in propellant tank. Crew loss—"

"—scenario. Right," she muttered. *Now what?*

Shuttle was old, but it wasn't supposed to fail. It was loaded up with redundant systems to keep it functioning, if minimally, for years.

In the end, though, everything failed. If it hadn't been this storm, the lightning strikes Shuttle had taken, it would have been some other damn thing, on some other remote world.

Wake was on her own, out here at the rim of human expansion. Her training had hammered home that, in the end, she couldn't rely on the equipment. It was up to her to keep herself alive. *If A fails, try B! If B fails, try C!*

If she couldn't get back to orbit, she'd land. She would need raw materials, for repairs, fuel. She couldn't see the surface, had no real idea what kind of conditions she was dropping into here. She'd have to deal with that later.

Lightning leapt before Shuttle, flashing in Wake's face, dazzling her. Shuttle took a sickening dive to starboard.

"Give me the coordinates of the Alpha One landmass."

"Affirm."

The grey, ragged clouds parted, revealing an ocean of beaten grey steel. On the horizon sat an island, mountainous, irregular. She was skimming just a couple of hundred metres above peaking waves.

Christ. And it's only an hour since I was in the sauna on Mother.

"Secondary systems shutdown imminent."

"Advise emergency procedure."

"Crew loss scenario."

"Oh, for God's sake—"

Shuttle was now, frankly, falling out of the sky. *One option left.* She got out of her seat and staggered towards Pod. Shuttle's floor tipped under her in a compound, violent motion; she lurched, clattering against consoles and equipment boxes.

She reached the long, hexagonal coffin and slid inside. Cold sub-dermals snaked over her skin.

"Instructions," Pod said.

"Use your heuristic algorithms. Assess the situation. Ensure minimal danger. Prepare damage reports, locality surveys, survival scenarios . . ."

"Affirm."

The lid closed over her. She closed her hands over the locket at her neck and thought of Ben.

She felt a kick in the back as Pod threw itself out of Shuttle.

She'd orbited the fifth planet of this dim star, a hundred light years from Earth, for two days, before deciding to come in for a closer look. It looked vaguely Earth-like: thick cloud cover over transparent oxygen-nitrogen air, oceans of water. The only landmass of any significance was the largest island of an archipelago straddling the equator. There were traces of green on the island, but her sensors didn't betray any hint of chlorophyll. She couldn't see any sign of Eetee organisation—no industrial smog, no large structures, no radio or other signals.

She was pretty sure the planet wouldn't be directly habitable, and there would be no Contact here. But maybe it could be terraformed.

Wake was paid by a complicated system to do with the number of useful worlds she turned up in each survey sweep, and how useful each world was. *Possibly terraformable* was pretty low down the list of desirables and wouldn't pay her much.

Maybe just enough to justify a landing, she'd decided at last.

The day after this landing, she'd been due to ship out and head home. In fact she was only three days from Earth, using Mother's Alcubierre FTL drive.

She surfaced through a sea of anaesthetics.

"Status report."

"Crew survival not assured."

Terrific. She struggled to sit up. Pod was tilted, so her head was maybe twenty degrees below her feet, and the crystal canopy was obscured by something—the drapes of the parachute, she realised belatedly. Through the uncovered half of the canopy she made out a blindingly green-blue sky.

Green? Of course. From the scattering of the orange light of this G8-class sun—

"Where's Mother?"

"Orbital elements are one hundred twenty-three point four by—"

"Show me."

Fine reticules appeared in the glass of the canopy. Guided by them she picked out a silver point steady in the south-west sky, brilliant despite the daylight: Mother, in its stationary orbit, over this landmass. She felt a surge of relief.

Pod's report said the air outside was close enough to Earth's to sustain her for a few hours, but there were some mild toxins. She could spend no more than a couple of hours at a time out of Pod. She couldn't move far, then.

Temperature thirty Celsius. *A bright summer's day on Alpha One.*

Right now Mother would be sending out "Crew Loss" buoys. If

Wake could get to Shuttle she could instruct Mother to start emitting mayday FTL buoys, telling the Universe she was still alive. There was no guarantee anyone would respond, but it was a better chance than nothing.

And if she did get to Shuttle, of course, she might do better than that; maybe she could figure out a way to get back to orbit, to Mother.

She pushed at the canopy; it opened with a sigh of hydraulics, shrugging off the parachute.

Pod had come down in the foothills of an eroded mountain range. She stood on a grass-covered plateau. *Well, it looks like grass.* Beyond the lip of the plateau a green valley fell away, widening towards a ribbon of ocean to the south. A quicksilver thread of river twisted across the valley bottom. *U-shaped valley. Glaciated, probably.* There were plants, something like trees: short, thick-boled, with a haze of crimson leaves. The sun sat on the horizon, huge, too orange.

The panorama was sufficiently *different* to send a shiver down her spine.

She touched the locket around her neck. From within the heart-shaped crystal Ben smiled. Ben's two girls—Wake's granddaughters, microgravity-slender—held on to his arm and waved. The hologram had been taken in the Shelter, the big, bright, grass-walled chamber at the heart of the L5 colony, the place children were brought up. The Earth colours, the chlorophyll green of the grass and trees, were strikingly different from Alpha One. As if this planet was a poor mock-up.

She kneeled down and picked a few blades of the "grass." It was more like a six-fold clover leaf. And the green tint was like copper oxide, not chlorophyll-bright.

"Pod. Tell me about the biota."

"Most numerous atoms are silicon, hydrogen, oxygen. Silicon bonds form the basic architecture of—"

She stopped listening. *Oh, great. I've discovered silicon-based life.* That was supposed to be impossible. Silicon couldn't form double bonds like carbon; silicon couldn't form the metastable compounds which encouraged the development of large, complex molecules . . . Evidently, nature here had found a way.

It didn't matter a damn to her. Basic science was part of her contract, but it paid hardly anything. What was most significant was the fact that not even Pod's smart digestive sacs would be able to turn these silicon-based raw materials into food for her.

She interrupted Pod's lecture. "Tell me about supplies."

"Five days at nominal intake."

Five days of gloop fed to her intravenously by the sub-dermals. *I need to find that damn Shuttle.*

Pod gave her a bearing for Shuttle's crash site. It was a kilometre to the south, down the valley.

She walked over soft, grass-carpeted ground, plucking diamond-shaped leaves from the trees. The green wasn't quite right, and neither was the sky, but it was almost impossible to believe that there was nothing here she could eat.

The crash site was a scar in the hillside, all but grown over. She found what might have been the comms deck; its case was corroded and broken open, and a kind of lichen spilled out when she tried to lift it.

She went back to Pod. "How long have I been down here?"

"Two local years." Which was about one Earth year.

"A *year*? Why so long?"

"Pod seeking crew survival assurance. Not attainable. Opened at limit of heuristic algorithms for further direction."

She squatted down on the grass and hugged her knees. She hadn't anticipated such a gap. She hadn't even thought to ask Pod how long she'd been inert. *Too damn long;* so long she'd already lost Shuttle, in the accelerated entropy of this spacetime pit.

She figured options.

She could try to signal. But, hell, she didn't have enough power to send anything that would be picked up at interstellar distances. And besides, it would take decades for a lightspeed signal to reach anywhere inhabited.

She could try to build a Shuttle, get back to orbit. Yeah. But she knew Pod didn't have the resources to enable her to turn unmined iron ore into a spacegoing craft. And besides, she was no engineer.

She was trapped here, in this gravity pit, alone, out of touch, and everybody who knew her must have been told she was dead.

She let go, just for a second.

Then she straightened up. *To hell with that.* She needed some options.

. . . At the foot of the valley, two or three kilometres away, a thin thread of smoke rose into the air.

She hurried back to Pod. She slipped a vocoder headset over her head, fixing the microphone before her mouth, and then she fastened a laser pistol to her belt.

The sun had climbed from the horizon. *It's local morning, then.* Another thing she hadn't thought to inquire of Pod. I have to get more observant, less self-obsessed, if I'm to live through this. She walked down the steep hillside into the valley.

There were fields in the valley bottom. They were delimited by low walls of boulders, glacial deposit hauled away from the soil. She made out more threads of smoke, a collection of tiny, mud-coloured huts. *Eetees.*

She passed small, brown quadrupeds: ruminants browsing on the grass-analogue. Silicon-based birds pulsed through the air around her, their chirps high and piercing. The whole place was just a feast of convergent evolution, she thought.

After a kilometre she found a path worn into the hillside. She followed the twisting, copper-coloured track to the valley bottom.

The first dwelling she came to, a timber and adobe shack on stilts, was on the other side of a field planted with orderly rows of what looked like beet. There were crude ploughs, made of some wood-analogue, standing around in the field. *Not technologically advanced, then.* This could be the sticks, of course. She needed to find a city, industrial advancement.

She was forming a tentative plan. It would take the resources of a partially industrialised society, at least, to project her back to orbit. Maybe these Eetees had space technology. If so, she had to find it.

It wasn't a good plan, but it was all she had.

There was movement in the field before her.

The Eetee was kneeling beside a row of the beet stuff, facing away from her. It straightened, and stared up into the empty sky.

Reptile, she thought immediately: specifically, a frog. A silicon-based frog. The thing was bilaterally symmetric: two arms, two legs. Its portly torso stood on spindly legs; its skin colour was a lustrous brown, almost as if lacquered. It wore a length of dun cloth over its loins area. Modesty? A tool belt?

The Eetee turned around. Its domed head was even more frog-like: two bulbous eyes, a wide slit of a mouth—but the eyes were sheltered *under* the mouth. It looked as if its head was upside down. Its naked chest was patterned with three mustard-yellow chevrons.

When its gaze met Wake's, it froze, staring at her.

Slowly she raised her hand in salute. Any tool-making biped ought to respond to the gesture. Wake crossed the field, between the rows of leafy plants. Two metres from the Eetee she started to speak, making random greetings.

The Eetee was small, barely reaching her midriff. Its yellow eyes

triangulated on her face. The Eetee issued a series of sibilant bur-
bles. After a couple of minutes the vocoder blipped.

". . . my field? What do you want? Have you come to damage
the crops? What . . ."

"I am a traveller. My name is Katerina Wake." She pointed to
herself. "And you?"

The Eetee peered up from under its mouth, listening to words
that weren't synchronised with her oddly placed lips. "I am a planter
and grower of crops. I am—" A gurgle. The vocoder projected a
transliteration on to her eyeball. "F'han Lha."

"What do you call your people?"

It just looked back at her.

That was a bad sign. A lack of a name to distinguish the locals
meant the Eetee didn't know of anyone beyond its immediate
group. Even in theory. And if this Eetee thought that this squalid
little community contained the only people in the world, there
couldn't be much in the way of travel, trade, communication.

*Not likely to be any spaceships, either. I've landed in a silicon-
based Middle Ages.*

F'han's gaze dropped from Wake's face and regarded the locket
at her neck. She pulled the locket over her head and held it before
the Eetee's fascinated eyes, let the hologram cycle.

F'han reached out with three-fingered hands. No opposable
thumb, she noticed.

"For me?"

"No. I'm sorry." She slipped the locket back over her neck.

Three more Eetees came clambering down a ladder in the
underside of the stilted hut. They loped towards her, their gait low
and regular. "F'han!"

F'han ran through the field towards the others. The newcom-
ers must have been as tall as Wake; one of them clutched F'han's
head protectively. *I've been talking to a child.*

Quickly, the four Eetees climbed the rickety wood-analogue
ladder and disappeared into the dark underside of the dwelling.

She walked back up the valley wall to Pod.

She could stretch Pod's supplies to ten or fifteen days by going
to half-rations. And she could always spin out her time on the surface by going back into stasis, inside Pod. Pod was self-maintaining.
She could last down here for months, years, if she had to, living a
few hours at a time . . . But for what? So she could starve next year
instead of this?

Of course F'han was only a kid. It wouldn't know everything. Maybe there was a glittering city just beyond the hills . . . But she would have seen it from orbit. *Face it, Wake. This is all there is. Silicon-based subsistence farmers: nothing more or less.*

These Eetees had to be generations away from developing a technology sufficient to help her: to sustain her complex bio-chemical needs, to lift her back to orbit.

If A fails, try B! If B fails, try C! . . .

Well, if the Eetees couldn't help her *now*, she'd just have to wait until they could. She'd climb into Pod and wait it out as long as was necessary for these Eetees to scratch their way to some kind of technology; she could hold out a hell of a long time, in Pod.

Into the face of the rock behind Pod she lasered a low crevice, and then, over the next hour, she pushed Pod into the narrow over-hang. She banked up earth and rock against the length of Pod; now it would be protected from the weather, and, when the grass-analogue grew on the earthworks, hidden from easy observation.

She climbed into Pod.

"Instructions?"

How long? She needed to wait out enough time to see if the Eetees were on an upwards technological curve, or not. But not so long she stranded herself out of time.

Fifty years?

In fifty years, Ben would probably be dead. And the girls would be middle-aged women—as old as Wake was now. She found it hard to accept that in subjective seconds the people she loved most would have lived their lives without her.

But she didn't have a lot of choice, she thought bleakly.

"Fifty years. Earth standard."

She closed her eyes, and submitted to the embrace of the sub-dermals.

She awoke, and lay there waiting for the lid to open.

She felt no different, as if she'd barely closed her eyes. And the sky she could see, beyond the overhang, looked unchanged. To the south west she could see Mother, a spark of light unmoving in the green-blue sky.

She put on the vocoder and made her way down the valley. She took a footpath across a fallow field towards the farm where, fifty years ago, she'd spoken with F'han Lha.

A group of Eetees laboured in their stony fields. The spindly limbed frog people had their wood-analogue ploughs shackled to their backs, and they scraped furrows through the crimson earth. The workers looked up, observed her progress for a few seconds, then returned incuriously to their toil.

More labourers were standing in line by the silver river. As Wake watched, they passed containers fashioned from gourds along the line. The last workers tipped the water on to the earth. It was laborious, fantastically inefficient.

She could see no signs of change.

She felt a sharp contempt for the Eetees. For how many centuries had they lived like this, enduring their bucolic existence of birth, work in the fields, death?

The orange sun beat down on her head; she was hot, ragged, hungry, alone. *So much for my plan.* Well, then, she thought with a trace of angry desperation, she would just have to tip the damn Eetees out of their dull, comfortable equilibrium.

She went to stand in the shade of the stilted farmhouse, and waited.

What she was planning wasn't exactly ethical. But ethics, for a mankind spreading desperately across new planets, were a luxury.

Ethical behaviour wasn't even in her training.

When the sun got to its highest point, the workers trudged from the fields and the river. They shaded themselves under the farmhouse, and pushed mashed beet into the mouths on the tops of their skulls.

Wake stood before them. As the Eetees ate, they watched her blankly. "Where I come from we do things differently. Better. Easier." She picked up a sharp rock and began to scratch a crude diagram into the wood-analogue panels of the farmhouse. It was a tube curled into a spiral, around a central cylinder. If the diagram didn't work she'd make a couple of simple models.

One of the Eetees came closer, apparently curious, a tall, wispy individual with a ring of green spots on its carapace.

"We draw water with this. It is easier. This device is called an Archimedes screw . . ."

"Instructions."

She kissed the locket. "I'm sorry, Ben."

She was sliding deeper into this pit in space and time. But what choice was there? *I'm falling in, because there's nothing I can hold on to . . .*

This is one hell of a plan, Wake.

"Instructions," Pod repeated.

She closed her eyes. "Two hundred years. Earth standard." Maybe that would be long enough for the seed she'd planted to bear fruit.

If A fails, try B! If B fails, try C! . . .

She opened her eyes. Above her, the crystal cover was cracked.

She pushed open the canopy and climbed out. She was stiff, her limbs sore, her stomach constricted. It was night; the clouds above her head were thick, rain-laden, and a sulphur yellow glow illuminated their undersides.

Change, she thought immediately, and she exulted.

Her earthwork was gone, and Pod had been dragged out of its crevice and set on an apron of stone cobbles, surrounded by tall iron railings. Along Pod's silver flank there were scrapes and dents; it looked as if someone had tried to prise open the canopy.

Her heart beat faster. *I've induced curiosity, then.*

She crossed the cobbles, gripped the railings and peered through. She was still in the foothills—the worn mountains loomed behind her, dark, deserted—and to the south the valley, faintly outlined, fell away beyond this little compound. But now artificial lights glowed across the valley, in tight, yellow splashes. She saw that roadways criss-crossed what had been a wide, green plain. Stone dwellings filled the valley bottom, clustered about dark, oppressive buildings: mills, factories perhaps. The river had been straightened out, dammed; huge spiral devices that she recognised as remote descendants of her Archimedes screw lined the engineered valley, pumping water into rectilinear irrigation ditches. At the mouth of the valley, remote, she saw the lights of a town, densely packed streets, smog-laden air.

Through the hazy air she could just see a crude harbour at the edge of the ocean beyond.

She gazed into the south-west sky, looking for Mother. But the clouds were thick, and a haze of smog hung over the valley.

". . . Halt! Do not move."

The command, with Eetee sibilants overlaid by her vocoder's whisper, came from behind her. She raised her hands in the air, showing them empty.

"Turn. Slowly."

Again, she obeyed.

Two solid-looking Eetees, garbed in black, tight uniforms, stood outside the Pod compound. They were covering her with what looked like crossbows. She could see the bolts; they were sharp, massive, and grooved with a spiral rifling. Evidently, she thought wryly, her Archimedes-screw revolution had had a few unexpected spin-offs.

One of the Eetees opened a heavy gate and entered the compound. It raised its inverted head and glared at her with golden eyes. Then it crossed to Pod, and peered through the closed crystal canopy. It hissed something at its companion, too fast for the vocoder, then left the compound and started working at a squat machine at the brow of the valley. She heard the crackle of electricity. From the machine, sulphurous light glared out over the valley, in a dot-dash sequence. A *signal. They've been watching, waiting for me to emerge. And now that I have, they're signalling.*

After that, they waited. The Eetees wouldn't let her return to Pod, so she sat down on the cobbles, miming weariness.

After half an hour a growling rumble came up out of the valley. She stood, and the Eetees let her come to the railings.

A squat steam-truck was climbing the wall of the valley. Two Eetees in glittering ponchos sat on its roof, grandly, before a pair of funnels which spouted steam. The wheels were big, wood-spoked, iron-rimmed. Whatever boiler was hidden inside the boxy frame of the vehicle wasn't strong enough to haul the truck up the hill, and there was a crude harness arrangement in front of the truck. A dozen or more Eetees were strapped into the harness, dragging at the truck as it bumped over the uneven ground. A serf looked up at her vaguely, its mouth gaping open. It had a mustard yellow chevron on its bare chest, and—she was astonished to see— a crude locket, carved from wood, around its neck. The locket was obviously a clumsy imitation of her own. Perhaps, then, the serf was a descendant of F'han Lha; could the memory of her last brief emergence have been passed down the generations?

The two Eetees on top looked fat, sleek, and well-dressed. The harnessed serfs, by comparison, appeared scrawny, exhausted, bruised.

You've become a serpent in paradise, Wake, she thought.

The truck pulled up in front of the railings.

Two serfs helped one of the riding Eetees down to the ground. It approached Wake, waddling imperiously. Its poncho glowed crimson with copper inlays. She saw that its upper carapace had a marking, a circle of green dots, and it wore a pendant of its own, in the shape of an Archimedes spiral.

She felt overwhelmed. These people must have been ready for

stimulation. Receptive. They'd taken the fragments she'd given them and built whole subcultures; she felt as if aspects of her personality were being reflected back at her, extrapolated to absurd lengths.

She held her hands out, palm up, questioning. "What do you want?"

The Eetee pointed to her vocoder, her clothes, Pod. It said something; it was a crude attempt to pronounce "Archimedes."

She was starting to feel breathless; already she needed to get back to Pod. Damn it. There just wasn't *time* to think any of this through.

These people did not appear motivated to help her. They just wanted what she had. She had to find out if they were a positive threat.

She pointed at Pod. "Mine," she said bluntly. "Not yours."

The serfs, still strapped into their brutal harnesses, stirred at this. She was hardly an expert at Eetee body language, but it seemed to her they were finding some kind of inspiration in her words of defiance. *Interesting.* Maybe there was an angle there she could exploit.

Green-Ring gestured. A soldier type raised its spiral crossbow and aimed at her head.

Wake's heart hammered, and she felt saliva pool at the back of her throat. *So. A threat, indeed. What now, Wake?*

She had to adjust their attitude. *Make them focus on a goal we can all share.*

She said, "Key. For Pod—for my tomb." She held her hands up, and started to lower them slowly towards her belt, to the laser pistol there.

Green-Ring seemed to be hesitating. She could see the soldiers' triple fingers tightening around their crossbow triggers.

She got the pistol out. She held it up for them to see, gambling they wouldn't recognise it as a weapon. "Key. Okay?"

She turned, holding the pistol up above her head, and started to walk back to Pod.

Then, with one movement, she turned and thumbed the laser's power switch. A wand of red light, intense in the smoggy gloom, arced over her head, supernaturally straight. Before the Eetees could move she brought the beam slicing down over a soldier, neatly lopping away an arm. Its crossbow clattered to the ground.

The soldier stared down at the stump, which was pumping out

some dark blood-analogue. Then it fell backwards, its eyes rolling up, its remaining limbs in spasm.

She advanced on the Eetees. She held up the locket and let the hologram cycle, glittering Earth green and blue. "Hear me! I will return in—" she calculated quickly "—one hundred years. Then, I will give you, your children, this light, the contents of my tomb. But in return . . ." She stabbed the wand of light at the clouds. "In return, you will build a machine to lift me into the sky. Take me to the light which orbits." The vocoder couldn't translate that. "The star which shines, steady in the sky." Enough. They had generations to figure it out. "Do it, or I will call down more light from the sky, and destroy your fields and factories, and turn the rivers and seas to steam, and cut your children to small pieces . . ."

The serfs—the descendants of the peasant-boy F'han, maybe—were shouting at her now, waving their arms in the air, holding up their crudely carved copies of her locket. *Good grief*, she thought. *They think I'm a god.* She hadn't anticipated that. Would it help, or harm her?

This culture, this valley world, was like a tub of paraffin into which, periodically, she was throwing lighted matches. She couldn't predict how this was going to turn out, if this latest absurd gamble would pay off.

It was too late to do anything about it.

She turned her back and walked to Pod, stiffly, expecting a crossbow bolt between her shoulder blades at each step.

She accepted the embrace of the sub-dermals with relief.

Pod shook; muffled booms reached her cocooned cabin.

Beyond the canopy's starred glass there was a flare of light. Lightning? No, it burned orange red.

Like aircraft fuel.

She pushed open the canopy and sat up; she felt old, stiff, beaten up.

The sky was huge, aquamarine, clear again. She located Mother, a spark of light in its southwest station, sailing serene above it all. But the sky was marred by contrails, white puffs of explosions, remote bangs.

The ancient hills still rose behind her, but something about them was different: in several places their profile had been altered, notched. In one place she saw the distant glint of glass, of fused rock.

She walked to the lip of the valley. The cobbled pavement was cratered rubble, the railings a tangle of rusting iron. There was an extensive barricade around Pod's enclosure now: earthworks, and what looked like tank traps. The earthworks extended down into the valley bottom: miles of them, bristling with gun emplacements and something like barbed wire.

Bedraggled Eetee soldiers moved through the mud. She saw several injured: stumps of amputated limbs, crudely bandaged carapaces. Many of the wounds looked infected. Evidently medical science hadn't advanced as much as the art of war.

Beyond the earthworks the valley was desolated, the ground smashed, the small trees reduced to burned stumps. The port town she remembered in the distance had been flattened, reduced to a rectilinear grid of foundations. Fires burned, unattended, and she thought she could see ragged Eetees picking their way through rubble. The smog was gone, though. This war must have dragged on for years; there could have been no industry in this valley for a long time. Now, she could easily see all the way to the coast . . .

And there she made out a row of gantries, stark and grey, and at each there was a slender spire, glowing pearl white in the sun, wreathed with vapour.

Her breath caught. *More convergent evolution.* It might have been Canaveral or Tyuratam, Mergui or Tanega Shima: any of Earth's spaceports. *It worked, by God. They are preparing to loft me to orbit.*

A few hundred yards below her, a soldier in the earthworks spotted her. It started jabbering to its companions. More of them poked their carapaced heads above the trenches, and shouted. Then they began to clamber out, some of them awkward on injured limbs, and came towards her. Most of them were wearing amulets around their necks, and they held them up, aping the gesture she'd made yesterday . . . or fifty years before.

They began to chant, and the vocoder whispered. *I will call down light from the sky. I will destroy your fields and factories, and turn the rivers and seas to steam, and cut your children to small pieces* . . . They were gathering into a mob, and climbing the slope towards her.

She backed off, making sure she had a way back to Pod. So her scheme had worked. It was obvious these people worshipped her, to some degree; in fact they were defending Pod's site. (*From who?*) Maybe these were the descendants of the oppressed serfs she'd seen last time. Maybe, inspired by her memory, they'd thrown off their masters.

And this was their millennium: the second coming she had predicted, and was now fulfilling.

Right now, she was scared of being worshipped to death. And for all their fervour these people weren't much use to her anyhow. She had to get to that coastal launch complex . . .

The ground shuddered. Cobbles exploded into the air. She threw herself to the ground and covered her head with her arms; the Eetee troops fell back, screaming.

What now? Artillery? But she'd seen no flash, or smoke, and surely she would have heard any incoming projectile. A quake, then?

The shuddering went on and on. Smashed paving hailed down around her.

The ground broke open, not ten feet away. A metal snout shoved upward, out of the earth, gleaming silver, spinning with a whine of worn bearings. The craft hauled its way out of its pit, laboriously, and tipped forward on to the surface. It was a fat cylinder with a spiral screw blade wrapped around its hull, like an Archimedes screw writ large and lethal. The blade stopped turning, and round hatches in the flanks of the craft tipped outward. Troops spilled out of the steaming metal hull, shouting, bearing heavy rifles; they wore copper-coloured ponchos strapped tightly to their bodies, laden with ammunition and other equipment.

So the oppressing class is still around. In fact it made sense; it must be the "oppressors," more technically advanced than the soldiers in the trenches, who had developed that launch complex.

She got to her feet. The siege-busting Eetees spotted her immediately; they pointed and shouted.

Her mind whirled. Should she throw in her lot with these poncho types, let them take her to the launch complex on the coast?

But they didn't look all that friendly. She remembered the naked greed of Green-Ring. These people evidently didn't venerate her; they just wanted what she had. And, despite the existence of that launch complex, they might be prepared to rob her without fulfilling their half of their bargain. At least the serfs were trying to protect her.

What do I do? Which side do I pick?

There was a growl from the trenches beyond the lip of the plateau. The ponchos turned, raising their weapons. A broad, iron muzzle poked over the lip; huge tracked wheels sent earth spraying across the smashed cobbles. It was some kind of primitive tank, venting steam from a row of stacks, climbing up from the trench-works. Behind it, serf trench troops were clambering on to the cobbled platform, shouting and waving their weapons.

The muzzle of the tank's main gun swivelled to point at the earth burrower, and the ponchos ran forward to engage the trench troops. The burrower's spiral screw began to spin, as if it was trying to get away.

It was all happening too quickly for Wake. *When in doubt, follow your gut.*

She made her choice. She ran forward, reaching for the burrower's closing hatches.

Before she got to the burrower, light flashed from the coast, dazzling, white and orange. Wake threw herself to the ground once more. The tank, the battling troops, were thrown into grotesque silhouette.

The noise arrived then, an immense clatter, so violent it rattled her chest cavity.

She lifted up her face. *Rocket light.* She stood up and shoved her way forward, past the dazzled, mesmerised troops, to the lip of the plateau.

The rockets on the coast had been launched. White smoke billowed in great plumes from the launch pads. She counted three, four, five of the slim white needles, thrusting towards the greenish sky on droplets of intense yellow light.

She felt panic clutch at her chest. *Too early! They launched too early! I'm not aboard, damn it!*

Then she looked more closely. The rising rockets were of a crude design: mostly fuel tank, with a small cone for payload at the tip. Too small to carry a human, or an Eetee.

They weren't spaceships, she realised. They were missiles.

It was impossible to be sure with the naked eye, but it looked as if they were climbing up to meet Mother, the bright, steady star in the south west.

The pieces fell into place quickly. *These ponchos had no intention of helping me. They want to destroy Mother. So I won't be able to bring down fire on their children, as I threatened . . . And when Mother's gone, they'll come for me.*

One hell of a plan, Wake.

But these primitives surely couldn't damage Mother, even if the missiles reached their target.

She thought of the notched hills, the glassy crater.

Nukes. They have nukes. And they've used them already.

Mother couldn't survive a nuclear attack.

Mother was powered by a colour-force drive: chromodynamics, the strong nuclear force. An order of magnitude more energy-dense than the weak forces involved in fission explosions. If the Eetees managed to disrupt Mother's hull, if the colour drive went up, then this damn planet would be wiped clean.

The nuclear-tipped missiles had almost risen out of sight. She turned and ran to Pod. It was the only place she might be safe.

The bands of Eetees, their shock at the launches fading, had started to wade into each other once again. Some of them broke off to chase after her. The burrower was pulling itself back into its pit in the ground.

She threw herself into Pod and dragged shut the canopy. Eetees clustered around Pod, hammering on the starred and scuffed surface.

"Instructions."

"Heuristic algorithms," she said quickly.

Distorted frog faces pressed up against the crystal canopy. The sub-dermals embraced her.

A light blossomed above her, far brighter than the sun.

Thumbless hands scrabbled at the canopy, leaving trails of slime that blistered and burned dry.

Then even the shadows were burned away, and she was enfolded in light.

The lid lifted. Sunlight, bright orange, flooded Pod's interior, but a deep cold worked into her bones.

Wake pushed herself up. She felt weak, fragile. She pulled at the cloth of her flight suit; pieces of it came away in her fingers. *Rotted.*

She stood up. She had to stand still, as the sky spun around her. She felt as if she had been out for . . .

How long?

She stepped out of Pod. The sun hung in an empty, washed-out, green-blue sky, shedding no heat. No contrails.

No Mother.

Some of the floor cobbles survived, but they were smashed, eroded smooth as pebbles. No grass-analogue grew between them. Ice coated the exposed earth. There was ash, soot, mixed in with the ice, little grains of it.

She walked to the lip of the plateau. The atmosphere was thin, as if she was at high altitude; her lungs strained, trying to extract oxygen from the cold air.

The valley was a sculpture in white and brown. Here and there rock, fused and glassy, protruded through the compacted snow. It looked as if a glacier was forming here. There was no grass, no trees. Nothing moved. No bird sang. She could see no sign of the scar in the hillside left by Shuttle's crash.

She shielded her stinging eyes and looked out to the coast. The town was gone, the harbour. There was an angular form that looked like the stump of one of the launch gantries. Huge icicles dangled from it. On the sea, white glinted. Bergs.

The cold was astonishing.

She was gasping. The oxygen content was way down on what she'd observed before. She returned to Pod and pulled out an air mask, fitted it over her face. "Atmospheric content," she said to Pod. "Interpretation."

"Combustion of biota. Global. Free oxygen removed."

"But no replenishment?"

"Not observed. Oxygen levels continue to decline. Crew survival not assured."

"How long was I out?"

"Forty-two thousand, five hundred and—"

Jesus. Tens of millennia.

Long enough for the radioactive products of that last nuclear war and Mother's destruction to decay to harmlessness. Long enough for the ash of the burned biosphere to fall to the ground in rain and, later, snow; long enough for the ruined planet to tip to a new climatic equilibrium: permanent winter, coated with ice, reflecting most of the sun's heat back to space.

Nothing left alive. I've killed the children of F'han Lha. I've even killed the forests and the algae and the plankton, or whatever silicon-based equivalent used to pump oxygen into this air.

Crew survival not assured, indeed.

She still had the locket around her neck. She took hold of the little pendant, held it up, turned it. It was dark. The hologram had failed, its tiny internal battery emptied.

She grieved.

Now what?

The random thought made her laugh, gasping into the mask.

I've stranded myself in this spacetime pit: a hundred light years from home, and forty thousand years out of my time. Longer than my species existed on Earth, before my own birth.

Now here's my plan.

＊   ＊   ＊

Actually, she discovered after a while, she *did* have a plan.

Of course it was absurd. But the alternative was to give up.

She spent a day of consciousness, a whole precious day, working through her scheme.

She dug a hole in the frozen ground with her laser. She buried a heater in the permafrost, and stretched a power line between the heater and Pod.

She cannibalised Pod's digestive sac. She set it to process the inert soil into amino acids, nucleotide bases, sugars: aminos for proteins, bases and sugars for nucleic acids, the building blocks of terrestrial life.

She took a sample of her own stomach bacteria and stored it cryogenically. She set the capsule to release gut bacteria samples, at timed intervals.

Her scheme was simple, elemental. She would propagate terrestrial life on this planet.

She'd nurture life, for as long as it took, and repopulate the world. Next time she climbed out of Pod there should be carbon-based biomass that Pod could process to feed her.

It was a fine plan. All she had to do was create life, evolve a sentient race, and educate them to take her home: whatever she might find there, anyhow, after forty millennia.

Simple. *If A fails, try B! If B fails, try C!*

While the machinery was setting up, she sat on the frozen ground, her knees tucked up against her chest, and thought about F'han Lha. F'han, whose descendants she had wiped out of history. All to save herself.

The morality of it was too big for her. All she'd been doing was following her training, damn it.

Wake was no hero. She wouldn't pretend to be. She'd been out here doing a job, for a fixed term, for a salary. Now things had gone wrong, and she just wanted to go home. Lying down and dying wasn't in her job description.

That ought to be enough morality for anybody.

It hurt her to think about it.

She climbed, without regret, back into Pod.

"Instructions."

"Open on request." *From the rescue team, golden, wise advanced.* "Or on reverse of oxygen trend. Or on detection of significant terrestrial biomass. Or—"

She hesitated.

Pod waited, infinitely patient.

"Or, after five million years."

She enfolded the locket in her hand. She was shamed to realise that its tiny failure upset her more than the death of this alien world. She rested her closed fist on her chest.

She closed her eyes.

She was immersed in white. Pod's canopy was so badly scarred and frosted over she couldn't see out of it.

She lifted her hand from her chest. Dust trickled out of her closed fist. That had been the locket. *Oh, shit.*

"How long?"

Pod's voice was blurred by phasing. "Five million—"

The canopy opened, but with a creak. Thick, ancient ice snapped away from the hinge. Air flooded in, needle-cold.

It was day, again, in this remote future. The sky was still green-blue. She stood. Save for her boots she was naked, her flight suit long rotted away.

The ground was still ice-bound, locked by permafrost. There were layers upon layers of ice now, the ash of burned biomass long buried. The valley—desolate, empty—fell away from her towards a white-flecked sea, apparently unchanged. She felt her lungs drag at the air. She could check with Pod, but she was sure the oxygen content hadn't increased.

Before Pod, there was a neat disk of melted mud, a hundred feet wide, set in the white-coated ground. As she watched, a huge bubble rose and broke, belching, from its interior.

She took a multiprobe from Pod and stepped, stiffly, out of the compartment.

She could feel the cold of the ground through her boots. Her lungs ached already. She couldn't feel her bare skin, but she could see the goosebumps down her arms, see the frosting of her breath. She couldn't stay out here for long.

She reached the melted circle, and thrust in the probe.

There were aminos and nucleotides and sugars in there. There were organisms which had evolved, significantly, from her gut bacteria. *How about that. Maybe the plan is going to pay off.*

Naked, alone in the spacetime pit, shivering over the muddy, primeval pond, she laughed at herself.

It was late afternoon, here, five million years deep in the future.

She decided to use up another few precious hours of consciousness, to see the night fall. She climbed back into Pod and tried to
get warm, wrapping her arms round her bare body.

She plumbed Pod's memory for details of photosynthesis. That
was what her little colony needed, to become self-sustaining, to
feed from the plentiful sunlight. Pod told her that the first photo-
synthetic organisms on Earth were colonies of bacteria. They left
behind fossils the size of basketballs, called stromatolites . . .

Wake tried to listen, but could take in very little of this, could
make no plans on the basis of the information. She didn't have any
resources, anyhow. Her gut-bacteria children would have to make
their own way.

Night fell. The stars came out. She inspected the sky. Five million years was enough time to colonise the Galaxy. So close to
Earth as this, she'd expect to see *signs:* stars rearranged to suit
human needs, encased in immense structures, Dyson spheres.

The constellations she saw were random, the spaces between
them empty, unstructured.

Was humanity extinct, then? Or fallen back to Earth, its
grandiose ambitions lost?

She was alone here.

She lay back in her couch, and let the sub-dermals crawl over
her, unfeeling.

"Instructions."

When you're in a pit, and you can't climb out, what do you do?
You keep digging, she told herself.

"Half a billion years," she said.

Rain pelted against the canopy, thick, heavy drops. Beyond Pod was
darkness.

Her boots had gone, and so had most of the soft material in
Pod; only hard surfaces remained.

She climbed out. The rain fell against her face. It was warm.
When she touched her scalp she found no hair. No eyebrows,
lashes, pubic hair.

It looked like day, but the clouds were thick, heavy. She
couldn't see anything of the valley, but the basic geology seemed
more or less unchanged. On this little plateau the ice was gone,
the ground turned uniformly to mud. Her feet sank into the
ground; she found it hard to pull her ankles free for each new
step.

She couldn't even tell where her primeval-life pond had been.

She let the rain run into her mouth. It was silty, muddy, salty. Sea-bottom mud.

This planet had suffered an impact: a comet, an asteroid maybe.

It happened, in every stellar system, if you hung around long enough. Life on Earth had been obliterated dozens of times, by impacts in the primeval Solar System, before catching hold. Maybe it had happened here.

She dug around in Pod, in the intervals she could function outside the canopy, trying to see if she could recreate her nutrient pond. But most of Pod's systems had failed, or were rotting away. Pod had been smart, she saw, in cannibalising its own components in order to keep the basic life support functions operating. *Good design, by some anonymous engineer a half-billion years dead. Stretching my handful of days across aeons, always diminishing but never finishing, like a paradox of infinite convergent series . . .* She wasn't expert enough to see what she could take out of this mess and use, that wouldn't finally wreck Pod.

Maybe it didn't matter. If her gut-bacteria babies had survived the impact, maybe they were flourishing, scattered, breeding, somewhere on this warm, wet world. There was nothing more she could do, anyhow.

She brushed the rain off her flesh, as best she could, and climbed back into Pod.

"Instructions."

She listened to the rain against the canopy. It reminded her of L5: the artificial rain storms beating against the walls, when she'd cradled Ben until he'd slept.

She was taking great strides into her pit now, leaping from home in huge logarithmic strides.

"Let's see if the series converges," she said.

"Instructions."

"I'm sorry, Pod. Five billion years."

She couldn't get out of Pod.

Out there it was hot enough now to melt lead, so hot she'd be immediately killed. And besides there was no oxygen.

The clouds overhead were thick, unbroken. A diffuse yellow light shone over baked, shattered ground. Even the geology had evolved: the emptied ocean bed was lifted up, the old mountains eroded and dipped.

Now Pod rested on a plain of shattered, broken plates.

Pod had been forced to repair essential subsystems with raw

materials taken from the planet. She could see, through the canopy, that it looked as if Pod's base had melted, flowed across square metres of the landscape, seeping into the fabric of this world.

All the oxygen in the air was gone, and carbon dioxide had baked out of the vanished ocean, the rocks, to form a blanket over the planet. The planet had become a Venus; it had fallen into the other classic stable-climate model, for a dead terrestrial world.

Her life seed had failed.

So much for the plan.

Pod showed her images it had gathered, through breaks in the clouds, and from non-optical sensors. The sun had grown huge, and it hovered on the south-western horizon. This battered old world had become tidally locked to its parent.

And there were fewer stars in the sky, it seemed to her.

She'd come so far, the galaxy itself was starting to die.

She lay down. The sub-dermals were faulty, and she had to lift them into place.

"Instructions."

She felt a morbid curiosity. *I want to see how it finishes.*

"Go on. Indefinitely."

"Instructions."

"Until something changes, damn it."

Maybe something would turn up, as the laws of physics unravelled.

Sure. Her situation was ridiculous. It was still less than a week, subjectively, since she'd taken that sauna in Mother, before descending on this routine survey. Now, she was probably the only human left alive, anywhere.

I wish I'd died, when Shuttle came down. At least those damn Eetees would have enjoyed a little life.

She closed her eyes.

There was a dull red glow beyond the canopy. She sat up, entrapped like some homunculus in a bell-jar. Through the crystal's protection she could feel the temperature. Too damn hot. Pod was failing at last.

It was almost a relief.

The red glow was nothing to do with the Venusian clouds, which had burned away. So had the rest of the atmosphere, in fact. The planet was more like the Moon now: cracked, battered, ancient. Pod had half-melted into the regolith coating the planet, a thin dust gardened by aeons of micrometeorite strikes.

The red glow was the G8-class sun. It was leaving the Main Sequence. Its core, exhausted of hydrogen, had collapsed; helium was fusing now, pumping energy into the outer layers, ballooning them out in a last, extravagant gesture. Soon, all the system's inner planets would be consumed. Including this one.

The warmth was pleasant. It reminded her of the Shelter on L5. When Ben had been small, and still hers.

"Crew loss scenario," said Pod thickly.

"It's all right," she said. "Don't be frightened."

The canopy dissolved, and light enfolded her.

Hunting the Slarque

UNTER OPENED HIS EYES AND DIMLY REGISTERED a crystal dome above him. Beyond, he made out a thousand rainbows vaulting through the sky like the ribs of a cathedral ceiling. Below the rainbows, as if supporting them, mile-high trees rose, dwellings of various design lodged within their branches. Large insects, on closer inspection Hunter recognised them as *Vespula Vulgaris Denebian*, shuttled back and forth between the trees. He guessed he was on Deneb XVII, The-World-of-a-Million-Wonders.

He was on Million? He was *alive*? It was a miracle. Or was this a dream? Was he dying, was this some cruel jest played by his embattled consciousness as he slipped into oblivion? Would this vision soon cease, to be replaced by total nothingness? The concept frightened him, even though he told himself that he had nothing to fear: dead, he would not have the awareness with which to apprehend the terrible fact of his extinction.

Now, however, he had. He tried to scream.

He could not open his mouth. Nor for that matter, he realised, could he move any other part of his body. Come to that, he could feel nothing. He tried to move his head, shift his gaze. He remained staring through the dome at the rainbow sky.

Following his pang of mental turmoil, he seemed to sense his surroundings with greater clarity. The prismatic parabolas overhead struck him like visual blows, and for the first time he made out sound: the strummed music of troubadours, the cool laughter of a waterfall, and muted chatter, as contented crowds promenaded far below.

Such fidelity could not be the product of a dwindling consciousness, surely? But the alternative, that he was indeed alive, was almost as hard to believe.

How could anyone have survived an attack of such ferocity?

In his mind's eye, dimly, like a half-remembered image from a dream, he recalled the attack: claws and teeth and stingers; he had experienced pain both physical—he had been torn savagely limb from limb—and mental, as he had known he was going to die.

And beyond that instant of mental terror?

Where had the attack taken place. How long ago? Had he been alone, or . . . ?

He wanted more than anything to call her name, less to verify the fact of his own existence than to seek assurance of her safety.

"*Sam!*" But the sound would not form.

He felt his grasp on reality slacken. The colours faded, the sounds ebbed. He fell away, slipped—not into oblivion, as he had feared—but into an ocean of unconsciousness inhabited by the great, dim shapes of half-remembered visions, like basking cetaceans. Hunter dreamed.

At length he felt himself resurface. The rainbows again, the stringed music and babble of water. He still could not shift his vision, not that this overly troubled him. He was more occupied by trying to shuffle into some semblance of order the images revealed in his dream.

He had been on Tartarus Major, he recalled—that great, ancient, smouldering world sentenced to death by the mutinous primary which for millennia had granted the planet its very life. He had been commissioned to catalogue and holopix Tartarean fauna, much of which had never been registered by the Galactic Zoological Centre, Paris, Earth—in the hope that some of the unique examples of the planet's wildlife might be saved from extinction, removed off-world, before the supernova blew.

He had been with Sam, his wife, his life and joy—Sam, carrying his child. He recalled her warning scream, and he had turned, too late to lift his laser. A charging nightmare: teeth and claws, and pain . . . Oh, the pain!

And, above everything, Sam's screams.

And his fear, as he died, for her safety.

Now he wanted to sob, but he had not the physical wherewithal to do so; he felt as though his soul were sobbing for what might have become of Sam.

Unconsciousness claimed him, mercifully.

When next he awoke, what seemed like aeons later, the trapezoid lozenges of sky between the cross-hatched rainbows were cerise with sunset, and marked with early stars. The achingly beautiful notes of a musical instrument, perhaps a clariphone, floated up from the thoroughfares below.

He tried to shift his gaze, move his head, but it was impossible. He had absolutely no sensation in any part of his body.

A cold dread surged through his mind like liquid nitrogen.

He had no body—that was the answer. He was but a brain, a pair of eyes. Only that much of him had survived the attack. He was the guinea pig of some diabolical experiment, his eyes fixed forever on the heavens, the stars he would never again visit.

Hunter. He was Hunter. For as long as he recalled, he had gone by that simple appellation. He had roved the stars, hunting down the more bizarre examples of galactic fauna, amassing a vast hololibrary, as well as extensive case-notes, that were regarded as invaluable by the legion of zoologists and biologists from Earth to Zigma-Zeta. He was a scholar, an intrepid adventurer *non pareil*. He had often gone where lesser men feared to go, like Tartarus . . . He wondered how his death had been taken by the galaxy at large, how his friends had mourned, jealous colleagues smiled that at last his need to prove himself had instead proved to be his undoing.

Tartarus, a double danger: to go among beasts unknown, on a world in imminent danger of stellar annihilation. He should have swallowed his pride and left well alone. Instead, he had dragged Sam along with him.

He recalled, with a keening melancholy deep within him like a dying scream, that Sam had tried to talk him out of the trip. He recalled his stubbornness. "I can't be seen to back out now, Samantha."

He recalled her insistence that, if he did make the journey, then she would accompany him. He recalled his smug, self-righteous satisfaction at her decision.

As unconsciousness took him once again, he was aware of a stabbing pain within his heart.

*   *   *

Someone was watching him, peering down at where he was imprisoned. He had no idea how long he had been staring up at the lattice of rainbows, mulling over his memories and regrets, before he noticed the blue, piercing eyes, the odd, bald head at the periphery of his vision.

The man obligingly centred himself in Hunter's line of sight.

He stared at his tormentor, tried to order his outrage. He boiled with anger. *Do you know who I am?* he wanted to ask the man. *I am Hunter, famed and feted the galaxy over! How dare you do this to me!*

Hands braced on knees, the man looked down on him. Something about his foppish appearance sent a shiver of revulsion through Hunter. His captor wore the white cavalier boots of a nobleman, ballooning pantaloons, and a sleeveless overcoat of some snow-white fur. His face was thin, bloodless—almost as pale as his vestments.

He reminded Hunter of an albino wasp: the concave chest, the slim waist, the soft abdomen swelling obscenely beneath it.

Without taking his gaze off Hunter, the man addressed whispered words to someone out of sight. Hunter made out a muttered reply. The man nodded.

"My name is Alvarez," he said. "Do not be alarmed. You are in no danger. We are looking after you."

Oddly, far from reassuring him, the words put an end to the notion that he might still be dreaming, and convinced him of the reality of this situation.

He tried to speak but could not.

Alvarez was addressing his companion again, who had moved into Hunter's view: a fat man garbed in robes of gold and crimson.

Alvarez disappeared, returned seconds later with a rectangular, opaqued screen on castors. He positioned it before Hunter, so that it eclipsed his view of the sky. Hunter judged, from the position of the screen and his captors, that he was lying on the floor, Alvarez and the fat man standing on a platform above him.

He stared at the screen as Alvarez flicked a switch on its side.

A work of art? A macabre hologram that might have had some significance to the jaded citizens of The-World-of-a-Million-Wonders, who had seen *everything* before?

The 'gram showed the figure of a man, suspended—but the figure of a man as Hunter had never before witnessed. It was as if the unfortunate subject of the artwork had been flayed alive, skinned to reveal purple and puce slabs of muscle shot through with filaments of tendons, veins, and arteries—like some medical student's computer graphic which built up, layer on layer, from skeleton to fully fleshed human being.

At first, Hunter thought that the figure was a mere representation, a still hologram—then he saw a movement behind the figure, a bubble rising through the fluid in which it was suspended. And, then, he made out the slight, ticking pulse at its throat.

He could not comprehend why they were showing him this monster.

Alvarez leaned forward. "You have no reason to worry," he said. "You are progressing well, Mr Hunter, considering the condition you were in when you arrived."

Realisation crashed through Hunter. He stared again at the reflection of himself, at the monstrosity he had become.

Alvarez opaqued the screen, wheeled it away. He returned and leaned forward. "We are delighted with your progress, Mr Hunter." He nodded to his fat companion. "Dr Fischer."

The doctor touched some control in his hand and Hunter slipped into blessed oblivion.

When he came to his senses it took him some minutes before he realised that his circumstances were altered. The view through the dome was substantially the same—rainbows, towering trees—but shifted slightly, moved a few degrees to the right.

He watched a vast, majestic star-galleon edge slowly past the dome, its dozen angled, multi-coloured sails bellying in the breeze. He monitored its royal progress through the evening sky until it was lost to sight—and then he realised that he had, in order to track its passage, moved his head.

For the first time he became aware of his immediate surroundings.

He was in a small, comfortable room formed from a slice of the dome: two walls hung with tapestries, the third the outer wall of diamond facets.

With trepidation, he raised his head and peered down the length of his body. He was naked, but not as naked as he had been on the last occasion when he had seen himself. This time he was covered with skin—tanned, healthy looking skin over well-developed muscles. He remembered the attack in the southern jungle of Tartarus, relived the terrible awareness of being riven limb from limb.

And now he was whole again.

He was in a rejuvenation pod, its canoe-shaped length supporting a web of finely woven fibres which cradled him with the lightest of touches. It was as if he were floating on air. Leads and electrodes covered him, snaking over the side of the pod and disappearing into monitors underneath.

He tried to sit up, but it was all he could do to raise his arm. The slightest exertion filled him with exhaustion. But what did he expect, having newly risen from the dead?

He experienced then a strange ambivalence of emotion. Of course he was grateful to be alive—the fear of oblivion he had experienced upon first awakening was still fresh enough in his memory to fill him with an odd, retrospective dread, and a profound gratitude for his new lease of life. But something, some nagging insistence at the back of his mind, hectored him with the improbability of his being resurrected.

Very well—he was famous, was respected in his field, but even he had to admit that his death would have been no great loss to the galaxy at large. So why had Alvarez, or the people for whom Alvarez worked, seen fit to outlay millions on bringing him back to life? For certain, Sam could not have raised the funds to finance the procedure, even if she had realised their joint assets. He was rich, but not *that* rich. Why, the very sailship journey from the rim world of Tartarus to the Core planet of Million would have bankrupted him.

He was alive, but *why* he was alive worried him.

He felt himself drifting as a sedative sluiced through his system.

Hunter opened his eyes.

He was in a room much larger than the first, a full quadrant of the dome this time. He was no longer attached to the rejuvenation pod, but lying in a bed. Apart from a slight ache in his chest, a tightness, he felt well. Tentatively, he sat up, swung his legs from the bed. He wore a short, white gown like a kimono. He examined his legs, his arms. They seemed to be as he remembered them, but curiously younger, without the marks of age, the discolorations and small scars he'd picked up during a lifetime of tracking fauna through every imaginable landscape. He filled his chest with a deep breath, exhaled. He felt good.

He stood and crossed to the wall of the dome, climbed the three steps and paused on the raised gallery. A magnificent star-galleon sailed by outside, so close that Hunter could make out figures on the deck, a curious assortment of humans and aliens. A few stopped work to look at him. One young girl even waved. Hunter raised his arm in salute and watched the ship sail away, conscious of the gesture, the blood pumping through his veins. In that instant, he was suddenly aware of the possibilities, of the wondrous gift of life renewed.

"Mr Hunter," the voice called from behind him. "I'm so pleased to see you up and about."

Alvarez stood on the threshold, smiling across the room at him. He seemed smaller than before, somehow reduced. Within the swaddles of his fine clothing—rich gold robes, frilled shirts—he was even more insectlike than Hunter recalled.

"I have so many questions I don't really know where to begin," Hunter said.

Alvarez waved, the cuff of his gown hanging a good half-metre from his sticklike wrist. "All in good time, my dear Mr Hunter. Perhaps you would care for a drink?" He moved to a table beneath the curve of the dome, its surface marked with a press-select panel of beverages.

"A fruit juice."

"I'll join you," Alvarez said, and seconds later passed Hunter a tall glass of yellow liquid.

His thoughts returned to the jungle of Tartarus. "My wife . . . ?" he began.

Alvarez was quick to reassure him. "Samantha is fit and well. No need to worry yourself on that score."

"I'd like to see her."

"That is being arranged. Within the next three or four days, you should be re-united."

Hunter nodded, reluctant to show Alvarez his relief or gratitude. His wife was well, he was blessed with a new body, renewed life . . . so why did he experience a pang of apprehension like a shadow cast across his soul?

"Mr Hunter," Alvarez asked, "what are your last recollections before awakening here?"

Hunter looked from Alvarez to the tall trees receding into the distance. "Tartarus," he said. "The jungle."

"Can you recall the . . . the actual attack?"

"I remember, but vaguely. I can't recall what led up to it, just the attack itself. It's as if it happened years ago."

Alvarez was staring at him. "It did, Mr Hunter. Three years ago, to be precise."

Again, Hunter did not allow his reaction to show: shock, this time. Three years! But Sam had been carrying their child, his daughter. He had missed her birth, the first years of her life . . .

"You owe your survival to your wife," Alvarez continued. "She fired flares to frighten the beast that killed you, then gathered your remains." He made an expression of distaste. "There was not much left. Your head, torso . . . She stored them in the freeze-unit at your camp, then returned through the jungle to Apollinaire, and from there to the port at Baudelaire, where she arranged passage off-planet."

Hunter closed his eyes. He imagined Sam's terror, her despair, her frantic hope. It should have been enough to drive her mad.

Alvarez went on, "She applied for aid to a number of resurrection foundations. My company examined you. They reported your case to me. I decided to sanction your rebirth."

Hunter was shaking his head. "But how did Sam raise the fare to Million?" he asked. "And the cost of the resurrection itself? There's just no way . . ." What, he wondered, had she done to finance his recovery?

"She had to arrange a loan to get the both of you here. She arrived virtually penniless."

"Then how—?"

Alvarez raised a hand. There was something about the man that Hunter did not like: his swift, imperious gestures, his thin face which combined the aspects of asceticism and superiority. In an age when everyone enjoyed the means to ensure perfect health, Alvarez's affectation of ill health was macabre.

"Your situation interested me, Mr Hunter. I knew of you. I followed your work, admired your success. I cannot claim to be a naturalist in the same league as yourself, but I dabble . . .

"I run many novel enterprises on Million," Alvarez went on. "My very favourite, indeed the most popular and lucrative, is my Xeno-biological Exhibit Centre, here in the capital. It attracts millions of visitors every year from all across the galaxy. Perhaps you have heard of it, Mr Hunter?"

Hunter shook his head, minimally. "I have no interest in, nor sympathy with, zoos, Mr Alvarez."

"Such an outdated, crude description, I do think. My Exhibit Centre is quite unlike the zoos of old. The centre furnishes species from around the galaxy with a realistic simulacrum of their native habitats, often extending for kilometres. Where the species exhibited are endangered on their own worlds, we have instituted successful breeding programmes. In more than one instance I have saved species from certain extinction." He paused, staring at Hunter. "Although usually I hire operators from the planet in question to capture and transport the animals I require to update my exhibit, on this occasion—"

Hunter laid his drink aside, untouched. "I am a cameraman, Mr Alvarez. I hunt animals in order to film them. I have no expertise in capturing animals."

"What I need is someone skilled in the *tracking* of a certain animal. My team will perform the actual physical capture. On the planet in question, there are no resident experts, and as you are already *au fait* with the terrain . . ."

Hunter interrupted. "Where?" he asked.

"Where else?" Alvarez smiled. "Tartarus, of course."

It took some seconds for his words to sink in. Hunter stared across the room at the dandified zoo-keeper. "Tartarus?" He almost laughed. "Madness. Three years ago the scientists were forecasting the explosion of the supernova in two to three years at the latest."

Alvarez responded evenly. "The scientists have revised their estimates. They now think the planet is safe for another year."

Hunter sat down on the steps that curved around the room. He shook his head, looked up. "I'm sorry, Mr Alvarez. Tartarus holds too many bad memories for me. And anyway, it would be insane to go there with the supernova so imminent."

"I think you fail to understand the situation in which you find yourself, Mr Hunter. You and your wife are in debt to me to the tune of some five million credits. You are now, legally, in my employ—"

"I didn't ask to be resurrected. I signed nothing!"

Alvarez smiled. "Your wife signed all the relevant papers. She wanted you resurrected. She agreed to work for me."

Hunter experienced a strange, plummeting sensation deep within him. He whispered, "Where is she?"

"Six months ago, when it was obvious that your resurrection would be successful, she left for Tartarus to do some field-work, investigations, and preliminary tracking."

Hunter closed his eyes. Alvarez had him.

He thought of his child. Surely Sam would not take an infant to Tartarus. "Who's looking after our child while Sam is on Tartarus?" he asked.

Alvarez shook his head apologetically. "I never actually met your wife. Our negotiations were conducted via intermediaries. I know nothing of your wife's personal arrangements."

Hunter stood and contemplated the view, the tall trees marching away into the mist, the canopy of rainbows and the star-galleons. It was against everything that Hunter believed in to hunt and trap an animal for captivity. How many lucrative commissions had he turned down in the past?

But there was one obvious difference in this case. If the animal that Alvarez wanted capturing was not tracked and taken from Tartarus, then it faced annihilation come the supernova.

And there was the added incentive that soon he would be reunited with Sam.

"I seem to have little choice but to agree to your demands."

Alvarez smiled thinly. "Excellent. I knew you would see sense, eventually. We need a man of your calibre in order to track the creature I require as the prize of my collection."

"Which is?" Hunter asked.

Alvarez paused for a second, as if for dramatic emphasis. "The Slarque," he said.

Hunter mouthed the word to himself in disbelief. Millennia ago, long before humankind colonised Tartarus, a sentient alien race known as the Slarque were preeminent on the planet. They built cities on every continent, sailed ships across the oceans, and reached a stage of civilisation comparable to that of humanity in the sixteenth century. Then, over the period of a few hundred years, they became extinct—or so some theorists posited. Others, a crank minority, held that the Slarque still existed in some devolved form, sequestered in the mountainous jungle terrain of the southern continent. There had been reports of sightings, dubious "eye-witness" accounts of brief meetings with the fearsome, bipedal creatures, but no actual concrete evidence.

"Mr Hunter," Alvarez was saying, "do you have any idea what kind of creature was responsible for your death?"

Hunter gestured. "Of course not. It happened so fast. I didn't have a chance—" He stopped.

Alvarez crossed the room to a wall-screen. He inserted a small disc, adjusted dials. He turned to Hunter. "Your wife was filming at the time of your death. This is what she filmed."

The screen flared. Hunter took half a dozen paces forward, then stopped, as if transfixed by what he saw. The picture sent memories, emotions, flooding through his mind. He stared at the jungle scene, and he could almost smell the stringent, putrescent reek peculiar to Tartarus, the stench of vegetable matter rotting in the vastly increased heat of the southern climes. He heard the cries and screams of a hundred uncatalogued birds and beasts. He experienced again the mixture of anxiety and exhilaration at being in the unexplored jungle of a planet which at any moment might be ripped apart by its exploding sun.

"Watch closely, Mr Hunter," Alvarez said.

He saw himself, a small figure in the background, centre-screen. This was an establishing shot, which Sam would edit into the documentary she always made about their field-trips.

It was over in five seconds.

One instant he was gesturing at the blood-red sky through a rent in the jungle canopy—and the next something emerged through the undergrowth behind him, leapt upon his back and began tearing him apart.

Hunter peered at the grainy film, trying to make out his assailant. The attack was taking place in the undergrowth, largely obscured from the camera. All that could be seen was the rearing, curving tail of the animal—for all the world like that of a scorpion—flailing and thrashing and coming down again and again on the body of its victim . . .

The film finished there, as Sam fired flares to scare away the animal. The screen blanked.

"We have reason to believe," Alvarez said, "that this creature was the female of the last surviving pair of Slarque on Tartarus—"

"Ridiculous!" Hunter cried.

"They are devolved," Alvarez went on, "and living like wild animals." He paused. "Do you see what an opportunity this is, Mr Hunter? If we can capture, and save from certain extinction, the very last pair of a sentient alien race?"

Hunter gestured, aware that his hand was trembling. "This is hardly proof of its existence," he objected.

"The stinger corresponds with anatomical remains which are known to be of the Slarque. Which other species on Tartarus has such a distinctive feature?" Alvarez paused. "Also, your wife has been working hard on Tartarus. She has come up with some very interesting information."

From a pocket in his robe, he pulled out what Hunter recognised as an ear-phone. "A couple of months ago she dispatched this report of her progress. I'll leave it with you." He placed it on the tabletop beside the bed. "We embark for Tartarus in a little under three days, Mr Hunter. For now, farewell."

When Alvarez had left the room, Hunter quickly crossed to the bed and took up the 'phone. His heart leapt at the thought of listening to his wife's voice. He inserted the 'phone in his right ear, activated it.

Tears came to his eyes. Her words brought back a slew of poignant memories. He saw her before him, her calm oval face, dark hair drawn back, green eyes staring into space as she spoke into the recorder.

Hunter lay on the bed and closed his eyes.

Apollinaire Town. Mary's day, 33rd St Jerome's month, 1720 — Tartarean calendar.

By Galactic Standard it's . . . I don't know. I know I've been here for months, but it seems like years. Sometimes I find it hard to believe that anything exists beyond this damned planet. The sun dominates everything. During the day it fills the sky, bloated and festering. Even at night the sky is crimson with its light. It's strange to think that everything around me, the everyday reality of Tartarus I take for granted, will be incinerated in less than a year. This fact overwhelms life here, affecting everyone. There's a strange air of apathy and lassitude about the place, as people go about their business, marking time before the wholesale evacuation begins. The crime rate has increased; violence is commonplace. Bizarre cults have sprung up — and I mean even weirder than the official Church of the Ultimate Sacrifice.

Alvarez, I want you to pass this recording on to Hunter when he's fit and well. I know you want a progress report, and you'll get one. But I want to talk to my husband, if you don't mind.

I'm staying at the Halbeck House hotel, Hunter — in the double room overlooking the canal. I'm dictating this on the balcony where we did the editing for the last film. I'm watching the sun set as I speak. It's unpleasantly hot, but at least there's a slight breeze starting up. In the trees beside the canal, a flock of nightgulls are gathering. You'll be able to hear their songs a little later, when night falls. A troupe of Lefervre's mandrills is watching me from the far balcony rail. I know you never liked the creatures, Hunter — but I find something inexpressibly melancholy in their eyes. Do you think they know their time is almost up?

(Oh, by the way, the hotel still serves the most superb lemon beer in Apollinaire. Mmm.)

Okay, Alvarez, I know — you want to hear how I'm progressing.

Three days ago I got back from a month-long trip into the interior. I'd been getting nowhere in either Apollinaire or Baudelaire.

The leads I wanted to follow up all ran out—people were reluctant to talk. A couple of people I wanted to interview—the freelance film-maker who recorded *something* ten years ago, and the uranium prospector who claimed he'd seen a Slarque . . . well, the film-maker left Tartarus a couple of years back, and the prospector is dead. I tried to make an appointment with the Director of the Natural History museum, but he was away and wasn't due back for a week. I left a message for him, then decided to take a trek into the interior.

Hunter, the ornithopter service no longer runs from Apollinaire. Gabriella's sold up and left the planet, and the new owner has re-sited the operation in Baudelaire. It's understandable, of course. These days there are few naturalists, geologists, or prospectors interested in the southern interior. The only visitors to the area are the members of one of the crackpot cults I mentioned, the so-called *Slarquists*, who come here on their way to the alien temples down the coast. I don't know what they do there. There are rumours that they make sacrifices to the all-powerful God of the Slarque. Don't ask me what kind of sacrifices.

Anyway, with no ornithopters flying, I hired a tracked bison and two armed guards, and set off inland.

It took four days to reach the site of our first camp, Hunter—the rock pool beneath the waterfall, remember? From there it was another two days to the foot of the plateau, to the place where you . . . where the attack happened. It was just how I remembered it—the opening in the smaller salsé trees, the taller, surrounding trees providing a high level canopy that blotted out the sun . . . I left the guards in the bison and just stood on the edge of the clearing and relived the horror of what happened three years ago.

I can hear you asking why I went back there, why did I torture myself? Well, if you recall, I'd set up a few remote cameras to record some of the more timorous examples of the area's wildlife while we went trekking. After the attack . . . I'd left the cameras and equipment in my haste to get to Baudelaire. It struck me that perhaps if the Slarque—if Slarque they were—had returned, then they might be captured on film.

That night in the clearing I viewed all the considerable footage. Plenty of shots of nocturnal fauna and grazing quadrupeds, but no Slarque.

The following day I took forensic samples from the area where the attack happened—broken undergrowth, disturbed soil, etc., for Alvarez's people to examine when they get here. Then I set up more cameras, this time fixed to relay images back to my base in Apollinaire.

I decided to make a few exploratory forays into the surrounding jungle. We had food and water for a couple of weeks, and as the guards were being paid by the hour they had no reason to complain. Every other day we made circular treks into the jungle, finishing back at the campsite in the evening. I reckon we covered a good two hundred square kilometres like this. I filmed constantly, took dung samples, samples of hair and bone . . . Needless to say, I didn't come across the Slarque.

Just short of a month after leaving Apollinaire, we made the journey back. I felt depressed. I'd achieved nothing, not even laid the terror of that terrible day. It's strange, but I returned to Tartarus on this mission for Alvarez with extreme reluctance—if not for the fact that I was working for him to cover the cost of your treatment, I would have been happy to leave Tartarus well alone and let the Slarque fry when the sun blew. That was then. Now, and even after just a few days on the planet, I wanted to know what had killed you, if it were a Slarque. I wanted to find out more about this strange, devolved race.

I left the interior having found out nothing, and that hurt.

When I got back to Halbeck House, there was a message for me from the Director of the Natural History Museum at Apollinaire. He'd seen and enjoyed a couple of our films and agreed to meet me.

Monsieur Dernier was in his early eighties, so learned and dignified I felt like a kid in his company. I told him about the attack, that I was eager to trace the animal responsible. It happened that he'd heard about the incident on the newscasts—he was happy to help me. Now that it came to it, I was reluctant to broach the subject of the Slarque, in case Dernier thought me a complete crank—one of the many crazy cultists abroad in Apollinaire. I edged around the issue for a time, mentioned at last that some people, on viewing the film, had commented on how the beast did bear a certain superficial resemblance to fossil remains of the Slarque. Of course, I hastened to add, I didn't believe this myself.

He gave me a strange look, told me that he himself subscribed to the belief, unpopular though it was, that devolved descendants of the Slarque still inhabited the interior of the southern continent.

He'd paused there, then asked me if I'd ever heard of Rogers and Codey? I admitted that I hadn't.

Dernier told me that they had been starship pilots back in the eighties. Their shuttle had suffered engine failure and come down in the central mountains, crash-landed in a remote snow-bound valley and never been discovered. They were given up for dead — until a year later when Rogers staggered into Apollinaire, half-delirious and severely frost-bitten. The only survivor of the crash, he'd crossed a high mountain pass and half the continent — it made big news even on Earth, thirty years ago. When he was sufficiently recovered to leave hospital, Rogers had sought out M. Dernier, a well-known advocate of the extant Slarque theory.

Lieutenant Rogers claimed to have had contact with the Slarque in their interior mountain fastness.

Apparently, Rogers had repeated, over and over, that he had seen the Slarque, and that the meeting had been terrible — and he would say no more. Rogers had needed to confess, Dernier felt, but, when he came to do so, the burden of his experience had been too harrowing to relive.

I asked Dernier if he believed Rogers's story.

He told me that he did. Rogers hadn't sought to publicise his claim, to gain from it. He had no reason to lie about meeting the creatures. Whatever had happened in the interior had clearly left the lieutenant in a weakened mental state.

I asked him if he knew what had become of Lt Rogers, if he was still on Tartarus.

"Thirty years ago," Dernier said, "Lt Rogers converted, became a novice in the Church of the Ultimate Sacrifice. If he's survived this long in the bloody organisation, then he'll still be on Tartarus. You might try the monastery at Barabas, along the coast."

So yesterday I took the barge on the inland waterway, then a pony and trap up to the clifftop Monastery of St Cyprian of Carthage.

I was met inside the ornate main gate by a blind monk. He listened to my explanations in silence. I said that I wished to talk a certain Anthony Rogers, formerly Lt Rogers of the Tartarean Space Fleet. The monk told me that father Rogers would be pleased to see me. He was taking his last visitors this week. Three days ago he had undergone extensive penitent surgery, preparatory to total withdrawal.

The monk led me through ancient cloisters. I was more than a little apprehensive. I'd seen devotees of the Ultimate Sacrifice only at a distance before. You know how squeamish I am, Hunter.

The monk left me in a beautiful garden overlooking the ocean.

I sat on a wooden bench and stared out across the waters. The sky was white hot, the sun huge above the horizon as it made its long fall towards evening.

The monk returned, pushing a . . . a *bundle* in a crude, wooden wheelchair. Its occupant, without arms or legs, jogged from side to side as he was trundled down the incline, prevented from falling forward by a leather strap buckled around his midriff.

The monk positioned the carriage before me and murmured that he'd leave us to talk.

I . . . even now I find it difficult to express what I thought, or rather *felt*, on meeting Father Rogers in the monastery garden. His physical degradation, the voluntary amputation of his limbs, gave him the unthreatening and pathetic appearance of a swaddled infant—so perhaps the reason I felt threatened was that I could not bring myself to intellectually understand the degree of his commitment in undergoing such mutilation.

Also what troubled me was that I could still see, in his crew cut, his deep tan and keen blue eyes, the astronaut that he had once been.

We exchanged guarded pleasantries for a time, he suspicious of my motives, myself unsure as to how to begin to broach the subject of his purported meeting with the aliens.

I recorded our conversation. I've edited it into this report. I've cut the section where Fr Rogers rambled—he's in his nineties now and he seemed much of the time to be elsewhere. From time to time he'd stop talking altogether, stare into the distance, as if reliving the ordeal he'd survived in the mountains. In the following account I've included a few of my own comments and explanations.

I began by telling him that, almost three years ago, I lost my husband in what I suspect was a Slarque attack.

Fr Rogers: Slarque? Did you say Slarque?

Sam: I wasn't one hundred per cent sure. I might be mistaken. I've been trying to find someone with first-hand experience of . . .

Fr Rogers: The Slarque . . . Lord Jesus Christ have mercy on their wayward souls. It's such a long time ago, such a long time. I sometimes wonder . . . No, I know it happened. It can't have been a dream, a nightmare. It happened. It's the reason I'm here. If not for what happened out there in the mountains, I might never have seen the light.

Sam: What happened, Father?

Fr Rogers: Mmm? What happened? What *happened*? You

wouldn't believe me if I told you. You'd be like all the others, dis-believers all—

Sam: I have seen a Slarque, too.

Fr Rogers: So you say, so you say . . . I haven't told anyone for a long time. Became tired of being disbelieved, you see. They thought I'd gone mad . . . But I didn't tell anyone what really hap-pened. I didn't want the authorities to go and find Codey, arrest him.

Sam: Codey, your co-pilot? But I thought he died in the crash-landing?

Fr Rogers: That's what I told everyone. Easier that way. He wanted people to think he hadn't survived, the sinner.

Sam: Father, can you tell me what happened?

Fr Rogers: It's . . . how long ago? Thirty years? More? There's little chance Codey will still be alive. Oh, he had supplies aplenty, but up here . . . up here he was sick and getting worse. He made me promise that I'd keep quiet about what he did—and until now I have. But what harm can it do now, with Codey surely long dead?

(He stopped here and stared off into the distance and the gothic monastery rearing against the twilight sky. Tears appeared in his eyes. I felt sorry for him. Part of me regretted what I was put-ting him through, but I was intrigued by the little he'd told me so far. I *had* to find out what he'd experienced, all those years ago.)

Sam: Father . . . ?

Fr Rogers: Eh? Oh, the crash-landing. We came down too soon. Don't ask me why. I can't remember. Miracle we survived. We found ourselves in a high valley in the central mountains, shut in by snow-covered peaks all around. We were a small ship, a shuttle. The radio was wrecked and we had no other means of communi-cation with the outside world. We didn't reckon the Fleet would waste much time trying to find us. We had supplies enough for years, and the part of the ship not completely stove in we used as living quarters. I made a few expeditions into the surrounding hills, trying to find a way out, a navigable pass that'd get us to the sea level jungle below the central range . . . But the going was too tough, the snow impassable.

It was on one of these abortive expeditions that I saw the first Slarque. I was coming back to the ship, wading through a waist-high snowdrift, frozen to the bone, and sick with the thought that I'd never get away from this frozen hell.

The Slarque was on a spur of rock overlooking the valley. It was on all fours, though later I saw them standing upright. It was watching me. It was a long way off, and in silhouette, so I couldn't really make out much detail. I recognised the arched tail, though, whipping around above its back.

So when I returned to the ship I told Codey what I'd seen. He just stared at me for a long time—and I assumed he thought I'd gone mad—but then he began nodding, and he said, "I know. They've been communicating with me for the past three days." Then it was *my* turn to think *he'd* flipped.

(His gaze slipped out of focus again. He no longer saw the monastery. He was back in the mountain valley.)

Fr Rogers: Codey was strangely calm, like a man blessed with a vision. I asked him what he meant by "communicating." Looking straight through me, he just pointed to his head. "They put thoughts into here—not words, but thoughts: emotions, facts . . ."

I said, "Codey, you've finally gone, man. Don't give me any of that shit!" But Codey just went on staring through me like I wasn't there, and he began talking, telling me about the Slarque, and there was so much of it, so many details Codey just couldn't have known or made up, that by the end of it all I was scared, real scared, not wanting to believe a word of it, but at the same time finding myself half-believing . . .

Codey said that there were just two Slarque left. They were old, a couple of hundred years old. They had lived near the coast in their early years, but with the arrival of humans on the southern continent they'd retreated further south, into the snowfields of the central mountains. Codey told me that the Slarque had dwindled because a certain species of animal, on which they were dependent, had become extinct long ago. Codey said that the female Slarque was bearing a litter of young, that she was due to birth soon . . . He told me many other things that night, as the snow fell and the wind howled outside—but either I've forgotten what else he said, or I never heard it at the time through fear . . . I went straight out into that gale and rigged up an electric fence around the ship, and I didn't stop work until I was sure it'd keep out the most fearsome predator.

The next day or two, I kept out of Codey's way, like he was contaminated . . . I ate in my own cabin, tried not to dwell on what he'd told me.

One night he came to my cabin, knocked on the door. He just stood there, staring at me. "They want one of us," he told me. As soon as he spoke, it was as if this was what I'd been fearing all along. I had no doubt who "they" were. I think I went berserk then. I attacked Codey, beat him back out of my cabin. I was frightened. Oh, Christ was I frightened.

In the morning he came to me again, strangely subdued, remote. He said he wanted to show me something in the hold. I was wary, expecting a trick. I armed myself and followed him down the corridor of the broken-backed ship and into the hold. He crossed to a suspension unit, opened the lid and said, "Look."

So I looked. We were carrying a prisoner, a criminal suspended for the trip between Tartarus and Earth, where he was due to go on trial for the assassination of a Tartarean government official. I hadn't known what we were carrying—I hadn't bothered to check the manifest before take-off. But Codey had.

He said, "He'd only be executed on Earth."

"No," I said.

Codey stared at me. "It's either him or you, Rogers." He had his laser out and aimed at my head. I lifted my own pistol, saw that the charge was empty. Codey just smiled.

I said, "But . . . but when they've done with him—how long will he keep them satisfied? How long before they want one of us?"

Codey shook his head. "Not for a long while, believe me."

I ranted and raved at him, cried and swore, but the terrible inevitability of his logic wore me down—it was either the prisoner or me. And so at last I helped him drag the suspension unit from the ship, through the snow to the far end of the valley, where we left it with the lid open for the Slarque . . . I—I have never forgiven myself to this day. I wish now that I'd had the strength to sacrifice myself.

(He broke down then, bowed his head and wept. I soothed him as best I could, murmured platitudes, my hand on the stump of his shoulder.)

Fr Rogers: That night I watched two shadowy ghosts appear at the end of the valley, haul the prisoner from the unit and drag him off through the snow. At first light next morning I kitted up, took my share of provisions and told Codey I was going to find a way out, that I'd rather die trying than remain here with him. I reckoned that with the Slarque busy with the prisoner, I had a slim chance of getting away from the valley. After that . . . who could tell?

Codey didn't say a word. I tried to persuade him to come with me, but he kept shaking his head and saying that I didn't understand, that they needed him . . . So I left him and trekked north, fearful of the aliens, the snow, the cold. All I recall is getting clear of the valley and the Slarque, and the tremendous feeling of relief when I did. I don't remember much else. The terror of what I was leaving was worse than the thought of dying alone in the mountains. They tell me it's one and a half thousand kilometres from the central range to the coast. I don't know. I just walked and kept on walking.

(He was silent for a long, long time after that. At last he spoke, almost to himself.)

Fr Rogers: Poor Codey. Poor, poor Codey . . .

Sam: And . . . then you joined the Church?

Fr Rogers: Almost as soon as I got back. It seemed . . . the only thing to do. I had to make amends, to thank God for my survival and at the same time to make reparations for the fact that I did survive.

We sat for a time in silence, Father Rogers contemplating the past while I considered the future. I knew what I was going to do. I unfolded the map of the southern continent I had brought with me and spread it across the arms of the invalid carriage. I asked him where the shuttle had come down. He stared at the map for a long time, frowning, and finally quoted an approximate grid reference coordinate. I marked the valley with a cross.

I sat and talked with Father Rogers for a while, and then left him sitting in the garden overlooking the sea, and made my way back to Apollinaire.

That was yesterday. Today I've been preparing for the expedition. Unfortunately I've found no one willing to act as my bodyguard this time—because of the duration of the planned trip and the sun's lack of stability. I set off tomorrow in a tracked bison, with plenty of food, water, and arms. I've calculated that it'll take me a couple of months to cover the one and a half thousand kays to the valley where the ship crash-landed. Fortunately, with the rise of the global temperature, the snow on the high ground of the central mountains has melted, so that leg of the journey should be relatively easy. With luck, the sun should hold steady for a while yet, though it does seem to be getting hotter every day. The latest forecast I've heard is that we're safe for another six to nine months . . .

I don't know what I'll find when I get to the valley. Certainly not Codey. As Father Rogers said, after thirty years he should be long dead. Maybe I'll hit lucky and find the Slarque? I'll leave transmitter beacons along my route, so you can follow me when you get here, whenever that might be.

Okay, Alvarez, that's about it. If you don't mind, I'd like the next bit to remain private, between Hunter and me, okay?

Hunter, the thought that sooner or later we'll be together again has kept me going. Don't worry about me, I have everything under control. Freya is with me; I'm taking her into the interior tomorrow. And before you protest—don't! She's perfectly safe. Hunter, I can't wait until we're reunited, until we can watch our daughter grow, share her discoveries . . . I love you, Hunter. Take care.

Hunter sat on the balcony of Halbeck House, where weeks before Sam had made the recording. He had tried to contact her by radio upon his arrival, but of course the activity of the solar flares made such communication impossible.

He sipped an iced lemon beer and stared out across what had once been a pretty, provincial town. Now the increased temperature of the past few months had taken its toll. The trees lining the canal were scorched and dying, and the water in the canal itself had evaporated, leaving a bed of evil-smelling mud. Even the three-storey timber buildings of the town seemed weary, dried out, and warped by the incessant heat. Although the sun had set one hour ago, pulling in its wake a gaudy, pyrotechnical display of flaring lights above the crowded rooftops, the twilight song of the night-gulls was not to be heard. Nor was there any sign of Lefervre's mandrills, usually to be seen swinging crazily through the wrought-ironwork of the balcony. An eerie silence hung in the air, a funereal calm presaging the planet's inevitable demise.

Hunter, Alvarez, and his entourage had arrived on Tartarus by the very last scheduled sailship; they would entrust their departure to one of the illegal pirate lines still ferrying adventurers, thrill-seekers, or just plain fools, to and from the planet.

They had arrived in Apollinaire that morning, to find the town deserted but for a handful of citizens determined to leave their flight to the very last weeks.

Three days ago, the sun had sent out a searing pulse of flame, a great flaring tongue, as if in derision of the citizens who remained. The people of Baudelaire and Apollinaire had panicked. There had been riots, much looting and burning—and another great exodus off-world. The regular shipping lines had been inundated by frantic souls desperate to flee, and the surplus had been taken by the opportunistic pirate ships that had just happened to be orbiting like flies around a corpse.

Technically, Halbeck House was no longer open for business, but its proprietor had greeted Hunter like a long-lost brother and insisted that he, Alvarez, and the rest of the team make themselves at home. Then he had taken the last boat to Baudelaire, leaving a supply of iced beer and a table set for the evening meal.

Hunter drank his beer and considered Father Rogers's story, which he had listened to again and again on the voyage to Tartarus. Although the old astronaut's words had about them a kind of insane veracity which suggested he believed his own story, even if no one else did, it was stretching the limits of credulity to believe that not only did a last pair of Slarque still exist in the central mountains, but that they had been in mental contact with Codey. And the beast that had attacked and killed Hunter? Sam's footage of the incident was not conclusive proof that the Slarque existed, despite Alvarez's assumptions otherwise.

The more he thought about it, the more he came to the conclusion that the trip into the interior would prove fruitless. He looked forward to the time when he would be reunited with Sam, and meet his daughter Freya for the very first time.

He had expected Sam to have left some message for him at the hotel—maybe even a pix of Freya. But nothing had awaited him, and when he asked the proprietor about his daughter, the man had looked puzzled. "But your wife had no little girl with her, Monsieur Hunter."

Dinner that evening was taken on the patio beside the empty canal. The meal was a subdued affair, stifled by the oppressing humidity and the collective realisation of the enormity of the mission they were about to embark upon. Hunter ate sparingly and said little, speaking only to answer questions concerning the planet's natural history. The chest pains which had bothered him on Million had increased in severity over the past few days; that afternoon he had lain on his bed, wracked with what he thought was a heart attack. Now he felt the familiar tightness in his chest. He was reassured that Dr Fischer was on hand.

The rest of their party, other than himself, Alvarez, and the doctor, consisted of a team of four drivers-cum-guards, men from Million in the employ of the Alvarez Foundation. They tended to keep to themselves, indeed were congregated at the far end of the table now, leaving the others to talk together.

Alvarez was saying: "I made a trip out to the St Cyprian monastery this afternoon, to see if I could get anything more from Rogers."

Hunter looked up from his plate of cold meat and salad. "And?"

He winced as a stabbing pain lanced through his lungs.

The entrepreneur was leaning back in his chair, turning a glass of wine in his fingers. He was dressed in a light-weight, white suit of extravagantly flamboyant design. "I found Rogers, and a number of the other monks."

Dr Fischer asked, "Did you learn anything more?"

Alvarez shook his head. "A couple of the monks were dead. Rogers was still alive, but only just. They were strapped to great, wooden stakes on the clifftop greensward, naked, reduced to torsos. Many had had their eyes and facial features removed. They were chanting. I must admit that in a perverse kind of way, there was something almost beautiful in the tableau."

"As an atheist," Hunter said, "I could not look upon such depredation with sufficient objectivity to appreciate any beauty. As far as I'm concerned, their cult is a sick tragedy."

"They could be helped," Dr Fischer said tentatively.

Hunter grunted a laugh. "I somehow doubt that your ministrations would meet with their approval."

The three men drank on in silence. At length, talk turned to the expedition.

Alvarez indicated the huge tracked bison he had transported from Million. The vehicle sat in the drive beside the hotel, loaded with provisions—food, water, weapons, and, Hunter noticed, a collapsible cage lashed to the side.

"All is ready," Alvarez said. "We set off at dawn. Your wife's radio beacons are transmitting, and all we have to do is follow their course through the jungle. Our progress should be considerably quicker than hers. We'll be following the route she has carved through the jungle, and as we have four drivers working in shifts we'll be able to journey throughout the night. I estimate that, if all goes well, we should arrive at the valley of the crash-landing within two weeks. Then you take over, Mr Hunter, and with luck on our side we should bring about the salvation of the Slarque."

Hunter restrained himself from commenting. The pain in his chest was mounting. He told himself that he should not worry— Dr Fischer had brought him back to life once; he could no doubt do so again, should it be necessary—but something instinctive deep within him brought Hunter out in hot and cold sweats of fear.

Alvarez leaned forward. "Hunter? Are you—?"

Hunter clasped his chest. Pain filled his lungs, constricting his breathing. Dr Fischer, with surprising agility for a man his size, rounded the table and bent over Hunter. He slipped an injector from a wallet and sank it into Hunter's neck. The cool spread of the drug down through his chest brought instant relief. He regained his breath little by little as the pain ebbed.

Dr Fischer said, "You've undergone a rapid resurrection programme, Mr Hunter. Some minor problems are to be expected. At the first sign of the slightest pain, please consult me." The Doctor exchanged a quick glance with Alvarez, who nodded.

Hunter excused himself and retired to his room.

He lay on his bed for a long time, unable to sleep. The night sky flared with bright pulses of orange and magenta light, sending shadows flagging across the walls of the room. He thought of Sam, and the daughter he had yet to meet, somewhere out there in the interior. He cursed the day he had first heard of Tartarus Major, regretted the three years it had robbed from his life, that long away from his daughter. He slept fitfully that night, troubled by dreams in which Sam was running from the teeth and claws of the creature that had killed him.

He was woken at dawn, after what seemed like the briefest of sleeps, by the ugly klaxon of the tracked bison. The vehicle was equipped to sleep eight—in small compartments little wider than the individual bunks they contained. It was invitation enough for Hunter. He spent the first six hours of the journey catching up on the sleep he'd lost during the night. He was eventually awoken by the bucketing yaw of the bison as it made the transition from the relatively smooth surface of a road to rough terrain.

Hunter washed the sweat from his face in the basin above his bunk, then staggered through the sliding door. A narrow corridor ran the length of the vehicle to the control cabin, where a driver wrestled with the wheel, accompanied by a navigator. A ladder lead up to a hatch in the roof. He climbed into the fierce, actinic sunlight and a blow-torch breeze. Alvarez and Fischer were seated on a bench, swaying with the motion of the truck.

Hunter exchanged brief greetings and settled to quietly watching the passing landscape. They had moved from the cultivated littoral to an indeterminate area of characterless scrubland, and were fast approaching the jungle-covered foothills that folded away, ever hazier, to a point in the distance where the crags of the central mountains seemed to float on a sea of cloud.

They were following a route through the scrub which he and Sam had pioneered years ago in their own bison. The landmarks, such as they were—towering insects' nests, and stunted, sun-warped trees—brought back memories that should have cheered him but which served only to remind him of Sam's absence.

As the huge sun surged overhead and the heat became furnacelike, Alvarez and Dr Fischer erected a heat-reflective awning. The three men sat in silence and drank iced beers.

They left the scrubland behind and accelerated into the jungle, barrelling down the narrow defile torn through the dense undergrowth by Sam's vehicle before them. It was minimally cooler in the shade of the jungle, out of the direct sunlight, but the absence of even a hot wind to stir the air served only to increase the humidity.

Around sunset they broke out the pre-packaged trays of food and bulbs of wine, and ate to the serenade of calls and cries from the surrounding jungle. Hunter recognised many of them, matching physical descriptions to the dozens of songs that shrilled through the twilight. When he tired of this he said goodnight to Alvarez and the Doctor and turned in. He lay awake for a long time until exhaustion, and the motion of the truck, sent him to sleep.

This routine set the pattern for the rest of the journey. Hunter would wake late, join Alvarez and the Doctor for a few beers, eat as the sun set, then retire and lie with his chaotic thoughts and fears until sleep pounced, unannounced. His chest pains continued, but, as Dr Fischer ordered, he reported them early, received the quelling injection and suffered no more.

To counter boredom, he pointed out various examples of Tartarean wildlife to his fellow travellers, giving accounts of the habits and peculiarities of the unique birds and beasts. Even this pastime, though, reminded him of Sam's absence: she would have told him to stop being so damned sententious.

Seven days out of Apollinaire, they came to the clearing where Hunter had lost his life. Alvarez called a halt for a couple of hours, as they'd made good time so far. The driver slewed the bison to a sudden stop. The comparative silence of the clearing, after the incessant noise of the engine, was like a balm.

Hunter jumped down and walked away from Alvarez and the others, wanting to be alone with his thoughts. The encampment was as Sam had left it on the day of the attack; the dome-tent located centrally, the battery of cameras set up peripherally to record the teeming wildlife. His heart pounding, Hunter crossed to where he judged the attack had taken place. There was nothing to distinguish the area; the disturbed earth had scabbed over with moss and plants, and the broken undergrowth in the margin of the jungle had regrown. He looked down the length of his new body, for the first time fully apprehending the miracle of his renewed existence. Overcome by an awareness of the danger, he hurried back to the truck.

Sam had been this way—the tracks of her bison had patterned the floor of the clearing—but if she had left any recorded message there was no sign, only the ubiquitous radio transmitter which she had dropped at intervals of a hundred kilometres along her route.

They ate their evening meal in the clearing—a novelty after having to contend with the constant bucking motion of the truck at mealtimes so far. No sooner had the sun set, flooding the jungle with an eerie crimson night light, than they were aboard the bison again and surging through the jungle into territory new to Hunter.

Over the next six days, the tracked bison climbed through the increasingly dense jungle, traversing steep inclines that would have defeated lesser vehicles. They halted once more, two days short of their destination, at a natural pass in the mountainside which had been blocked, obviously since Sam's passage, by a small rock fall.

While Alvarez's men cleared the obstruction, Hunter walked back along the track and stared out over the continent they had crossed. They were at a high elevation now, and the jungle falling away, the distant flat scrubland and cultivated seaboard margin, was set out below him like a planetary surveyor's scale model. Over the sea, the nebulous sphere of the dying sun was like a baleful eye, watching him, daring their mission to succeed before the inevitable explosion.

Alvarez called to Hunter, and they boarded the truck on the last leg of the journey.

The night before they reached the valley where the starship had crash-landed, Hunter dreamed of Sam. The nightmare was vague and surreal, lacking events and incidents but overburdened with mood. He experienced the weight of some inexpressible depression, saw again and again the distant image of Sam, calling for him.

He awoke suddenly, alerted by something. He lay on his back, blinking up at the ceiling. Then he realised what was wrong. The truck was no longer in motion; the engine was quiet. He splashed his face with cold water and pulled on his coverall. He left his cabin and climbed down into the fierce sunlight, his mood affected by some residual depression from the nightmare. He joined the others, gathered around the nose of the bison, and stared without a word into the valley spread out below.

In Father Rogers's story the valley had been snow-filled, inhospitable, but over the intervening years the snow had melted, evaporated by the increased temperature, and plant life in abundance had returned to this high region. A carpet of grass covered the valley floor, dotted with a colourful display of wild flowers. Over

the edges of the lower peaks which surrounded the valley, vines
and creepers were encroaching like invaders over a battlement.

Hunter was suddenly aware of his heartbeat as he stared into
the valley and made out the sleek, broken-backed shape of a starship, its nose buried in a semi-circular mound it had ploughed
all those years ago, grassed over now like some ancient earthwork.
Little of the original paintwork was observable through the cocoon
of grass and creepers that had captured the ship since the thaw.

Then he made out, in the short meadow grass of the valley, the
tracks of Sam's vehicle leading to the ship. Of her bison there was
no sign. He set off at a walk, then began running towards the
stranded starship.

He paused before the ramp that led up to the entrance, then
cautiously climbed inside. Creepers and moss had penetrated a
good way into the main corridor. He called his wife's name, his
voice echoing in the silence. The ship seemed deserted. He
returned outside, into the dazzling sunlight, and made a complete
circuit of the ship. Sam's truck wasn't there—but he did see, leading away up the valley, to a distant, higher valley, the parallel
imprint of vehicle tracks in the grass.

Beside the ramp was a radio beacon. Tied to the end of its aerial
was Sam's red-and-white polka-dotted bandanna. Hunter untied it
and discovered an ear-phone.

Up the valley, the others were approaching in the bison. Before
they reached him, Hunter sat on the ramp, activated the 'phone
and held it to his ear.

The sound of Sam's voice filled him with joy at first, then a
swift, stabbing sadness that he had only her voice.

*Somewhere in the interior . . . Luke's day, 26th, St Bede's month,
1720, Tartarean Calendar.*

I've decided to keep a regular record of my journey, more for
something to do before I sleep each night than anything else.

I set off from Apollinaire three days ago and made good time,
driving for ten, twelve hours a day. I preferred the days, even though
the driving was difficult. It didn't occur to me until I stopped on
that first evening that I'd never camped alone in the interior before.
It was a long time before I got to sleep—what with all the noise,
the animal cries. The following nights were a bit better, as I got
used to being alone. On the morning of the fourth day I was
awoken by a great flare from the sun. I nearly panicked. I thought
this was it, the supernova. Then I recalled all the other times it'd

done that, when you were with me, Hunter. It wasn't the end, then—but perhaps it was some kind of warning. Nothing much else to report at the moment. Long, hot days. Difficult driving. I stopped yesterday at the clearing where . . . *it* happened. It brings back terrible memories, Hunter. I'm missing you. I can't wait till you're with me again. Freya is well.

The interior. Mary's day, 34th, St Bede's month.
    I've spent the last few days trying to find the best route through the damned foothills. The map's useless. I've tried three different routes and I've had to turn back three times, wasting hours. Now I think I've found the best way through.

The Central Mountains. Mathew's day, 6th, St Botolph's month.
    Well, I'm in the mountains now. The going is slow. What with a map that's no damned good at all, and the terrain clogged with new jungle since the thaw . . . I'm making precious little progress. Sometimes just ten kays a day. I haven't had a proper wash for ages, but I'm eating and sleeping well. I'm okay.

Central Mountains. John's day, 13th, St Botolph's month.
    Another frustrating week. I suppose it's a miracle that I've been able to get this far, but the bison's a remarkable vehicle. It just keeps on going. I reckon I'm three weeks from Codey's Valley, as I've started to think of it. At this rate you won't be far behind me. I've decided to leave the recording on one of the radio beacons some-where, so you'll know in advance that I'm okay. So is Freya.

Central Mountains. Mark's day, 22nd, St Botolph's month.
    I've been making good progress, putting in sometimes fourteen hours at the wheel. I've had some good luck. Found navigable passes first time. I should make Codey's Valley in a week, if all goes well.

Central Mountains. Mary's day, 27th, St Botolph's month.
    I'm just two or three days from Codey's Valley, and whatever I'll find there. I must admit, I haven't really thought about what might be awaiting me—I've had too much to concentrate on just getting *here*, never mind worrying about the future. It'll probably just be a big anticlimax, whatever. I'll wait for you there, at the ship.
    It's dark outside. I'm beneath a great overhanging shelf of rock that's blocking out the night sky's lights. I can't hear or see a

single thing out there. I might be the only living soul for kilometres . . . I just want all this to be over. I want to get away from this damned planet. Promise me we'll go on a long, relaxing holiday when all this is over, Hunter, okay?

Codey's Valley. I don't know what date, St Cyprian's month.
    I . . . A lot has happened over the past couple of weeks. I hardly know where to begin. I've spent maybe ten, eleven days in a rejuvenation pod—but I'm not really sure how long. It seemed like ages. I'm okay, but still a bit woozy . . . I'm getting ahead of myself. I'll go back a bit—to the 28th, I think, when it happened.
    I was a day away from the valley, according to the map. I was feeling elated that I was nearly there, but at the same time . . . I don't know, I was apprehensive. I could think of nothing else but the Slarque, what they'd done to you. What they might do to me if they chose to . . . Anyway, perhaps I wasn't concentrating for thinking about this. I was driving up a ravine, crossing the steep slope. I'd had little trouble with the bison until then, so I think what happened was my fault. I lost control. You know how you feel in that terrible split-second when you realise something life-threatening is about to happen, well . . . the truck rolled and I couldn't do a thing about it. I was knocked unconscious.
    I don't know how long I was out, maybe a day or two. The pain brought me around a few times, then put me under again, it was that bad. I thought I'd cracked my skull, and there was something wrong with my pelvis. I couldn't move. The bison was on its side, with all the loose contents of the cab piled up around me. I knew that if only I could get to the controls, I'd be able to right the bison and set off again. But when I tried to move—the pain! Then wonderful oblivion.
    When I came to my senses, the truck was no longer on its side. It was upright again—and I wasn't where I'd been, in the cab. I was stretched out in the corridor, something soft cradling my head.
    Then the truck started up and roared off up the side of the ravine, the motion wracking me with pain. I was delirious. I didn't know what the hell was happening. I cried out for the truck to stop, but I couldn't make myself heard over the noise of the engine.
    When I regained consciousness again, night was falling. I'd been out for hours. The truck was moving, but along a flat surface that didn't cause me pain. I tried to look down the length of my body, into the cab, and as I did so the driver turned in his seat and peered down at me.
    I knew it was Codey.

Spacers never lose that look. He was short and thick-set, crop-headed. I reckoned he was about seventy—Codey's age—and though his body looked younger, that of someone half his age, his face was old and lined, as if he'd lived through a hundred years of hardship.

I passed out again. When I came to, I thought I'd dreamed of Codey. The truck was stopped, its engine ticking in the silence. Then the side door opened and Codey, wearing old Fleet regulation silvers, climbed up and knelt beside me. He held an injector.

He told me not to worry, that he was going to take me to the ship, where he had a rejuvenation pod. My pelvis was broken, but I'd soon be okay . . . He placed the cold nozzle to my bicep and plunged.

I felt nothing as he lifted me and carried me from the bison, across to the ship. He eased me down long corridors, into a chamber I recognised as an astrodome—the glass all covered and cloaked with creepers—and lay me in the rejuvenation pod. As I slipped into sleep, he stared down at me. He looked worried and unsure.

Yesterday, I awoke feeling . . . well, *rejuvenated*. The pelvis was fine. Codey assisted me from the pod and led me to a small room containing a bunk, told me to make myself at home. The first thing I did was to hurry out to the truck and root around among its tumbled contents until I found the container, then carried it back to my new quarters. Codey watched me closely, asked me what it was. I didn't tell him.

I remembered what Fr Rogers had said about him, that he thought Codey had flipped. And that was *then*. For the past thirty years he'd lived up here, *alone*. When I looked into his face I saw the consequence of that ordeal in his eyes.

Codey's Valley. Mark's day, 16th, St Cyprian's month.

Early this morning I left my cabin, went out to the truck, and armed myself. If the story Father Rogers had told me in the monastery garden was true, about Codey and the Slarque . . .

I remained outside the ship, trying to admire the beauty of the valley.

Later, Codey came out carrying a pre-heated tray of food. He offered it to me and said that he'd grown the vegetables in his own garden. I sat on the ramp and ate, Codey watching me. He seemed nervous, avoided eye contact. He'd not known human company in thirty years.

We'd hardly spoken until that point. Codey hadn't seemed curious about me or why I was here, and I hadn't worked out the best way to go about verifying Father Rogers's story.

I said that Rogers had told me about the crash-landing.

I recorded the following dialogue:

Codey: Rogers? He survived? He made it to Apollinaire?

Sam: He made it. He's still there—

Codey: I didn't give him a chance of surviving . . . They monitored him as far as the next valley down, then lost him—

Sam: *They?*

Codey: The Slarque, who else? Didn't Rogers tell you they were in contact with me?

Sam: Yes—yes, he did. I didn't know whether to believe him. Are you . . . are you still in contact?

Codey: *They're* in contact with me . . . You don't believe me, girl?

Sam: I . . . I don't know—

Codey: How the hell you think I found you, ten klicks down the next valley? They read your presence.

Sam: They can read my mind?

Codey: Well, let's just say that they're sympathetic to your thoughts, shall we?

Sam: Then they know why I'm here?

Codey: Of course.

Sam: So . . . If they're in contact with you, you'll know why I'm here . . .

(Codey stood up suddenly and strode off, as if I'd angered him. He stood with his back to me, his head in his hands. I thought he was sobbing. When he turned around, he was grinning . . . insanely.)

Codey: They told me. They told me why you're here!

Sam: . . . They *did?*

Codey: They don't want your help. They don't want to be saved. They have no wish to leave Tartarus. They belong here. This is their home. They believe that only if they die with their planet will their souls be saved.

Sam: But . . . but we can offer them a habitat identical to Tartarus—practically unbounded freedom—

Codey: Their religious beliefs would not allow them to leave. It'd be an act of disgrace in the eyes of their forefathers if they fled the planet now.

Sam: They . . . they have a religion? But I thought they were animals . . .

Codey: They might have devolved, but they're still intelligent.

Their kind have worshipped the supernova for generations. They await the day of glory with hope . . .

Sam: And you?

Codey: I . . . I belong here, too. I couldn't live among humans again. I belong with the Slarque.

Sam: Why? Why do they tolerate *you*? One . . . one of them killed my husband—

Codey: I performed a service for them, thirty years ago, the first of two such. In return they keep me company . . . in my head . . . and sometimes bring me food.

Sam: Thirty years ago . . . ? You gave them the prisoner?

Codey: They commanded me to do it! If I'd refused . . . Don't you see, they would have taken me or Rogers. I had no choice, don't you understand?

Sam: My God. Three years ago . . . my husband? Did you guide them to him?

Codey: I . . . please . . . I was monitoring your broadcasts, the footage you beamed to Apollinaire. You were out of range of the Slarque up here, and they were desperate. I had to do it, don't you see? If not . . . they would have taken me.

Sam: But why? Why? If *they* bring *you* food, then why do they need humans?

Codey broke down then. He fled sobbing up the ramp and into the ship. I didn't know whether to go after him, comfort him, try to learn the truth. In the event I remained where I was, too emotionally drained to make a move.

It's evening now. I've locked myself in my cabin. I don't trust Codey—and I don't trust the Slarque. I'm armed and ready, but I don't know if I can keep awake all night.

Oh my God. Oh, Jesus. I don't believe it. I can't—

He must have overrode the locking system, got in during the night as I slept. But how did he know? The Slarque, of course. If they read my mind, knew my secret . . .

I didn't tell you, Hunter. I wanted it to be a surprise.

I wanted you to be there when Freya was growing up. I wanted you to see her develop from birth, to share with you her infancy, her growth, to cherish her with you.

Two and a half years ago, Hunter, I gave birth to our daughter. Immediately I had her suspended. For the past two years I've carried her everywhere I've been, in a stasis container. When we were reunited, we would cease the suspension, watch our daughter grow.

Last night, Codey stole Freya. Took the stasis container. I'm so sorry, Hunter. I'm so . . .

I've got to think straight. Codey took his crawler and headed up the valley to the next one. I can see the tracks in the grass.

I'm going to follow him in my truck. I'm going to get our daughter back.

I'll leave this recording here, for when you come. Forgive me, Hunter . . . Please, forgive me.

He sat on the ramp of the starship with his head in his hands, the sound of his pulse surging in his ears as Alvarez passed Sam's recording to Dr Fischer. Hunter was aware of a mounting pain in his chest. He found himself on the verge of hysterical laughter at the irony of crossing the galaxy to meet his daughter, only to have her snatched from his grasp at the very last minute.

He looked up at Alvarez. "But why . . . ? What can they want with her?"

Alvarez avoided his gaze. "I wish I knew—"

"We've got to go after them!"

Alvarez nodded, turned, and addressed his men. Hunter watched, removed from the reality of the scene before him, as Alvarez's minions armed themselves with lasers and stun rifles and boarded the truck.

Hunter rode on the roof with Alvarez and Dr Fischer. As they raced up the incline of the valley, towards the V-shaped cutting perhaps a kilometre distant, he scanned the rocky horizon for any sign of the vehicles belonging to Sam or Codey.

His wife's words rang in his ears, the consequences of what she'd told him filling him with dread. For whatever reasons, Codey had supplied the Slarque with humans on two other occasions. Obviously Sam had failed to see that she had been led into a trap, with Freya as the bait.

They passed from the lower valley, accelerated into one almost identical, but smaller and enclosed by steep battlements of jagged rock.

There, located in the centre of the greensward, were Codey's crawler and Sam's truck.

They motored cautiously towards the immobile vehicles.

Twenty metres away, Hunter could wait no longer. He leapt from the truck and set off at a sprint, Alvarez calling after him to stop. The pain in his chest chose that second to bite, winding him.

Codey's crawler was empty. He ran from the vehicle and hauled himself aboard Sam's truck. It, too, was empty.

Alvarez's men had caught up with him. One took his upper arm in a strong yet gentle grip, led him back to Alvarez who was standing on the greensward, peering up at the surrounding peaks.

Two of his men had erected the collapsible cage, then joined the others at strategic positions around the valley. They knelt behind the cover of rocks, stun rifles ready.

An amplified voice rang through the air. "Hunter!"

"Codey . . ." Alvarez said.

"Step forward, Hunter. Show yourself." The command echoed around the valley, but seemed to issue from high in the peaks straight ahead.

Hunter walked forward ten paces, paused, and called through cupped hands, "What do you want, Codey? Where's Sam and my daughter?"

"The Slarque want you, Hunter," Codey's voice boomed. "They want what is theirs."

Hunter turned to Alvarez, as if for explanation.

"Believe me," Alvarez said, "It was the only foolproof way we had of luring the Slarque—"

Hunter was aware of the heat of the sun, ringing blows down on his head. "I don't understand," he said. "Why me? What do they want?"

Alvarez stared at Hunter. "Three years ago," he said, "when the Slarque attacked and killed you, it laid the embryos of its young within your remains, as has been their way since time immemorial. The primates they used in times past began to die out millennia ago; hence the fall of the Slarque. It so happened that humans are also a suitable repository . . . Of course, when Sam rescued your remains and had them suspended, the embryos too were frozen. We discovered them when we examined your remains on Million."

Hunter was shaking his head. "You used me . . ."

"It was part of the deal, Hunter. For your resurrection, you would lead us to the Slarque."

"But if you wanted the Slarque, you had them! Why didn't you raise the embryos for your exhibition?"

"The young would not survive more than a few months. We examined the embryos and found they'd been weakened by inbreeding, by cumulative genetic defects. I suspect that the brood incubated in the body of the prisoner thirty years ago did not survive. We need the only existing pair of adult Slarque."

Something moved within Hunter's chest. He winced.

Dr Fischer approached. "A pain-killer."

Hunter was unable to move, horrified at what Alvarez had told him and at the same time in need of the analgesic to quell the slicing pain. He just stood as Fischer plunged the injector into his neck.

Codey's voice rang out again. "Step forward, Hunter! Approach the south end of the valley. A simple trade: for the Slarque young, your wife and daughter."

Hunter stepped forward, began walking.

Behind him, Alvarez said, "Stop right there, Hunter. Let the Slarque come to you . . . Remember our deal?"

Hunter hesitated, caught between obeying the one man capable of granting him life, and the demands of the Slarque who held his wife and daughter.

The pain in his chest was almost unbearable, as if his innards were being lacerated by swift slashes of a razor blade. My God, if this was the pain with the sedative . . .

He cried out, staggered forward.

"Hunter!" Alvarez cried.

He turned. He saw Alvarez raise the laser to his shoulder, take aim. He dived as Alvarez fired, the cobalt bolt lancing past him with a scream of ionised air.

He looked up the valley, detecting movement. Two figures emerged from behind a jagged rock. They were at once grotesquely alien and oddly humanoid: scaled, silver creatures with evil, scorpion tails. What invested them with humanity, Hunter thought, was their simple desire to rescue their young. And even as he realised this, he was overcome by the terror of their initial attack, three years ago.

Behind him, he heard Alvarez give the order to his men. He turned in time to see them raise their stun-guns and take aim at the Slarque.

"No!" he cried.

A quick volley of laser fire issued from a single point in the rocks high above. The first vector hit Alvarez, reducing him to a charred corpse. The succeeding blasts accounted for the others, picking them off one by one.

Only Dr Fischer remained, hands in the air, terrified.

Hunter hauled himself to his feet and cried Sam's name, trying to ignore the pain in his chest.

The Slarque approached him. As they advanced, Hunter tried to tell himself that he should not feel fear: their interest in him was entirely understandable.

"Sam!" he cried again.

In his last few seconds of consciousness, Hunter saw his wife run from the cover of the rocks and dash past the Slarque. He was suddenly struck by the improbable juxtaposition of ugliness and extreme beauty. Behind her, he saw a thin, bedraggled human figure—the madman Codey, hefting a rifle. In that second he remembered the death of Alvarez, and wondered if Codey's action in killing the doctor meant that he, Hunter, would die on this infernal planet without hope of resurrection.

He keeled over before Sam reached him, and then she was cradling him, repeating his name. Hunter lay in her arms, stared up at her face eclipsing the swollen sun.

He felt the lifeforms within him begin to struggle, a sharp, painful tugging as they writhed from his chest and through his entrails, the tissue of his stomach an easier exit point than his ribcage.

"Sam," he said weakly. "Freya . . . ?"

Sam smiled reassurance through her tears. Behind her, Hunter saw the monstrous heads of the Slarque as they waited. He tried to raise his face to Sam's, but he was losing consciousness, fading fast. He was aware of a sudden loosening of his stomach muscles as the alien litter fought to be free.

Then he cried out, and died for the second time.

Aboard the Angel of Mercy, *orbiting* Tartarus Major, *1st, May, 23,210—Galactic Reckoning.*

I need to make this last entry, to round things off, to talk.

With Dr Fischer I collected the remains—the bodies of Alvarez and his men—and your body, Hunter. Fischer claims he'll be able to resurrect Alvarez and the other men lasered by Codey, but he didn't sound so sure. Personally, I hope he fails with Alvarez, after what he put you through. The man doesn't deserve to live.

I've negotiated a price for our story with NewsCorp—they've promised enough to pay for your resurrection. It'll be another three years before you're alive again. It's a long time to wait, and I'll miss you, but I guess I shouldn't complain. Of course, I'll keep Freya suspended. I look forward to the day when together we can watch her grow.

The final exodus has begun. I can look through the viewscreen of my cabin and see Tartarus and the giant sphere of the sun, looming over it. Against the sun, a hundred dark specks rise like ashes —the ships that carry the citizens to safety. There's something sad and ugly about the scene, but at the same time there's something achingly beautiful about it, too.

By the time we're together again, Hunter, Tartarus will be no more. But the exploding star will be in the heavens still, marking the place in space where the Slarque and poor Codey, and the other lost souls who wished for whatever reasons to stay on Tartarus, perished in the apocalypse.

I can't erase from my mind the thought of the Slarque, those sad, desperate creatures who wanted only the right to die with their young in the supernova, and who, thanks to Codey and you, will now be able to do so.

Two thousand copies of this book have been printed by the Maple-Vail Book Manufacturing Group, Binghamton, NY, for Golden Gryphon Press, Urbana, IL. The typeset is Electra with Flamme display, printed on 55# Sebago. Typesetting by The Composing Room, Inc., Kimberly, WI.